The author has been writing for over thirty years and has self-published a number of books for children and adults. His last self-published book in America was *Saintly Intervention*. He is, at present, writing a number of New Zealand historical novels. He is a retired school principal.

I would like *The Willows* to be dedicated to my late wife, Pamela.

Kevin Beardsley

# THE WILLOWS

AUSTIN MACAULEY PUBLISHERS™

LONDON * CAMBRIDGE * NEW YORK * SHARJAH

A CIP catalogue record for this title is available from the British Library.

ISBN 9781398458987 (Paperback)
ISBN 9781398458994 (ePub e-book)

www.austinmacauley.com

First Published 2022
Austin Macauley Publishers Ltd®
1 Canada Square
Canary Wharf
London
E14 5AA

'Rusty corrugated iron, two rotting planks of wood and a few bits of driftwood,' simple things and simple words in themselves, but what a connotation they could have for me. They arouse pangs of anguish and guilt that overcome me. How long had he lain there and what part, if any, I had played in his death? I have agonised over the implication those few words could have for me. Now sleep eludes me, leaving me tossing and turning in my bed, leaving me to ponder long into the night. I must find out more but why was I being denied this information and by whom?

Jack Waldron, February 2019.

# 1

# Daphne

It must have been three weeks ago, when Uncle Ernie came in Jack Waldron's bedroom and told him to get dressed and put his few clothes in a bag and to get a move on. "Your father is in an ugly mood and we want you out of here, before he comes back," Uncle Ernie had said. Uncle didn't come around to Jack's place very often and Aunty never, yet she was in the car when Jack got in the back seat of Uncle Riley's Kestrel. They said nothing when he asked if his mother was alright. That was too much to expect, seeing that his mother had been taken to hospital after his father had bashed her up again last Friday. Jack Waldron has been living now for just over three weeks with his aunty and uncle in the beach holiday village of Waireka, North of Christchurch City. And tonight, it is a special Friday in 1965, as it might be Jack's birthday, Jack looks forward to Friday night's meal. It is always different from other nights' meals, more of it, and always a pudding. And this Friday night, because it was his birthday there was to be a very special meal with a huge rabbit pie, and a pudding, and what a pudding! His eyes grew wide when he saw what was in the safe when Aunt Kate asked him to bring her milk from the safe. There is a raspberry red jelly wobbling in the biggest dish that Aunt has, a lovely Spanish cream pudding next to it, a smaller dish of stewed peaches and a full jug of rich, thick cream next to the jug of milk.

"Come on, boy. Don't dandy like a wet Sunday." Aunt snaps as he stares wide eyed at the contents of the safe.

He takes the jug of milk and puts it on the table.

"Not there, you idiot, not on the floorboard." She flings her floured hand out to slap him across his ear, but he has learnt from previous experience to avoid her half-hearted gesture.

He recognises her expression, her chin thrust out, her lower lip protruding over the upper lip and her hard, even, fixed gaze that would freeze anything, even freshly caught fish. He learnt quickly that it was better not to cross her in any way. All afternoon he'd chopped, and carried in wood, and placed it carefully in a neat heap by the stove and hung around at a safe distance watching her preparing the meal. Surely, Uncle Earnest would not be late on this Friday. He is on some Fridays, and they don't eat until he comes home. Jack, whose last meal on those days was his cheese and fish pate sandwiches at lunch time, feels he is dying of starvation. More than once out of desperation he'd thought of sneaking a scone or a biscuit from the tins in the kitchen, but the consequences of being caught were too much to bear. It was better to suffer a grumbling tummy than to complain that he was hungry when Uncle was coming home late.

Uncle Earnest, if he comes home at all during the week, it was only on Fridays. Sometimes, he doesn't want to eat straight after he arrives, but preferred to sit in the chair by the fire in the sitting room and closes his eyes, saying he had a busy week, and is too tired to eat until later and Jack has to suffer in agony listening to his uncle's loud snoring. Jack's Aunt seems to be impervious to his appealing eyes, and the noise of his rumbling tummy. On these nights, Uncle's breath smells strongly of something, that Aunty Kate would never say, but it is obvious to Jack who knows it is the same that he used to smell on his mother's breath. This Friday night is to be different with it being, what he thinks might be, his birthday, and all this wonderful food, waiting for Uncle to come home and enjoy with them. After all Aunty had gone to town this week, and she would have told Uncle about the special meal, and to make sure he was home early.

Old Bert Saunders had given the two hares that were to be the feature of the meal to Jack this morning. "They are skinned, gutted and ready for the pot," he'd said.

"My pleasure." Bert said when he handed them over. "Don't drop them and get sand in them all. Take them straight home and tell your aunt they are from a well-wisher."

Jack felt the weight of the two rabbits in his hand. "Oh, thank you so much, Mr Saunders."

"My pleasure now as I said. She's a fine woman, and as women go, she goes further than most. Worth more than all the women put together in this place. Knows her mind, and no mucking about. Knows a good thing when she sees it, and how to use it, and even though she has a sharp tongue, she keeps it well-honed and hits her target bulls eye every time."

Jack's mouth sags open. He'd never thought his aunt could, or would, throw stones. She was too big and slow moving. He didn't know what Bert Saunders was saying. Still, he'd given them the rabbits. He'd given him two trouts once to take to his aunt. Strange he thought that Bert hadn't given them to his aunt himself. Bert lived in a ramshackle hut near the river.

"Don't go near the lagoon and keep well away from Bert Saunder's place by the river, I'm warning you!" Aunt had warned him.

To Jack there is nothing sinister about Bert. He may have been a big man once, but now he has shrivelled and is not much taller than Jack. Even his hair has thinned to a spindly cluster hardly noticeable until the wind spreads it across his furrowed temple. His eyes have a vacant look nestled deeply like two mountains, tarns below his protruding hairy eyebrows, his mouth nothing more than a lipless slash and his hollowed cheeks deeply crevassed by wrinkles give him an almost benign appearance.

Jack hears his uncle's car pull up outside the holiday home. It is earlier than he expects. He rushes out to greet him as Uncle climbs out of the car. Uncle seems amused to see Jack's enthusiastic welcome and he rumples his hair. "Whoa boy, what's the rush," he exclaims.

"Aunty has cooked a bonsa meal for us tonight. There's pie and jelly and all."

"Has she now, I look forward to it, but don't rush me off my feet." Aunty Kate stands in the doorway of the Bach her arms folded, her expression severe, which doesn't change when her husband approaches. He holds a bottle of whisky in his hand.

"Come on, old thing let's celebrate. The boy here tells me you have prepared something grand for tea tonight." He pushes passed her and enters the room and goes to the cupboard to take out two glasses. He pulls the cork out from the bottle and pours two whiskies.

She glares at him. "You know I don't touch the stuff, and you shouldn't either. At least, you haven't been drinking already."

The boy senses the tension between the two. "Aunty, I told Uncle Earnest that you have cooked a special meal tonight," he says.

"All in good time, Boy. I'm sure Uncle Ernie wants to have his drink first, and we have some talking to do. Run along, now to your room, and I'll call you when I serve."

Jack is on his bed, reading his one and only comic that he possesses, when he hears raised voices coming from the sitting room. His heart races, his face flushes, and he becomes agitated when he recognises the tone of the voices. It was like it was, when he remembers such arguments between his mother and father, when he was younger. The raised voices, the shouting, and the noise of things being thrown in the kitchen. Then, he had put his hands over his ears, and his head under the pillow to try and drown out the ever increasing crescendo of the voices, and the dull thuds of punches being thrown by his father at his mother. It's happening again this time between his uncle and aunt. Uncle's voice is shrill and high pitched, hers is dominant and overpowering.

Jack isn't going to hide this time. He slips off the bed and goes to the door that leads from his bedroom to the sitting room where the other two are arguing, and he puts his ear to the door and listens.

"I've had enough of what's going on," his aunt shouts. She bangs her fists on the table.

"Easy there, old girl. You nearly spilled my drink."

"Damn your drink, Ernie. It's all you care about, isn't it?"

"I wouldn't say that, old scone. Look what I've had done here this year, had an extra room built on for the boy."

"For God's sake Ernie! You don't expect me to stay out here and look after the brat, do you?"

"And why not, I ask?"

"I'll tell you why not. I took the bus to town on Tuesday and after what I saw, I'm determined to come back to town to live, to keep an eye on you. After all, this is only a holiday place which we only use in the summer for a week or two, and you don't spend hardly any time out here, do you?"

"What's the hurry to get back to town to live then?"

"On Wednesday I went to your rooms when I saw you go over to the dentist rooms across the road."

"What's wrong with that. I make dentures for his patients."

"While I was in your rooms, I had a look in the back room, where you say you sleep during the week. The bed hadn't been slept in for weeks. Last time I was there, I put a piece of paper between the sheets. It was still there."

"Christ you, scheming hussy. You don't trust me, do you?"

"Trust you! I saw you go for lunch at Collins Quick lunch place, and you were with a woman."

Uncle is slurring his words now. "Nothing wrong there, old thing. I often sit beside a woman if it's the only place left to sit. We talk and what's wrong with that?"

"And do you always hold their hand and kiss them when they leave. I saw you do that. I followed that hussy of yours. All dolled up, make up and high heels. She works behind the counter at Ballantynes, but you know that. You've been sleeping with her because she is available. Well, I've got news for you Ernie Bennett. I'm going to become available now. I'm moving back to our home in town. All the alterations to the house must be finished by now."

There was a long silence and Jack is about to go back to bed when he hears his uncle say in drawn out words. "Available, you say. You won't be moving. I've sold that house. Need the money for my business."

There is the noise of a chair being moved and then the crash when it obviously fell on the floor. Jack opens the door just a little to see his aunt standing over his uncle who is cowed in his chair, his hands held in front of his face as if to defend himself from a blow.

"And you think that I'm going to stay here looking after that boy. No way. He's your sister's boy. You take him. I want nothing more to do with this."

Ernie gets to his feet and stands with his back to the wall. "Can't, and you know that. His mother has T.B. and is very low. And that husband of hers has long gone, off to Australia, or somewhere like that. He's no good, a loser anyhow. My sister, well she hasn't got long to live now, the doctor told me and anyhow even if she did recover and that's not likely, she's got nowhere to live. I have sold her house too. She's been put in the sanatorium now."

Neither would have heard the loud sob from Jack and his sharp intake of breath, or the click of the door as it shut. Jack pulls out his school bag from under the bed, puts in it his five lead soldiers, his comic, and his model tin car. He flings the bag over his shoulder and opens the bedroom window wide and jumps to the ground outside. He runs along the road and over the small bridge across the lagoon and dropping to a canter he makes his way along the road leading to the main north road that would take him towards Christchurch. When he hears an approaching car and sees its lights coming towards him, he dives under the wire fence at the side of the road and crouches low behind a gorse bush and stays there until the car has passed.

Once on the main road he reckons someone going to Christchurch might stop and give him a ride. The few cars on the road pass him without stopping. He had got as far as the Rope factory across the road when a car pulls up a few yards ahead of him. He runs towards it when the driver gets out of the car. In the fading light it isn't until he has almost reached the car that he recognises his uncle who seems to be hanging on to the door as if he needs its support to remain upright. He lurches towards Jack and grabs his arm and pushes him against the car his face close to Jacks. The smell of alcohol is overpowering. "What's this, Boy? Going out on a night like this when you should be tucked up in your bed. Your aunt is sick with worry," he slurs and squeezes Jack's arm even tighter until it hurts. Jack struggles and yells out in pain. "You are hurting me."

"Hurting you, hurting you, little devil. I'll show you what hurting is." He swings his arm as if to strike Jack but hits the side of the car when Jack ducks. "Smart hey. Then take this! Ernie Bennett doesn't miss a second time." He cuffs Jack a stinging slap on his ear, and he wraps his arms around Jack and drags him into the car on the driver's side. "Scramble over to the other side," he says as he gets in himself, and then collapses heavily in the seat with his head resting against the driving wheel. Jack pushes his uncle's arm, but he didn't move. Maybe, he was dead. "Uncle," he screams.

Uncle sits up suddenly. "What's now, Boy. Think you can drive the car, is that it?"

"No," says Jack in a small voice. He is shaking and his mouth is opening and closing uncontrollably.

"What do you mean by clearing out? Your poor Aunt is beside herself with grief."

Uncle starts the engine and swings the wheel violently to turn back the way he had come. There is a squeal of brakes, the sound of a horn and a car coming from behind swerves over to the other side of the road to avoid hitting them.

"Do you see that, Boy. Bloody fool of a driver. Thinks he's the only one on the road. Should never be allowed anywhere near a car. By Christ, Boy I won't half slay you when we get back. You running off like that nearly caused an accident."

He swings the car around and turns down the road leading back to Waireka Beach settlement. He starts to sing to himself as the car swerves from side to side of the road on their way back. When they reach the village instead of turning right over the bridge, he pulls up opposite the Community hall.

"I'm not going over that damn bridge. It's getting narrower and narrower every time I come out here. I think you and I will be lucky to get across tonight. It's hardly wide enough for one person at a time let alone two of us. Follow me Boy and keep close behind me now." He gets out of the car and leaving the door wide open puts his hand on the bonnet for support as he lurches forward. He would have fallen flat on his face if Jack hadn't grabbed his arm.

"Easy, Boy. No need to hang on to me for support. Uncle will lead the way."

His uncle's weight is too much for Jack to support and they fall in a heap on the road with Jack underneath.

"What's you pulling me down like that, Boy." He gets to his feet, leans on Jack's shoulder, and dusts himself down. "What did I tell you. That blasted bridge is now too narrow for even one of us to cross.

"Uncle." Jack's feeble voice is hardly audible.

"What is it, Boy?"

"The car's lights are still on and the door is wide open."

"Nonsense, Boy. What's got into you tonight. Got into Kate's gin, hey. Know where she hides it, hey!"

He leans against the railing of the bridge when Jack, free from his uncle's weight goes back to the car, switches off the lights, turns the engine off and takes the keys out before closing the driver's door. The journey back to the holiday home is long and tortuous before they are able to stagger in through the door where Kate waits arms folded her eyes half closed, her mouth turned down in a scowl.

Uncle must have forgotten about his threat to thrash Jack, but Aunty is unrelenting.

"There's no tea for you, Boy. Off you go to your bed and don't think you can clear out again. I've locked your bedroom window," she scolds.

Jack's heart sinks. Even if Uncle has already forgotten about his threat to thrash him. Aunty Kate's is the worst possible punishment he could have.

It's mid-morning in 1965, and the village is still under a white sea mist. The dim outlines of the bachs on the high sandhills seem to float in the air above the playing field. Beyond them, darker shapes loom of the tall pines, but Jack could not see where they began, or where the sandy road led. Big drops of moisture plop on the ground now and then from the overhanging branches of the trees in the playing field and the grass is weighed down with moisture. He can hear the sea, somewhere beyond but could not determine how far away it was.

Jack had been staying with his aunt since his mother was in hospital and now had been admitted to the Sanatorium with T. B.

Three weeks with no other kids to play with, throws Jack on his own resources. Summer school holidays wouldn't start for at least a fortnight until these interminable days of loneliness pass. There is little else to do with nothing much happening in the village. Most mornings three old men sit sunning themselves outside the shop in River Road waiting for the mail van to arrive bringing the morning paper. The middle-aged couple staying at 'The Willows', walking their dog, hardly acknowledged the old men's greeting, and they completely ignore Jack. Now and again, there is the excitement of a car arriving or leaving. And now there was this mist that makes him feel even more miserable. He feels a cold breeze on his face and then, as if on some preconceived signal, the mist starts to lift slowly revealing the playing field, the swing, the slide, and the cottages on raised ground which appear at first to be floating in the air. And then the mist is clearing revealing the tall trees behind the cottages to lord it over the village again.

Over by the river the fading mist reveals old Bert Saunders in the wide riverbed doing his rounds of his rabbit traps. Jack thinks he might join him, but on reflection he nearly gives up the idea, but blow it all, there is nothing else to do. He would put up with old Bert's bad temper. Bert is surly and discourages him.

"What do you want boy. When the rabbits see you around, they'll scamper off to their burrows in quick time mark my words. This is a job for one only and that any more than that would scare the rabbits."

"But they have long gone back to their burrows by this time of the morning. The only ones above ground are what you have caught already in your traps surely, Mr Saunders."

"Scat Boy. I told you this was a job for one only. Now get home to your aunt or I'll fetch you one across the ear."

Jack confused and despondent, slips away with his tail between his legs. This wasn't the Bert he had known when he gave Jack rabbits and fish last week.

It isn't much better back in the village. The large green playing field in the centre is deserted, except for a dog which is unfriendly and runs away as Jack approaches. The long row of bachs spread out along the high sand hill on the seaward side of the playing field stare with blank windows across the field to 'The Willows' which stands alone on a promontory above the river. Jack and a few others in the village regard the people in those bachs as being up themselves, thinking their places were much more grand than the few others scattered elsewhere and certainly much more important than the ones over the bridge where he is staying. But they are all insignificant compared to the grandeur of 'The Willows'.

'The Willows' is to let for a week or more at a time during the summer and is always fully booked then. During the winter, and up to Christmas it is often empty except for a few elderly couples who stay for not much longer than a week. At present it is occupied by the cranky middle-aged couple and their dog. They are leaving tomorrow, and the place will be empty like many of the bachs until the Christmas holidays when the village becomes full of life.

Like many other boys of ten or eleven Jack resorts to living in his own world of his imagination. There he builds castles among the beach sand hills, look out towers from the top branches of the pine trees that stand guard over his castles, and he rides his horse, a long stick, slashing his sword at imaginary foes. There is no one around to witness his mighty deeds. He has ventured out in the sea but finds the water still too cold for swimming. His aunt doesn't seem to mind what he was up to as long as he keeps out of her way during the day.

'The Willows' intrigues him. After all it was once, in his mind, a mighty castle to be captured only it needed a well thought out plan and timing to assault it. While it was occupied, he kept his distance, but now that the couple who were staying there were out on their walk along the beach, he has time to reconnoitre.

There is a fence to cross, and an old caste iron gate that makes a noise when it swings in the wind. However, there are gaps in the paling fence where some of the palings have fallen and lie on the ground. They must have been there for some time, for long grass grows over them and much of the wood has rotted away. Perhaps, an army had once tried to take the castle and had broken through the walls. The Castle doesn't look so grand close up. There are gaps in the veranda floorboards and the paint has peeled away on the red front door. Spider webs are undisturbed over the windows. He wipes the webs and the dust from one of the windows and peers inside. There is little he can make out. A mat covers a small patch of the dark stained floorboards, and there is a sofa in front of a brick fireplace on the far wall. He creeps along the length of the side the house and looks up at a window in the second storey. It seems so high up like a

16

castle wall and is far out of his reach. He is about to try the back door when he hears a dog barking and realises the couple are returning. He slides down the slope at the back of the house, and keeping low below the scattered lupins that grow in the riverbed he makes his way to the lagoon and hides behind a large stand of reeds.

The day they came Jack hears the booming sound of their large, black car and the popping of the exhaust as the driver slows to turn up River Road. The middle-aged couple who had been renting 'The Willows' had left with their dog two days earlier and this could be the arrival of new occupants. Jack runs along the road to watch their arrival, but by the time he reaches their car, which they have parked outside on the road they have gone inside 'The Willows'. He hears doors being opened and closed as the new occupants move from room to room. Their car is larger than any he had seen in the village before. Suitcases and bags are tied on the back rack and the boot lid is forced partly open by other luggage in the boot. Whoever, the newcomers are there must be a few of them and it looks as if they intend to stay for some time. They must have travelled a long distance because he hears pinging noises from the hot engine and steam is rising from the radiator. The name on the radiator is 'Bugatti', a car that Jack has not heard of before and he prides himself by knowing the names of many cars.

He hears voices and a short and well-built man appears on the veranda. He is wearing a green voluminous shirt outside his wide shorts that reached just below his knees. He walks across the veranda, changes his mind, and goes back inside. It's time for Jack to leave, but before he does, he hears the shrill voices of children and their hurried steps on the stairs. He hesitates, too late, the man has returned and is opening the front door of the car. He sees Jack and winks at him. Closer up, Jack notices his speckled beard and hair.

"Blast it," he says. "Must have dropped it somewhere. Haven't seen my pipe, have you?" Jack shakes his head and slowly walks away. He can still hear the children's voices as they rush about the house. New people for 'The Willows', he mutters to himself and kids too. Someone to play with at last.

There is no sign of the newcomers for two days, perhaps they were busy settling in. Then on the third day the Bugatti car drives passed the shop where Jack is standing. The bearded man is driving, his head thrown back in laughter. Beside him sits a woman whose her long hair is blown back by the gusts of wind from the open window, she is smoking a cigarette and wearing sunglasses. The roar of the exhaust must have drowned anything that she had said. The car slows as it approaches the sharp corner of the road by the bridge and leaving blue exhaust smoke behind it disappears.

As Jack walks along River Road towards 'The Willows', he hears the screeching sound of the rusty gate. A boy of about his own age is drooped over the gate pushing it backwards and forwards with his foot. He glares at Jack with the sort of expression that kids have on their first encounter, hostile but enquiring. Jack returns the stare and nods. The boy pulls a grotesque face with his tongue out and his eyes rolling. Jack keeps walking at the same pace aware of the mocking eyes on him.

Had the adults left him at home on his own. But where was the other kid he'd heard in the house when they first arrived.

Later that day, Jack sees the boy again. He and an older girl come out of the shop eating ice-cream cones. She is older than Jack, has long legs and ponytail. She is dressed in black shorts and a loose-fitting blouse. The boy pulls a face at him, and the girl with him grins with her head thrown back. Her swaggering walk annoys Jack. She makes some remark to the boy, and they both look at Jack and laugh. He colours and tries to hide his embarrassment by returning their stare, standing with his feet apart and his hands on his hips. The girl swirls her ponytail as she looks away. They turn their backs on Jack, and walk away licking their ice-creams.

He has been thoroughly snubbed this time, but that wouldn't put him off in seeking their companionship. He can't afford to offer them ice creams on the threepence that Aunt gives him now and then, but he can show them around all his forts and tracks.

Later when Jack buys a threepenny ice cream, he overhears Mr Cameron, the storekeeper, telling his wife that the new people in 'The Willows' were called the Goldings.

It is on the beach, on a bright windy day that Jack first sees all the inhabitants of 'The Willows' together. They are sitting in a narrow recess among the dunes out of the wind. Mr Golding sits on a small folding wooden chair, his feet stretched out in front of him, his hat pulled down low over his forehead. Smoke from his pipe hangs in the air until a sudden draught of wind blows it away. The boy is playing with a toy truck, loading it with sand, and tipping it out to make a pile beyond his father's seat. Every now and then a gust blows the sand from the pile over his father's legs.

"Must you Nathan, make your tower of sand somewhere else," his father says. A little further off lying on a beach towel is a young woman in a blue swimming costume. She is turning the pages of a magazine. She wears a broad brimmed hat which hides her features.

The woman who Jack had seen in the car earlier, who must be Mrs Golding, has come out of the water and joins the others. She tosses her flaxen hair and shakes her shoulders as she walks. Jack is fascinated by her. The sun glistens on the water on her costume and wet shoulders. She is well built with strong, solid legs. She takes up a towel and drops down in the chair beside her husband.

"I'm parched. Do fetch me a drink if you don't mind Vera," she says addressing the young woman lounging on the beach towel.

Vera props herself up and reaches over to the basket in front of her. She takes out a bottle of wine and two glasses.

"Don't mind if I join you," said the man. She pours the wine and gives a glass to them both. "Will you join us?" asks the woman. The young woman shakes her head and replaces the bottle in the basket.

From his observation post on a sand dune further along the beach Jack becomes aware of someone creeping on all fours on top of one of the sand dunes above the family group. When she stands poised above the others, Jack recognises her as being the girl he'd seen earlier with the boy eating ice-creams. She lets out a shrill whoop, and launches herself in the air, and crashes down in front of the others sending sand over Vera, the young woman lying on the beach towel.

"Daphne look what you have done," remonstrates Vera, "sending sand over the sandwiches in the basket. "

The man smiles and his wife goes on drying her hair with the towel as if she hadn't seen the whole thing.

Jack feels the pangs of hunger watching the Goldings unpack their lunch from the basket and open the wrapped sandwiches and cakes. There seems to be piles of them all beautifully enclosed in lunch paper. Daphne and Nathan waste no time making their selection, although, there was some dispute about the tomato sandwiches between the pair. Mr Golding doesn't seem all that interested in the food and asks Vera to pour him another wine. Mrs Golding finishes her cigarette before she reaches for a sandwich. It is all too much for Jack to watch as they eat and then unwrap the biscuits and cake. His own lunch had been a piece of bread with peach jam and an apple. He can't help noticing how the mother eats her food so delicately taking time to chew her mouthful before taking another bite whereas the kids eat like pigs. Aunty Kate would never allow him to eat like that.

After lunch when the brother and sister go for a swim Jack thinks of joining them but gives up the idea when their mother joins them. Daphne and her mother swim out beyond the breakers while Nathan remains in water that rarely reaches his knees. Later they play throwing a ball to each other. Nathan looks uncoordinated and finds it difficult to catch the ball when it is thrown gently to him. He appears to hold his hands in a position to catch after the ball has passed him. Daphne on the other hand is very athletic and lithe in her movements catching the ball every time while her mother makes strenuous attempts to catch the ball even when the ball is thrown above her head. She leaps in the air and collapses, laughing when she is unsuccessful. To Jack it seemed improper for her to cavort like this. Even her husband puts down his book and watches applauding her efforts although he makes no attempt to join in the game, instead laughing and clapping when his wife falls on her back in an effort to catch the ball. Jack looks on in disgust. Are all fathers like him? He can hardly remember his own father. The only memory he has of his own father was when he hit his mother and blackened her eyes and his punches left dark bruises on her arms. Would Mr Golding hit his wife like that? If he did Jack would run down, there and hit him hard like he had seen Daphne hit Nathan the other day. He would protect Mrs Golding like he tried to protect his own mother. Only now he is older and stronger and can hit harder. He thinks of Mrs Golding as a mother that he has never had. His own mother is only a hazy memory now, cowed and badly beaten, unable to look after him. She had become so sick that she sometimes never left her bed for days.

If it hadn't been for Mrs Kelly next door he would have starved. She brought over Shepherds' pie and sausages and showed him how to cook them in the wood fired stove's oven. He and his mother never had enough money and what there was must have come from Uncle Earnest. Uncle Earnest came to their house now and then and left money on the table. Mrs Kelly took that and bought some food.

It wasn't as if he starved now, he is at Aunty Kate's place. The food is all right, but nothing like the feast the Goldings had partaken this afternoon. They not only had sandwiches, piles of them and biscuits and cakes, but cold meat, salads and a pie. Jack has never seen, little alone imagined, that anyone ate like that. If only Mrs Golding could be his mother. She is like a Goddess. Those kids didn't know how lucky they are and he envies them.

They have stopped playing with the ball and are packing up their picnic. As they walk along the beach and down the track through the sand dunes that leads to the village Jack overhears Daphne say, "Look there's that kid. He's been up there watching us all day. Spying on us."

"Maybe he is lonely and would like to play with you," her mother replies.

"Really, Mother, play with him! He's only a little kid, and a boy too."

Before tea that day, Jack is sent to the shop to buy bread and potatoes. As he is leaving the shop, Daphne approaches him. Her direct manner confuses him when she asks his name. He mutters his name in such a low voice that she asks again.

"Jack," he answers.

"And where do you live Jack?"

"With my aunt over the bridge."

"Over there." Her manner of reply leaves him in no doubt that she thought of anyone living over the bridge was a nobody worth knowing.

"How old are you?"

"Ten, but I will soon be eleven."

"I'm nearly thirteen. You can play with Nathan, He's nearly twelve, Mum says you can come over tomorrow, and we might go for a swim."

Jack's heart leaps when he hears these words. She might be a little stuck up and Nathan, well he seems a little queer, but at least he might have found some companions. And he would meet Mrs Golding, his new mother figure.

For Jack this was an exciting time in his life. He is up early in the mornings, gulping his porridge, making his bed with lightning speed and out the door before Aunt Kate can call him back to make a better job and to tidy his room, what joy, what excitement, all beyond his highest expectations, even if he has to wait outside 'The Willows', for he often arrives before the Goldings were out of bed. To while away the time, he'd hide behind the hedge and plan what they would do that day.

Then, when he hears the heavy footsteps of Nathan on the stairs, and the slamming doors, Jack would be at the front door counting to twenty before he knocks. Nathan is always first to answer.

"God! You are up early. We haven't had breakfast yet," Nathan would say. Jack would sit on the veranda watching the morning sun rise above the tops of the pine trees.

Nathan comes out first after breakfast and they sit and wait the arrival of Daphne. Some days she comes out soon after, but on other days she makes them wait for what seemed like for ever until tired of waiting Nathan would suggest they go on without her, but Jack would never hear of it. He is getting used to her moods and her sudden sulks if things didn't go her way. Jack would make excuses for her. It wasn't the long waits he minded, but the thought of not being with her that disappoints him.

Sometimes while they waited, and the sun was climbing higher, Mrs Golding would come out and sit on the veranda with them.

"You are a patient boy Jack. Why don't you and Nathan go on. Daphne will come in good time. She doesn't like being alone in the house. Give her time. She'll come around." Her bright, warm smile is everything to Jack. He feels her motherly presence beside him and longs to snuggle up against her and rest his head against her shoulder. When she rises and puts her hand on Jack's shoulder, he feels a sensation he's never experienced before, something strange, yet comforting and supportive. Was this what it was like to be touched by a mother. His own mother, as far as he could remember, didn't touch him much, then she was always either too sick or had drunk too much and Aunt Kate only touched him when she slapped him and that didn't count. This is a new sensation and one that he wants to stay him for the rest of the day.

The first few days they were together Jack is in his element. He knows where to go to show them all the different tracks through the sand hills and the tall pine trees and where he has his secret hide-aways. He shows them how to get to the lagoon and follow the stream until it flowed out to the river.

Daphne, obviously put out that Jack was the leader soon asserts her authority.

"Look I'm not so interested on that little boy stuff let's do something adventurous like seeing how far you can swim out to sea and who can collect the most birds' nests and the most pipis. Dad likes to eat them, and Mum doesn't mind cooking them."

Jack agrees but Nathan is less enthusiastic. "You always pick the things you can win don't you," he says.

"What of it. I'm older than you. Let's see if Jack can beat me. Let's have a competition. How about a swim. We all have our costumes under our shorts."

"We don't have any towels," says Jack.

"Who needs towels. We can lie in the sun on the sand dunes to dry," she replies.

Jack races across the sand to the sea and although he is going as fast as he can Daphne soon catches up and passes him. She races in the surf raising her knees high to avoid slowing and dives through the first breaking wave and starts swimming out to sea. Jack slows when the water is up to his waist and hesitates before he too dives under a breaking wave. By the time he comes up again Daphne is well ahead and swimming strongly. He is not a fast swimmer and has never before gone out much further than the first breaking wave. His strength is ebbing as he struggles to swim further. His arms are aching, and his legs are sinking further in the water. He floats on an incoming wave that hasn't broken and then makes a strenuous effort to swim out to join Daphne only to find himself sinking further below the surface. There is nothing for it, but to turn and return to the beach. Panic is starting to take over. He misjudges an oncoming wave and is soon floundering under water. He comes to the surface gasping for air and flaying his arms about to try and keep afloat. Then she is there beside him.

"Come on," she says. "Let's catch a wave and surf in." And she was gone, head and shoulders in front of the breaking wave, carrying her to the shore.

Exhausted as he is, Jack flays his arms around as he turns towards the shore, and as luck would have it, he is caught by a breaking wave which carries him surfing effortlessly to the shore. When he picks himself up where the wave dumped him on the sand, he feels his legs are too weak to support him. "Beat you," she says. "First blood to me," and she races away to the sand dunes and throws herself down on the warm sand.

Jack is relieved when Nathan, who has not entered the sea, walks with him at a slow pace to the sand dunes to where Daphne lies.

That mindless thrill of that mad leap from the top of the highest sand dune into the air to be borne up by the steady blowing easterly, up over the beach below, across the sea, soaring every higher, gliding like the big black backed gull, lasted but seconds until the predictable crash headfirst in the sand at the bottom of the dune. Has he jumped further than Daphne is Jack's first thought. He has been trying all afternoon to beat the mark measured by the stick in the sand. He shakes his head and wipes the sand from this face and opens his eyes. There in front of him is the stick still there as if mocking him. Daphne hasn't bothered to watch his efforts. She, disdainful of his efforts, has gone pipi gathering. She has won the race along the beach and the cross country over the sand dunes and now to his dismay she'd out jumped him.

"Don't feel too bad about it," she says. "You are only a kid. I'm over two years older than you and you are, after all, only a boy and boys are useless. I take my hat off to you for trying and not giving up. Come on let's swim."

Beaten by her in most physical efforts Jack, rather begrudgingly admits he isn't yet up to her standards and doesn't feel too upset. What really matters to him is that she obviously enjoys his company as much as he enjoys hers. Nathan isn't much of a companion. He has a limp and can't keep up with them. He didn't swim and couldn't take much of a part in what they did even though he tried to.

Then there was Vera, a real spoil sport, always in the background spying on them and calling Daphne and Nathan to come home and do their studies. They reluctantly leave the beach and returned to 'The Willows', to do their lessons. During the late mornings and early afternoons, they have their school lessons with Vera.

Lately after they were released from their studies, Vera accompanies them keeping her distance, but never losing sight of them for long. Vera is a sort of governess who not only keeps a watchful eye on her chargers but is responsible for their lessons. The Goldings travel not only in New Zealand, but overseas as well. Vera, from Jack's view is old, nearly twenty or something. She was far too old to play or swim with them. When not taking the school lessons, she spends her time with the Golding couple on the beach lying on a rug pretending to be reading a book, while watching the younger ones at play.

Jack is at ease in the presence of the family except for Vera. She seems distant and gives the impression that she didn't trust Jack and resents his presence.

"Why aren't you at school? I thought all children should be at school or be home taught like Daphne and Nathan?" she asks as she stands looking down at him from what appears to Jack from a great height. She is taller than any of the others.

Jack flushes and feeling guilty stammers. "My Aunt Kate said it wasn't worth while sending me to the local school for a few weeks before Christmas."

"Stuff and nonsense, your aunt should've known better. I bet you are pulling the wool over her eyes and playing the wag."

Mrs Fiona Golding interrupts. "I'm sure Jack isn't playing the wag. His mother is very sick in hospital. Leave the boy alone Vera. My two children enjoy his company after they have finished their schooling for the day."

"Maybe, but I don't want him to be distraction for them while they study."

Fiona turns to Jack. "How would you like to come to town with us tomorrow? We are taking Nathan to the hospital for his treatment. It usually takes a couple of hours or more and I promised Daphne that next time I would allow her to go to the pictures."

"The pictures, goody, good. Can Jack come too?" Daphne leaps to her feet and moves from foot to foot in excitement.

"But of course, he can." Mr Golding pushes his glasses down over his nose and lowers his newspaper. "Capital. Well, that's settled," he says.

Next morning Jack finds it difficult to sit still in the back seat with Daphne and Nathan in the big Bugatti car as they travel to the city.

Daphne and he are dropped off in the Square by the Plaza theatre. Daphne buys the tickets with the money her father has given her, and they go inside. Jack holds his breath with excitement as they are ushered to the fourth row from the front. The usher holds her torch to light their way and takes their tickets as they settle down in their seats. This is the first time Jack has been to the films. He is entranced as he looks around him in the half light in the theatre, at the light on the huge red curtains in front of the screen and marvels at the huge auditorium with the ceiling high above him. Then the lights dim, and the curtain moves to the side and the National anthem brings them to their feet. When they settle again in their seats the film starts. It is a cowboy and Indians film with Hopalong Cassidy and his Indian companion. Jack stares open mouthed as the excitement increases. He hardly notices that Daphne, almost as excited as him, has drawn closer to him and until their bodies touch. He feels her hand seek his hand until they touch, and they hold hands. Her head is close to his and he feels a slight pressure on his cheek and a slight dampness where her mouth has touched. This is a sensation that he has never felt before. Then just as suddenly she withdraws and is sitting away from him. The excitement of the moment has gone, and his attention turns once again to the screen.

Gladys, she said her name was, a little girl of nine years shy and withdrawn, dressed in old fashion skirt that almost reached to her feet, a cardigan over her blouse and what looks like a scarf tied under her chin. Jack notices her standing outside the shop, wringing her hands, and moving from foot to foot and he asks what her name is.

"You just visiting?" She shakes her head.

"Are you staying here then?"

She looks down at her feet and points in the direction of the line of smart bachs on the rise. "Why do you wear those old fashion clothes?'

She shrugs her shoulders and seems surprised at his question.

"You want to play with us? The others will be along soon, and we can play in the sand dunes or go for a swim."

She is aghast at his suggestion and turns away from him.

"Don't you talk?" he asks as if taunting her.

She pulls a face. "God! You aren't half shy."

Daphne and Nathan come out of the shop. "Who's this?" asks Daphne.

"Go on tell them your name," says Jack.

"It's Gladys."

"She says she is staying here in one of those posh bachs on the hill," said Jack.

Gladys shakes her head. "Not in one of those. In the caravan, in the camping ground behind them," she replies.

"Who's with you then?" asked Daphne.

"My dad, that's who."

"Where's your mother then?"

"In Cust. That's where."

Satisfied with her answers the three companions moved away. "Coming with us to play?" asks Daphne. Gladys shakes her head.

"Please yourself then."

Daphne and Jack spend the morning in and out of the sea, sometimes surfing in on the waves or swimming out as far as they could go. Gladys who has been watching from the top of a sand dune comes down on the beach and stands just above the high tide mark but keeps her distance from them. Nathan takes no notice of her while he digs in the sand with a large shell he has found on the beach.

As the morning ages, Jack no longer tries to match Daphne's long swims beyond the breakers, but is contented by either surfing with the waves closer to the shore and lying in the shallows allowing flowing water, now a slow trickle, to wash over him. Not until he comes out of the water, does he realise that there is a cool wind blowing and wrapping his towel around him he goes over to Nathan who is now digging deeper in the wet sand.

"No pipis this far up from the water," he says. "What are you digging for? Gold!"

"Na, there's no gold here. I'm going to build a castle before the tide comes in. Give's a hand."

The two boys are too busy making the castle to notice that Gladys is standing close to them.

"Don't just stand there," says Jack. "Give us a hand to build the walls before the tide reaches us."

Gladys hesitates, approaches closer as if she might join them, and then she runs back to the dunes. "Too scared to get her feet wet and to get her clothes all sandy." Jack stands up." God I nearly forgot the milk. I'll be skinned alive. You go on with the castle Nathan. Maybe Daphne might help you when she comes out of the sea." He'd left his billy on the seat outside the store and is relieved to find it still there when he returns. The farm where he gets the milk each morning is up the road towards the Main Road. It is only a few minutes' walk up the road.

Felix Golding loves nothing better than on a fine day to take his folding wooden chair, his bag over his shoulder in which he carried the morning paper, his reading glasses, his tobacco pouch, pipe, and hip flask of whisky and then find a spot out of the breeze among the sand dunes where he can see the sea and there he would sit until the pangs of hunger come upon him, usually earlier on colder days, but no later than lunch time. His old war wounds are playing up today and it takes some effort to get in the chair and stretch his stiff leg out in front of him. There with his pipe well-lit and newspaper on his knee he watches the coming of the waves growing higher and higher until their crest topples forward, starting at one end and travelling the length of the wave to the other end, crashing down with a fine display of white foam and thunderous roar this windy day, to advance upon the beach, tumbling and displaying its irresistible power and then flows so gently as if soothing the beach, only to retreat in a hurry drawing with it sand that reveals the pipi beds and leaving behind debris what it has no use for, dead fish, pieces rope, driftwood and anything else that has been cast upon its surface. Felix finds this all so relaxing and soothing. A full pipe, his hat pulled forward, his paper on his lap, he feels today that he could stay there for ever watching this unending sequence as the tide comes ever closer to where he is sitting.

This morning was particularly satisfying. He'd gone over the papers that his brother had sent from England. The Firm is doing well, perhaps particularly well now that he is away from it. During the war the family Firm had made various munitions and after the war has adapted with great speed back to what it had made before the war. Much of this success is due to his brother Stanley although he likes to think that he has made considerable contributions as well. His war injuries persist, making him lame, if he was on his feet for too long, and the bullet wound in the head has healed, but left him with severe headaches from time to time. Long holidays to places far away like New Zealand restore his energy. This is the third holiday like this that he has taken since he returned to the Firm eight years ago. The further away from war damaged Europe the better.

His wife, Fiona, enjoys these breaks and the children have Vera as governess to ensure they don't miss too much school. Nathan is a worry with his poor health and a congenital condition. Felix, because back in England he was away at work and often stayed at the club some evenings, had little to do with his son. On holiday Felix is beginning to realise how difficult it is for Fiona. He has come to dislike Nathan with his clumsy ways and his incoherent speech. He spends as less time with him as he could while on holiday. Perhaps it is apparent to both Fiona and Vera that he favours Daphne for she is more like him, impulsive at times, but very direct in her manner.

A large black backed sea gull swoops down over the sand dunes gliding only a few feet from where he is sitting. Another comes from the other direction coming even lower over him. Then the sky is full of gliding, wheeling gulls, shrieking, evacuating their droppings on the ground near him. Startled and alarmed Felix tries to get to his feet, but loses his balance and falls out of his chair, and he lies on his side unable, for a moment to move, his heart beating quickly, his breathe short. His gammy leg has failed him again. His pipe is in the sand, his paper caught in the breeze flops about him. He reaches about him to grab the disarranged pages to avoid them from blowing away in the increasing wind. The birds have gone further down the beach. The sea as always continues its never ceasing assault on the land.

Felix, breaths deeply. It always pays to do this to gain control of oneself. It had aided him in times of great danger during the war and at times after when he felt his heart racing for no apparent reason. He stays on the ground a little longer before he pulls himself to his hands and knees and flops down again in his chair. Keeping control in moments like this is what was important he tells himself.

Perhaps it was an omen, all this swooping down on him by those big birds. Hardly. More like a shift in the wind had blown them in his direction. He didn't, or did he believe in omens. There were times during the war that he had liked to think they had saved his skin. He remembers the expression on the face of that Maori women Hilda who comes to clean and cook at 'The Willows' from time to time, when a fantail had come in the house and chased insects from room to room. "It's a bad omen," she had said her eyes wide open and rolling in fear. "Someone nearby is going to die."

Further down the beach a woman, her dress billowing in the wind, bends to pick up an object on the beach. She looks at it closely and then throws it away.

Fiona resents the presence of the electrician who is rewiring some of the rooms upstairs even if he is probably doing his best not to disturb her, by moving quietly through the sitting room carrying with him a step ladder, and coils of electric cable. With Felix out of the house, and the children outdoors, this was her quiet time when she could read poetry without interruption, when she could linger over the hidden meaning of many of the lines, where she could indulge herself in the atmosphere of a poem. There were times when she felt inspired to try and write a few lines of her own.

Vera is in the house, but she knows better than to intrude during these private mornings. A clatter of something falling down the stairs in the hall startles Fiona. A tangled pile of old wiring has fallen and lies on the floor outside the room. She puts her book down and for a moment is bewildered by the interruption to the Gerald Manley Hopkin's world of 'For rose-moles all in stipple upon trout that swim, Fresh fireball chestnut-falls; finches' wings'.

Vera's voice breaks the spell. "Morning tea Fiona. Shall I pour one for the electrician?"

"Yes of course. Invite him to join me in the sitting room." Vera had taken to calling her by her Christian name only when Felix is out of ear sound.

"I don't want to intrude," said the electrician when he enters. "I'll take my overalls off before I sit on your furniture."

"Nonsense, Mr Dab, is it."

"That's right, ma'am."

"You must be the father of that quiet little girl, Gladys."

"That's right. I am her father. We are living in a caravan in the camping ground at present." Vera pours the tea and offers a plate of buttered scones with raspberry jam.

Fiona notices that Mr Dab has no trouble in managing his tea and his plate with a scone.

Obviously, a man with some social graces. He'd lived in female company before. He is an ordinary looking man, red hair, cut short, protruding ears and a jutting jaw. His manner is reserved and withdrawn and Fiona, her morning interrupted, determined to find out more about him.

"You just living in the caravan while you work in this district."

"In a manner of speaking, yes, but we will stay there until we find something better."

"I imagine your wife would like something more permanent."

"She already has."

"I'm sorry. I didn't intend to be nosey."

"Not at all."

"Your daughter seems very shy. My children and Jack have tried to involve her in their games, but she is reluctant to join in."

Mr Dab puts his cup in the sauce and places it on the table beside him. "It will take time, but she will get over it."

"She is dressed in rather old fashion clothes, Mr Dab."

"That's how they all dress in the commune. The women and the girls make the clothes both for themselves, and the men members. I was once a member myself, but I pulled away and I brought Gladys with me. No daughter of mine was going to be brought up in that place with what goes on there. There is no freedom. They are controlled by Steadfast who runs the place. I couldn't half tell you what goes on in there. The women cook and bake, do housework, make clothes, while the men either work on the farm, or like me go out to work in the wider community. Every penny we own goes to the Commune. We got clothes, food and accommodation and preaching, and the rules to make us conform to the will of Steadfast and his like.

And your wife, is she with you now?"

"No, she stayed in the Commune. I tried to get her to leave but she is far too indoctrinated."

"I'm sorry for you both."

"My wife had always wanted to find a Commune like this, and 1 reluctantly followed her there years ago, but I soon found that the life didn't suit me, and I hated to think what influence it would have on my daughter.

"Do you see your wife now?"

"I take Gladys on Saturdays to see her. We have been caste out now and we are not allowed to go through the locked gate. My wife comes to the gate accompanied by one of the elders. They stand well back from the gate. My wife says little. She has accepted that we are now damned and are no longer one of the chosen. Gladys is finding these visits difficult. Her mother, for God's sake, denouncing her like that and can hardly bring herself to say a word to the child."

"I cannot understand how any mother would be like that to her own child. Look for what it is worth I have some dresses and other things that Daphne has grown out of and I'd like you to have them. Vera and I will sort them out and give them to you before you leave today."

Mr Dab lowers his head; a tear runs down his cheek. "Thank you so much I will be very grateful indeed."

Jack watches Aunty Kate pour another glass of sherry and put the bottle down on the table before her. Usually, she puts the cork back in the bottle and before she drinks, she would take the bottle and put it behind the books on the second shelf of the bookcase. Jack knows that is where she keeps it because he has seen her once before when she thought he wasn't looking. The next day when Aunty Kate is out of the bach he takes the bottle and pours a little in his cup. Yuk, the taste almost makes him puke. If this is what adults drink, he never wants to become an adult himself if he can help it.

When he was eight years old and living with his mother, he'd poured some of her gin from the bottle down the sink and filled it with water up to the mark it had been. His mother didn't seem to notice the difference and so far, neither did his aunt. She must have suspected that Jack might get up to something like this and made a pencil mark showing the level of the drink in the bottle before she put it away. He always filled it up to that mark with water. Gosh, he thought it must be some sort of strong stuff if she didn't detect any weakening of the spirit.

He doesn't consider its mischief he is getting up to by doing this. It is to save Aunty Kate from what had happened to his mother. If what happened to his mother, happened to Aunty Kate she would have to go to the sanatorium like his mother, and there would be no one to look after him. Then again, he thinks, Mrs Golding might take him on, as her new son, seeing that Nathan must be such a disappointment to her and Mr Golding.

His thoughts are rudely interrupted when Aunt pinches the flesh on his forearm.

"What are you looking at, Boy? Counting how many I have is that it? Good God a woman got to have something to keep her spirits up when she has a boy like you in the house to look after. A drop now and again is small compensation, I can tell you for all your dirty washing and the sand and the dirt you bring in with you."

Jack wonders what she means by all his washing. He wears a pair of shorts with elastic at the top, one of his three shirts he owns, and he has bare feet all day. He shakes any sand from his clothes at night before he enters the house. The only other clothes he owns are his school clothes and he hasn't worn them since he had been in Waireka. They are hanging in the wardrobe.

Aunt reaches over and gives him a sharp slap on the side of his head.

"Discipline that's what you need boy. There hasn't been any before you came here. Your father was a no hoper and a drunken and your mother is not much better. Look at that pathetic pile of wood you have brought in. You expect me to make your porridge in the morning and me to heat the copper for washing. Get out and get me a decent pile before I tan your hide."

Jack needs no more prompting. He is outside in a flash before she deals him a further blow. The light of the day is fading quickly and shadows from the trees are already creeping across the ground. He picks up a log and places it carefully on the block. The axe in his hand is heavy and he knows he can't control it if he attempts to split the log of pine. He slides his hands on the handle of the axe towards the heavy head to give him some control. He brings the axe down as hard as he can, but his aim is bad and as the blade of the axe hits the side of the log sends it flying to the ground. He tries again and again without success. The tomahawk of course, why hasn't he thought of that. Then his spirits sink when he remembers that Uncle Ernie had taken it away to be sharpened after he had tried to split the wood last weekend.

The pitiful heap of kindling that he has found in the grass and near the block would not be acceptable. There is nothing for it, but to go foraging under the lupins that grow near the lagoon, and maybe the broom bushes nearby and the elderberry trees nearer the dark, gloomy forest of pines that stretch for miles behind the sand dunes of the beach.

Already it is twilight and with it comes a steady breeze from the sea. The shadows are now deeper, more mysterious, more frightening and the sound of the wind in the trees or was it the sound of the bad spirits that live there, have come out with the coming of night. Jack freezes, his heart is beating louder, his breath shorter. He had never before dared to venture out at this time of night and certainly never in the dark forest of the Pines.

Tonight, he has no choice. He couldn't possibly go back with the few sticks of wood. He would get a hiding and be shut out of the bach until he'd gathered sufficient wood. There was nothing for it, now or never. He drops to his knees and crawls under the cover of the hanging branches of the lupins. There is wood to be found there, even if it is a little rotten, and would burn away too quickly it will make his pile of firewood looks bigger. The tall broom bushes are next but there is no dry wood there. The branches are strong and green, and he can't pull them out.

The elderberry trees give him some hope. Dead, dry branches fallen from the trees and the few he is able to break from the trees themselves will help. Still not enough. Pinecones of course, but that means a quick dash under the pines themselves where the shadows are deeper, and more frightening than ever. He makes a dash for it. Once under the trees the shadows seem less threatening, and the cones are easy to find without him going too deep in the forest. He gathers as many as he can carry and together with the few sticks of lupin and elderberry, he runs back to the bach as if all the bad spirits of the night are after him. He bursts in the room and drops his offerings on the floor by the stove.

Aunty Kate advances on him like a galleon of the sea her skirts swishing about her.

"What's this, she demands. "Bursting in here as if the Devil himself was after you. What's all this wood doing in here?" Her words are slurred, and she sways a little above him where he crouches.

"It's the wood for the washing and my porridge in the morning."

"Porridge and washing. Who ever mentioned them? There's no washing in the morning. I'm off to town and for breakfast there is corn flakes, you stupid boy. Get off to bed and don't forget to wash your face, behind your ears and your hands before you lie on my nice, clean sheets."

Who would have thought that Uncle Ernie would notice that the two boards that Jack had taken to build his underground hut had gone missing? Jack thought Uncle had forgotten all about them where he found them covered in tall grass and half covered in sand. Uncle hardly ever went to the back of the section and any how they couldn't have been any use to him.

The way Uncle went on you have thought he'd lost the crown jewels or something like that. He railed and ranted for some time accusing the mean thieves of Waireka for stealing them.

"Probably used for parts of some of those flash bachs on the other side," he said.

Jack had taken the boards early one morning when most of the residents had left for work or school. He'd taken them to the back of their section and had followed a route among the sand hills to avoid being detected. They were exactly what he wanted to lay across his underground hut he had built during the day in his kingdom of the Great Pines Forest. The two planks together with the drift word that had come down the river, which he'd dragged along the beach and two sticks of broom, formed the structure for the roof of his secret hide away. All that need to be done now was to find something in the village like a tarpaulin or perhaps and some old rusty roofing that might be lying about to complete his hut. He had been long planning his underground hut since he found a suitable depression in the ground. With some digging with the spade and shaping it a little it was just deep enough for him to crouch below ground level. When he found something to put on top of the roof, he'd cover the whole thing with dirt and pine needles, and no one would know it was there. He'd needs to hurry because schools would be over in less than a fortnight and the camping ground would soon fill up and the bach owners will be coming to stay over the Christmas holidays.

On the way back from his last trip he comes across old Bert Saunders who is sitting outside his front door with his dog, Wally, at his feet. Bert may not have seen Jack if Wally hadn't got up and starts barking.

"You're up and about early young man, Got ants in your pants or something."

"Just going for a walk."

"Don't give me that. You're up to some think I bet."

Jack colours and he stammers a denial that hardly sounds creditable.

"Don't worry Young man. One's got to be up to something to make life worth living, I say." Jack is on the point of admitting to Bert what he has been up to and then remembers just in time that it certainly wouldn't remain a secret for long if Bert has anything to do with it.

"Na, just mucking about that's all," he replies.

"Haven't seen you around with that Golding girl and her brother for a while. You know of course the Goldings have another girl staying with them now,

Elaine, I think is what she is called. There must be all sorts of goings on at 'The Willows' from the noise and shrieks that I hear when I'm passing by on the riverbed. That Nathan lad can't be much of a companion for you either. He's a queer one that lad, can't talk proper, hardly says a word. It's all shrieks, grunts, and horrible noises from him. Better keep your distance from him I'd say."

Bert is a grumpy old man, always finding fault in most things, but what he has to say this morning makes sense to Jack. The girls, Daphne, Gladys, and Elaine have made it quite clear they don't want anything to do with him now. He is very much on his own again. He'd let Nathan help him build the lookout on a high sand dune. Not that he was much help, but still having someone around instead of being alone was what mattered. Together they had dragged fallen pine and elderberry braces and some driftwood he didn't need for the underground hut, to the top of the dune and made a sort of fort from which they had a good view along the beach as far as they could see.

He gathers an armful of dry pine and lupin wood and drops it outside the back door. He wipes his hands against his shorts and sits on the back doorstep. It is on mornings like this with only the sound of the sea, the seagulls and now and then the unmistakable long, drawn-out song of the magpies, that Jack feels the pangs of loneliness, of not being wanted and having nothing much to do. Sometimes, it becomes a deep despair which he finds hard to deal with. The girls have spurned him, and it will be days before the schools close, and there might be a few more kids around. That thought lifts his spirits a little, even if he tries not to think, it might come to nothing. Most of the kids that come to the camping ground keep to themselves, and the local kids, well, they stick together and have never included him in their play.

He takes a handful of sand in his hand and lets it drop between his fingers. A fantail suddenly appears and darts about chasing the insects in the air. Jack runs to join it as it flits from branch to branch on the apple tree. It too disregards him and flies in its darting fashion deeper among the higher branches out of his reach and then disappears altogether. It is as if it has never been there at all. He kicks the sand at his feet sending it high in the air like a sandstorm before it settles.

What is there to do to overcome this boredom. There is the lagoon, but there isn't much to do there. The shop is not to be considered. Two days ago, he'd stolen an apple from the case outside the shop and although he prided himself on his dexterity in this act of stealing, he got the impression that Mr Cameron, the storekeeper was keeping an eagle eye on him when he collected the bread yesterday. It wouldn't do to press his luck too far there. The river of course, but Bert wouldn't be there this morning, and there is little else to do. The beach, of course. There was always something to do there, like beach combing to see what the high tide might have left on the beach and if he was lucky, he might see a ship far out near the horizon.

The girls are there on the beach, running holding long ribbons in their hands letting them flow out behind them as they run. A small, excited dog runs with them barking and jumping up now and then as if to catch the ribbons in the wind. Jack, unseen among the sand dunes, follows their progress along the beach. He will hide in the lookout and watch them from there. A movement behind the walls of the lookout catches his eye. Then a branch that forms one wall of the lookout tumbles down the sandy slope, followed by another. Nathan is in the lookout and is smashing it. As he pulls the dead branches from the walls he shrieks and hoots.

Jack climbs the sand dune shouting at the top of lungs calling him to stop. Seeing Jack suddenly appear Nathan pulls a smaller branch out and hurls it at him. It misses and Jack throws his arms around Nathan and puts out his foot and trips him sending him sliding down the dune. Then something heavy hits Jack on the back of his head and he falls forward on his face in the warm sliding, dry sand. Before he can recover his arms are pinned to the ground and a bony knee in his back holds him down.

"Hit my brother, would you?" he hears Daphne say above him. "We'll teach you; you bully."

"Get him. Is this the kid you told me about. Push his face in the sand."

"All right Elaine. We got him. Sit on his back so he can't get away," says Daphne. Jack tries to lift his head out of the sand only to feel a hand on the back of his neck forcing it down again. He spits the sand out of his mouth, and tries to close his eyes, but the sharp grains of sand in his eyes made it too painful.

"Et off, get off. I can't breathe," but his appeals are answered with jeering laughter. Then his shirt is being pulled up over his head and arms until it comes off and is thrown on the round near him.

"Come on Daphne. Let's do it," he hears the new girl, Elaine say followed by giggles and laughter as the hands of the girls slip inside the waist of his shorts and pulls them down. He tries to kick and heave himself up, but his legs are hampered by the shorts that are now around his ankles until they are wrenched free to fall on the sand by his shirt.

"Look he's all bare. Smack his little bum," Elaine shouts and he feels their hands on him, on his back, his bottom and his legs. They are trying to turn him over. He'd never been so humiliated and intensely embarrassment before as they slip their hands under him and try to turn him on his back. He resists their efforts with all his strength clutching at the sand with his hands but getting no support there the girls finally succeed in turning him over. He clutches his hands together and holds them over his groin, but too late.

"Look at his little diddle all covered in sand," cries Elaine in triumph. She picks up his shorts and runs down the dune waving them about. "Come on try and catch me."

Still holding his hands over his groin Jack sit ups. Daphne who has said nothing is looking at him as if a little embarrassed to see him in such a plight. Gladys, who hasn't taken part in stripping him runs down the slope, grabs his shorts from Elaine's hands and brings them back and hands them to Jack, who now so utterly humiliated and red in the face can't bear to look at her. The girls run down to the beach giggling and laughing with the dog which hasn't played any part in the affair, runs before them. It isn't just the sharp pangs of pain of sand in his eyes, or the dry sand in his mouth that hurt as much as the intense shame of being stripped naked and jeered at by those girls. Their ribald laughter still echoes in his ears. He would go in to hiding now and keep well aware from those horrible vixens.

With tears rolling down his checks, his eyes smarting and sand in his hair Jack takes a long route home to avoid meeting anyone. His progress is slow and uncertain. Once or twice, half blinded by the sand in his eyes, he stumbles and falls on all fours and doesn't see the low branch of a pine tree which swishes across his face as he leaves the shelter of the trees.

He avoids the road entrance to the bach and plunges back among the pines again and comes home by the back of the section.

He opens the back door and is confronted by Aunt Kate who must have seen him coming round the back. She stands in the open doorway her arms folded, a towering figure of disapproval.

"What's this?" she demands. "Since when has our front door not good enough for you. And just look at you boy, your hair full of sand and your face just look at it. Tears. I'll give you tears boy if you try to enter my home looking like that. Been fighting is it and come off worst I suspect."

She takes him by the shoulders and shakes him. Sand falls from his shirt and hair. She jostles his head with her hands. "Look at that, Boy. Have you been buried in sand? I won't put it passed you. You, silly boy. Don't you know you could be suffocated by sand? Get out of those clothes and to the bathroom with you."

The possibility of being naked again out in the open and in front of his aunt is too much. He tries to break away from her clutches, but the more he struggles, the firmer her grip on his shirt. His resistance broken he collapses against her.

"Have it your way. Get along to the bathroom and run a bath now." She propels him through the back door with a push that sends him tumbling through the kitchen towards the bathroom.

The lukewarm water is soothing, and he relaxes lying half submerged. Most of the sand is out of his eyes and mouth, but not his hair. He hates washing his hair. The door flung open, and Aunt enters. His attempt to cover his genitals fails when she pushes his hand away and pulls him to a sitting position in the bath.

"Put your head down," she demands and putting her hand behind his neck she pushes his head under water and starts to scrub his hair with a face cloth. Spluttering, struggling and screaming Jack fights for his breathe.

"Stop that bloody noise. Anyone would think your dying."

She doesn't leave the bathroom until she is satisfied that not a grain of sand remains in his hair.

He lies on his back, recovering from the ordeal he'd felt he'd undergone, but finding the coarse grains of sand now on the bottom of the bath are too uncomfortable to stay any longer, he climbs out of the bath and grabs the towel to dry himself. He expects that any moment she will return and take over the drying of not only his hair but his whole body, but she has finished with him and leaves him to care for himself.

The tears of shame splash on Jack's hand as he sits on the edge of his bed, the dreadful feeling of anguish of desertion and loneliness weigh heavily on him. This isn't the first time he'd felt so low, and it probably wouldn't be the last time either. Jack knows he would do what he had always done when this happened. He would withdraw to his own world where he can control things and use his imagination.

There must be more to life than what he has experienced in his short life so far. Other kids seem different from him. They laugh a lot and have fun which he longs for, but there is little to enthuse him so far. They make friends easily and play together, which even though he tries hard to emulate them, he finds it difficult. The ones he knows have toys and they don't understand why he has nothing to contribute in their games. It has never occurred to him that he is different in that way.

In the past at Christmas his mother had put a stocking on the end of his bed and filled it with an orange, a bar of chocolate and a bag of boiled and paper lollies. Once there was a half crown in the stocking which his uncle Ernie and given him. There were never any toys, except on one occasion when he was five, he remembers his father brought home a toy bakers van which was painted a bright red. He'd taken it out to play and some older kids had taken it from him. He never saw it again.

Because his father was in and out of work, they moved from one place to another, and he was never in one school long enough to form friendships. Then two years ago, when he was eight, he had found happiness for the first time that he could remember. That year before his mother had gone to the Sanatorium for the first time, they had both come to stay with Aunty Kate. There were plenty of other kids about his age in the camp who included him in their games. What fun, what excitement, the days were hardly long enough. His aunty had tried to keep him home on some days because she said he was over excited and noisy in the house and disturbed his mother who needed to rest. Really, she was pleased to see the last of him and let him out to play.

They played cops and robbers, cowboys, and Indians in the pine forests, making forts, finding sticks they used as guns, some long like rifles, others bent at one end like a pistol. That's all they needed. Their imagination did the rest and each of them had their favourite stick for a gun. If you were shot, you had to fall down and count to ten before you could return to the game. All day they played chasing each other among the pines, over the sand dunes and along the beach where they galloped on their horses of long sticks of broom which they held between their legs as they ran. There were days when he didn't return to the bach until after dark. Even the tellings-off and the threat that no tea would be kept for him didn't deter him. Aunty and Mother relented thankful, probably, that he wasn't under their feet during the day. The memories of those memorable days would be with him for ever.

This year is different. It is too early for the campers and he had thought he had found a true friend in Daphne until today. The shame of what happened to him today lies heavy on him and he sheds a few more tears. If there is no one to play with him he would make up his own fun, which he has always done when he was alone.

He has his underground hut and in it his prize possession, the rifle from two years ago.

John Bell's father had made the rifle for John and when he left, he gave it to Jack to look after. Its stock is cut from a piece of an apple box and the barrel is a piece of conduit pipe. He keeps it wrapped in an old tea towel and every day he unwraps it, wipes it with the tea towel, wraps it up again and puts it back in the hut. The Bells shifted to the North Island so it is unlikely that John would be back to claim the gun.

In a clearing in the pine forest Jack has a playground of his own. The clearing is mainly sand with a few large clumps of grass here and there. One side of the clearing a stand of elderberries and lupins grow. These provide all Jack needs to use his imagination to turn the place in to a war zone. The ripe berries of the elderberry are his army, and he picks them to defend his islands of clumps of grass. The end three leaves of the elderberry branches when picked form a swept back winged aeroplane. The enemy is the lupin flowers which try to invade the small islands formed by the grass by landing there from boats Jack makes out of hollowed flax to form a catamaran. His soldiers of berries together with air support from his aeroplanes resist the enemy. When the campaign is over, he takes his gun from the hut and hunts wild beasts and Indians in the forest. There are favourite trees that are his tram, lorry, or train according to their shape. In them, in his imagination, he travels many miles, sometimes to far off lands. Here he is alone and can't be spied on by anyone else. This is his world, and he doesn't really need anyone else, he likes to tell himself.

Nothing much changes here. At nearly eleven Jack is too young to be sensitive to the change in growth around him, the growth of tall weeds in, what had been for months, bare paddocks, the flowering of the cabbage trees, the mist storms of pollen from the pines and dying of the spring flowers in the village. He is tiring of playing his imaginary games of cops and robbers, stalking dangerous game in the alpine forest and his imaginary wars. The lupins still provide him with flowers and the elderberry trees with ripe berries for his soldiers, but his enthusiasm has dimmed for such games.

Now schools have closed for the summer holidays there are more kids about, but they ignore him. Some were too young for him to have anything to with anyhow and others who were older ignored him. Now the water is warmer he spends more time in the sea and on the beach. Sometimes he is the only one in the water, or on the beach. He leans over the railings on the bridge over the stream flowing from the lagoon watching the cars, vans and caravans that come to the village. There are more cars parked in front or in the driveways of the holiday homes and the camping ground was beginning to fill. Tents are going up and high hessian fences were erected enclosing two or three tents. Camping ground status was being established with those who had been camping in the same spot for years erecting their walls to preclude others of a lower rating. Caravans cluster close together as if for protection from the tent people. The smell of burning wood and charcoal BBQs pervades and their smoke drifts in the still air of the late afternoon.

A small group of children are hanging around the shop eating ice cream. Among them Jack recognises Daphne and her friend Elaine. Jack crosses the bridge to his side of the village, hoping they haven't seen him. Since that fateful afternoon in the sand dunes, he has kept his distance from those two girls. He could still hear their mocking laugher and certainly didn't want to hear it again in front of the other kids. He had no doubt that Elaine would have told the newcomers about his disgrace although he liked to think that Daphne would have held her tongue. Now there were many kids around he feels even more isolated than before.

When Jack wakes on Monday morning he is surprised to see his uncle's Riley Kestrel still parked outside. Uncle usually left for work early in the morning before Jack was out of bed. He must be ill or something for this had never happened before. At breakfast Aunty Kate was dressed in her best clothes and Uncle had his best suit on and is wearing a white shirt and tie. He had never worn his best suit to work before. They look so serious and there is little talk at the table. They must be going somewhere important probably in town and Jack thinks this was an opportunity for him to ask if he can come with them too.

"Can I come with you? I can change into my school clothes in a jiffy. Can I go and see Mother today? I'd like that. You could drop me off at the Sanatorium and I could sit on the grass outside her window and wave to her and she would smile at me and wave back and you can come back later and pick me up. Can we have lunch at Collin's Quick Lunch place?"

Aunty gets up from the table and clears her voice before she goes to the kitchen. Uncle doesn't look up, his spoon full of porridge held in his hand before his mouth as if he has suddenly frozen and can't move it any further.

41

"Can I?" Jack's tone hopeful, but uncertain.

Uncle lowers his spoon and not looking directly at Jack for a moment or two replies, "Not today Jack I'm afraid. Your aunty and I have some important business to attend to in town today."

"But you could let me off in town by the Museum. I could stay there until you have finished your business and we could have some afternoon tea in the cafe, Uncle."

Aunty Kate come back. She is wearing her hat; gloves and her handbag is hung over one arm.

"Don't bother your Uncle boy. You heard what he said. We must leave immediately. We can't wait for you to change. Wash the dishes and clean the ashes from the fireplace and make your bed. Don't forget to get the milk from the farm. I'll expect all that to be done before we return. Mark my words. There's bread in the bin. Get yourself some lunch and don't use too much butter on your bread."

Uncle has left the room and returns wearing his hat. He doesn't look at Jack as he leaves the house.

Jack stands at the open front door and watches as the car moves off and crosses the bridge before taking the road out to the main North Road towards Christchurch. He is miserable and lonely and neglected by everyone. Even Nathan avoids him. Why were Aunty and Uncle all dressed up like that and why were they so serious and didn't want to look at him at the breakfast table. Did he have some dreadful disease or something like a rash on his face. He goes to the bathroom and looks in the mirror. No, it isn't anything like that, but why is everyone avoiding him.

Jack's spirits rise a little when Jill, the farmer's dog comes running up the track to him his tail wagging and he jumps up almost knocking the billy out of Jack's hand. He pats the dog and breaks into a run with Jill running after him jumping up and barking. The morning which had been so gloomy and threatening has suddenly become brighter. There is nothing like a friendly dog to brighten his mood. There is no one at the dairy shed, nor can he see anyone in the paddocks beyond. The milking shed is empty for the morning milking would have been finished long ago. The farmer, Tom Fielding, is usually about at this time of the day to fill the billies of the campers who also come for milk.

He knocks on the door of the farmhouse hoping that Tom Fielding might be in. The door opens slightly and then more fully to reveal the portly body of a small, old woman. She looks at Jack her eyes blinking and her mouth opening and shutting without saying a word. She looks Jack up and down and then waves her arm and points to the hay shed behind the milking shed and then she closes the door.

Tom had seen Jack and comes over to him. "Late this morning old fellow," he says. "There's been a run on the milk this morning what with all those campers setting up at the camp ground. They don't half want milk by the gallon I'd reckon, but not to worry young man, I saved some for me regulars."

His uncle and aunty return in the late afternoon. They've bought fish and chips with them and they sit outside by the back door in the last of the day's sun with their parcels of fish and chips on their knees. They eat in silence until Jack, unable to remain quiet any longer, asks if they had done what they had set out to do that day. The two adults look at each other, and nod. "Yes," says Uncle. "We did what we had to do, Son."

They crunch their empty fish and chip papers in their hands and Aunty puts them in the fireplace. Uncle sits with his head bent forward, as if studying the ground at his feet.

"I think I'll go for a walk," he says. "On my own if you don't mind."

There are times when we are sensitive to changes of atmosphere about us, perhaps over sensitive, in our reaction to someone whom we know. This is more likely to occur, when there is tension in relationships, felt more keenly by adults, but becomes apparent to children as well. And Jack feels there is a change in how his aunty is treating him now. She speaks more kindly to him, scolds him less and is more tolerant, rarely telling him off for being late or not bringing enough wood for the fire. This change perplexes him, and he is uncomfortable in her presence. He doesn't know how to react and instead of feeling pleased he is miserable at times.

Gifts were something he never expects to receive having had very few in his life even at Christmas time and never for his birthday. Now Uncle promises to bring him a special gift at the end of the week and it isn't even Christmas. This is something he didn't expect even in his wildest dream and he can't bring himself to believe that it would be true. They had never mentioned buying him a present before. Why now he wonders is his uncle and aunt promising to give him a present. He'd had promises before from his mother and his aunt if he behaved himself, but those promises came to nothing even after he had made special efforts not to offend them in any way. Promises were rubbish, worth nothing and he didn't believe in them. Still, he waits with a feeling of excitement for his uncle to return from work on Friday. In spite of his disbelief in promises he waits impatiently by the bridge for his uncle's car two hours before he usually arrives. He sits against the trunk of the tree for what seemed to him hours. When a car he hears arriving at the township he jumps to his feet and runs to the bridge only to find that it isn't his uncle's car. He tells himself he mustn't get carried away and get too excited. It is after all a sham and he is wasting his time sitting around. He'd be better off going to his kingdom in the Pine Forest and hunt wild beasts than kidding himself that his uncle would really bring him a gift. Then there were the times when he noticed both Uncle and Aunty looking at him as if they pitied him, or something. He doesn't know why but he is aware of their looks. When he looks closely at them, they smile and look away. It is so uncomfortable. Why this sudden change? Is there something wrong with him which they are not going to tell him?

He hears Uncle's car long before it crosses the bridge. His heart is beating faster and his excitement mounts when the car pulls up outside the bach. He starts to run towards it before Uncle gets out and then he slows to a casual saunter to give the impression he isn't excited. Uncle gets out of the car and slams the door shut as he always did. He has nothing in his hands and Jack's heart sinks. He kicks the shingle on the road as he approaches and turns away and go to the beach until Uncle calls to him.

"There you are Jack. Be as good to fetch those things I left in the car and bring them up to the bach. That's a good boy."

Jack takes the two parcels he finds on the back seat and follows his uncle to the front door and hands them to his uncle.

"Nearly forgot. That would never do. Your aunt asked me to bring home some things from the grocer for tea tonight," he said. He sees the downcast expression on Jack's face and relents.

"Oh, by the way that parcel wrapped in brown paper is for you Jack. Put it on the table and we'll unwrap it and have a look inside."

Aunty Kate had cleared the table for Jack, and she stands beside him as he undoes the string and unwraps the paper. Inside is a long box with a coloured picture of a glider. Jack cannot believe his eyes. "A glider, a real glider," he exclaims. "Is this really for me?"

"That's it, Jack. Let's look inside, and I will help you assemble it before tea tonight," says Uncle as he ruffles Jack's hair.

It hasn't occurred to Jack that Aunty has cleared the table and delayed the meal, so that he and his uncle can spread the plans for building the glider on the table, and then carefully unpack the balsa wood framing, and put it on top of the plan in the appropriate place. Jack is so excited that Uncle has to ask him to take deep breaths and take care in assembling the plane. It is Uncle's skilled and steady fingers that assembled the body of the glider and lay out the frame for the wings. Together, they glue the pieces of balsa wood frames together and attach the propeller with the hook on one end to attach the thick rubber band that when wound up would help the glider to fly. Then came the thin tissue paper to cover the assembled frame and wings. With the wheels attached and the tail in place the glider, or plane which it really was, is ready to fly in no time. There it stands fully assembled on its wheels on the table for Aunty to admire. She doesn't show much enthusiasm, merely nods when he asks what she thought of it.

"Now, clear the table of all that rubbish and let me put the meal on the table before it gets cold," she says.

"But Aunt just one flight before it gets too dark." Jack looks at his uncle for support.

She regards this little boy with his wide-eyed expression and feels some compassion towards him. How could she not be moved? "All right one flight only, and then straight back here." Jack and his uncle take the glider to the grassed space by the lagoon. Jack winds the rubber band, until it will not go any tighter, and holding the glider above his shoulder and with some trepidation, he throws it up in front of him. For a moment, it looks as if it will nosedive and crash on the ground, then it lifts and with the propeller turning, it flies higher before it slowly glides down to land on its wheels, where Uncle Ernie stands.

"Test flight, OK."

"Just one more flight." Jack full of excitement dances in front of his uncle.

Ernie smiles. He'd never seen the child like this before, excited his face wreathed in smiles.

This wasn't the unsmiling, surly, little brat that he has known. Marvellous! What a gift will do.

Changes a kid as fast as you can say, 'Jack Robinson.'

"One more flight than, and that is it," he says. "You know what we promised your aunt. Tea's on the table. By the way, I wouldn't be too keen to fly the plane over on the playground. Too many kids around, and it might get damaged. Unless of course, you have that girl I've seen you with to help you. By the look of her, she can stand up to any of the kids around here, but I'm not so sure about that brother of hers."

After tea, Jack reverently puts the glider on the sideboard to admire it.

"It can't stay there," his aunt says. "Keep it in your room."

And that's what Jack did, putting it on the chest of drawers in his room, where he can see it from his bed. When he wakes in the morning, much earlier than usual, he can't believe it is still there looking so splendid. It wasn't a dream after all.

On future flights, although they were carefully planned when there were few other kids about, Jack can't help showing his glider off to the others. They follow him, whenever he takes his glider to fly either on the playing field, or on the beach, running to retrieve it only to find that Jack has followed the flight, and gets there first. No one else has a glider to fly, and some of the kids want to have a try to fly Jack's. If it hadn't been for Daphne, who must have seen what was going on, appearing as if from nowhere, and positioning herself where she thinks the glider will land, it might well have been broken by over eager kids wishing to fly it. She brings the glider back to Jack and hands it over without saying a word.

"Thanks," says Jack feeling a little shamefaced. "Where's that Elaine? Is she still with you?"

"Na, she's gone home. We didn't get on, after all. Sorry about what we did to you."

"That's nothing, forget it." Jack lies. "Would you like to help me fly my glider?"

She holds her head to one side, and regards him, as if trying to assess if he really means it. "I'll think about it," she replies. "If I'm not doing anything else. and I see you around I might come out to help if you like."

After tea, on Sunday night Uncle Ernie lies on the couch exhausted after helping Jack fly the glider on the beach. Aunty Kate is clearing the table when Jack announces that he would like to fly his glider up on the hills.

"I would like to show it to Mother and show her how it flies." Uncle sits up suddenly, and Aunty stops what she is doing. Jack is aware of the awkward tension in the room. The two adults exchange looks, and Uncle clears his voice.

"Afraid that's not possible any longer, Son." The chill blandness of his look alarms Jack.

Aunty Kate leaves the room not wanting to be part of what was to follow.

"Why? Mother would like to see my glider."

Uncle Ernie looks away and shifts his position on the couch.

"Well, it's like this Jack. I've been meaning to tell you earlier, but what with being busy at work, and the glider and all that I just haven't got around to it, but I'm sorry to say your mother died a little while back." His voice dropped to a whisper and he lowered his head to his chest. "Died. She can't have died Uncle. She's in the Sanatorium. I saw her there last time we went. She looked just the same then and spoke to me. How could she have died."

The realisation of what Uncle had said strikes Jack, and his voice dies away. Tears roll down his face, and his lips start to tremble, as he tries not to cry.

"Is it really true then?" he whispers.

Uncle Ernie leaves the couch and puts his arm around Jack's shoulder.

"I'm afraid it is, Son. Your aunt and I went to her funeral. She said before she died that she loved you Jack and knew you would take it like a man." Jack nestles his head on his uncle's shoulder and weeps.

"Did they put her in a box and bury her then?"

"There, there old Son. We can go to the cemetery, and you can fly the glider over her grave.

She would like that, I'm sure. Let's do it next weekend."

A week later, there is an air of ominous silence in the house when Jack comes home in the afternoon. What it is, or why he should be aware of it, worries him. Things were changing here, and he is more aware of tensions and long silences between his aunty and uncle.

He has come home late before, when Aunty has not been in, but somehow this was different. When he calls his aunt's name there is no reply. Her hat and coat are not hanging where they always hang behind the door in her bedroom. He hesitates before he enters her bedroom, feeling guilty for trespassing in her sanctum. She had made it clear to him that under no circumstances was he to enter her bedroom when she was not there. He tiptoes into the room looking about him, half expecting her to come out of the wardrobe, or from behind the door and grab him. He gingerly opens the wardrobe door, and kneeling he pushes aside the hems of her dresses hanging there and feels for her purse which he knew she kept on the floor behind them. It has gone. He closes the door of the wardrobe taking care not to make too much noise and with pounding heart he leaves the room. Someone is knocking on the front door. His thoughts race: It can't be Aunty. She would never knock. She would come straight in and biff him a blow that would crush him and call him a sneaky thief. Whoever it is must have seen him in the bedroom and caught him in the act. He rushes to the back door, opens it quietly, and before he can move the bulky body of Mrs McGregor from next door, bars his way.

"Wow there, young man. What's your hurry? Your aunt asked me to look for you. A car came and took her away. Your uncle has had an accident and is in hospital."

"Is he badly hurt? Can I go and see him?"

"How would I know. I know no more than you do now, and as for going to see him, we'll just have to wait."

"When will Aunt be back?"

"You and your questions young fella. I'm no quiz master. All I know is that you can come over for tea if you like."

Jack had learnt to be suspicious of anyone who tried to show him some kindness, for it never came to much.

"No thanks, Mrs McGregor. Aunt has left me some tea in the cupboard."

"Are you sure, but suit yourself. If your aunt isn't back by dark, come over and I'll fix you up somewhere to sleep for the night."

He sits by the front window watching the light of day slip away across the lagoon, until he can no longer determine the tall bulrushes that grow on its margin, or the clear definition of the two tall trees beyond it, and the paddock behind that has become a blur. The fear of darkness, and what might lurk there under its dark cover, and could be creeping up to the bach this very minute, strikes even a greater fear in him. He's never had to worry about being on his own in the bach before. Aunty was always there in another room, for even though, she was not much company and growled a lot, her physical presence was a comfort. He pulls the curtains across the windows, switches on all the lights and closes the door bolts on both outside doors. Nothing can get in now, not even ghosts. They could not stand the light, if he keeps the lights on all night. Anyhow his mother is a ghost now and she will see that no harm will come to him. He isn't hungry, and as there is no prepared tea for him, he eats a slice of bread and syrup and an apple. He curls up in a chair in the sitting room with a rug around him, and after listening intently for any noise outside, he relaxes. The night outside is still, no breeze rattles the loose fence plank outside or moans in the tall pines near the batch. He must have fallen asleep, for he wakes with a start. He gets up and pulls back the corner of a curtain and looks outside. The shadows of the night are creeping away and a grey pre-dawn light takes their place on the dunes and the road outside. He switches off the lights, tidies up the rug and the chair he's been sleeping in, and brushes away any crumbs on the table and the floor from his night's supper. It would never do for Aunty to come back and find all the lights still on and the place in a mess.

Aunty Kate doesn't come back to Waireka until the late afternoon. She comes in without saying anything and plonks herself in the chair by the fireplace. She looks dishevelled with her hat having fallen to one side, her coat is undone, and her face red, with the effort of having to walk from the main road.

"Don't just stand there boy, put the kettle on. Make yourself useful for once. Get a move on."

Even after drinking her tea and returning her cup to the saucer she offers no information about Uncle's accident. "What are you staring at?" she says. "The cat got your tongue."

Jack plucks up courage to ask, "Is Uncle Ernie alright?"

"What do you think Boy. How would you be if a car ran over you. Eh, think of that."

Obviously, Aunty is in no mood to say anything more. She gets up, and after going to the bathroom and the toilet, she goes to the kitchen and starts opening the cupboards.

"Eaten us out of house and home have you, while I was away. Not a bean left in the cupboard. Here take this ten-shilling note and buy two pies from the shop. Go on get going."

When he returns with the pies, Mrs Gregor is with his aunty in the sitting room. He places the pies on the bench in the kitchen and is about to go the sitting room when he hears his aunt say.

"Of course, he was drunk. The driver of the car probably was too. He was crossing the road outside the Grosvenor pub, too drunk for his own good. He and his partner in the Denture business had been imbibing for goodness knows how long. He's in a bad way, crushed chest, ribs broken, and lung collapsed. Poor bugger what a fix he's put us in now. Don't say a word to the boy. The less he knows the better."

Jack counts to twenty before he enters the room.

Christmas has come and gone before Uncle Ernie is allowed to come home. The ambulance that brings him causes a stir in the village with the kids hanging around to see what is happening. Jack feels important, as he stands with his aunt, and watches the ambulance men bring Uncle in on a stretcher. They carry him to his room and put him on the bed. He grimaces in pain, as they make him as comfortable as possible. To Jack he seems to have shrunk, his face gaunt and his eyes lacking their usual spark of good humour that Jack remembers.

"Well, old chap! There's a lot to do. But you should see the car that knocked me down. It's all in pieces and will never go again. Nothing kicks me about and gets away with it. I'll soon repair, but in the meantime, old chap you will have to help as much as you can about the place. Aunty Kate's going to need your help lad," he says.

The District Nurse came once a week for the next two weeks, and with the help of Mrs McGregor and Aunty, they tried to carry Uncle to the bathroom, but after strenuous attempts gave up, and gave him a bed bath instead. Jack did all he could to help by keeping the fire wood up for cooking, going to the shop with a list of groceries that Aunty made out for him to buy, and offering to hang the clothes, which wasn't accepted by Aunty, who scolded him for dropping a sheet to the ground when he tried to hang it on the line outside, Aunty was finding the effort of caring for Uncle too much, and she often threw herself down in her chair after tea in the evenings and was asleep in no time. Her manner towards Jack mellows, as if the effort to tell him off for anything he tries to do is too much effort for her now. This change of habit towards him confuses Jack and makes him feel uneasy. Uncle tries to appear in good humour by telling jokes that somehow didn't sound funny any longer. Then a few days later a stranger knocks on the door of the bach and introduces himself to Aunty.

"Hello there. I hear that your husband has been in a bad accident and that you are now home nursing him," he says.

Aunty regards him with suspicion, her eyes half closed her mouth clamped firmly and her hands on her hips. "That's so." she replies.

"Well now. You won't know me and I've never met your husband, but I'm willing to help in any way I can. By the way, the name is Len Hales, let's say the Good Samaritan. I could help to carry him to the bathroom and toilet."

Aunty relaxes, drops her hands from her hip and smiles. "That's very kind of you, Mr Hales."

"Let's say three times a week and see how it goes then. No charge you understand, although a cup of tea wouldn't go amiss. I'll see you on Monday. I'll be on my way now." Intrigued Jack follows him to his car.

"That's a Riley Kestrel. isn't it?" he asks. "like the one that Uncle Ernie drives and it's the same colour too."

The man pats him on his head and smiles, "Is it? Now that's a coincidence." He climbs in the car and waives his hand out of the window, as he drives away.

He calls three times a week for the next three weeks, always at the same time in the Riley Kestrel and always dressed in the same dark suit, white shirt, tie, and highly polished black shoes that shone so much that their reflection blinds Jack, if he looks at them for too long.

It is Jack's responsibility to fill the bath and have it at the right temperature that Mr Len Hales requires. Len lifts Uncle in his arms and carries him to the bathroom and bathes him.

Jack doesn't know what to make of a stranger being with his uncle in the bathroom. He stays close to the closed door and listens to the two men talking in soft voices. Len does most of the talking and there are long lapses during the conversation. When he hears Aunty Kate coming, he slinks away undetected to his own room nearby.

Len carries Uncle back to his bed and helps to dress him with Aunty standing by. Jack can see from his room what is happening in Uncle's room.

When Uncle is fully dressed, she sits on a chair beside Len by Uncle's bed and they join hands while Len offers up a prayer. Len finishes the session by putting his hand on Uncle's forehead and holding it there while he whispers something in Uncle's ear. Then they all say 'amen' and Aunty brings in a tray of cups and sauces, teapot, milk jug and a plate of newly baked scones. Jack begins to wonder if all this is because Uncle is going to die like his mother, and they are praying for his soul.

Visits to the beach, the river, and his underground hut in the woods are less frequent now because Aunty wants him to stay close to the bach. He sees Daphne now and then at the beach, and together with Nathan they swim and play in the sand hills or climb the tall pines growing nearby. She never once mentions anything about his shame or even hints that she has not forgotten that fateful day.

Nathan sort of tags along with them, taking part at times in their games and at other times going off on his own which makes Daphne anxious for his safety, and she would leave Jack and look for Nathan among the dunes. Things aren't the same any longer. Jack has the impression that Daphne goes along with him because she had nothing better to do. She is half hearted about wanting to do what Jack suggests they do, and Nathan, well he is even more of a nuisance than before, wandering off by himself and then when found, being moody and difficult to understand. Then there is Uncle's accident and Len Hales visits which are longer than before. Uncle is different, not as friendly as he used to be, rarely smiling and he seems to be under Len Hale's spell. Even Aunty has changed and Jack, who is used to things as they were before, is confused and uncertain how to take these changes.

Whenever he can, he'd sneak out to the Pine Forest and go to his underground hut.

This is his hut, and his alone, for he hasn't told anyone about its existence, not even Daphne.

When he returns home, he is surprised to see Uncle fully dressed sitting in a deck chair at the back of the bach. Len is kneeling beside him holding his hand and whispering something to him, and every now and then Uncle and Aunty who is standing behind him says 'amen'. When Jack appears, Len lets go of Uncle's hand and gets to his feet.

"Jack, your aunty tells me you have been a good Christian and helped in the house. Now we can all rejoice, for your uncle is now well enough by the grace of the Lord to come to church. Your uncle and aunty have seen the true way, and now we must not lose this way, but follow the true path to redemption to see the light. I will be here next Sunday with the car and take you all to our church."

He smiles and pulls Jack to him and tries to hug him. Jack, who has no experience of being hugged before, pulls away, but the more he resists, the firmer Len holds him.

"And think of this Jack. Your aunty is to take you to town to buy new clothes for you, new shoes, pants and jersey. Think of that and praise the Lord, for he will hold you tight on the road to redemption if you will let him."

From then on, Len calls for them every Sunday morning to take them to church where they hear long sermons on degradation and redemption. Jack is finding it more and more difficult to sit still. He is bored with having to sit on a hard chair in the church, although it isn't really a church with pews, a tower, and a pulpit, but a small hall in the countryside with uncomfortable chairs and a platform for the preacher. He'd never had to sit still for so long with nothing to do but look out of the window on to a rusty corrugated iron fence, and the tall thistles that grew beside it. When he wriggled or shifted his feet to get more comfortable his aunt would dig him in the ribs and glare at him. He tries to sit still, but he can't stop wriggling.

"Stop fidgeting." Aunty said as she slaps him on his leg. Then when he thinks he can no longer stand it his boredom is relieved by at long last by the preacher leaving the platform and walking down the aisle to talk to some of the parishioners.

What he says Jack doesn't hear but he notices that those who he has spoken to drop their heads as if in submission. There is a hush in the church with the only sound is the preacher's whispering and his shuffled footsteps. He goes to the church door and opens it and stands there with his arms outstretched. "Rejoice," he says, and the congregation leave their seats and follow him outside.

Jack's eyes light up when he sees the long tables of sandwiches, cakes, and jugs of soft drink. He tries to push through the throng of parishioners who have blocked his way. His aunty holds him back. "Don't be greedy. That food is for those who deserve it. Not for people who wriggle and don't listen to the preacher's wise words of praise," she says.

"Children to the far end of the table if you please," says the preacher and Jack needs no further bidding. He knows he has to move quickly, if he is to get as much as a sandwich, and a piece of cake.

The people start to drift away to their cars or sit on the seats outside to chatter to each other. There is to be another service soon after lunch. Some of the people have left, and a few others are arriving. Any hope Jack had of Len joining those leaving are dashed when Len helps Uncle back inside the church. It was as if the interminable afternoon will never end for Jack, who is even more restless than before during the service.

"If you can't sit still, we will leave you behind on Sundays and then what will become of you. The Devil's fodder no doubt," says Aunty in a tone of voice that Jack recognises is meant to frighten him, but he can really rejoice if she really means he will be left at home on Sundays.

Two Sundays later, there is some respite when Uncle says he is too tired and sore to go to evening church. Aunty is a little put out and tries to convince Uncle that it is for his own good that he should make the effort to attend, if he wants his health back. "It is for your redemption," she says. She leaves him in bad grace and accompanies Len in the evening, and Jack was asked to stay and look after Uncle's needs. Uncle lies on his bed, closes his eyes and falls asleep. Jack is about to tip toe out of the room when Uncle wakes and sits up with a start.

"There you are Boy. For a moment, I thought you had gone out. Glad to get out of evening church, I suspect. Don't worry once a day is more than enough for a boy of your age. You want to be active and that's only natural. You can't be active this afternoon though can you, what with me to look after."

All day squally showers have come in from the sea on a steady easterly wind.

"Here Boy! Look under my bed and you will find a box full of old 'Westerns' I used to read. Browse through them and pick out a few you would like to read. With your imagination, you will find yourself in the Wild West shooting it out with the best of them."

Jack can't believe his luck. Uncle always comes to his rescue. This is much better than listening to that old preacher groaning away, and the congregation trying to sing those musty old hymns. He feels so much more at home with the strong, salty smell of the sea and the pungent aroma from the broom and elderberry, than he could ever be with the dusty, damp smells in the church hall.

There are days during the week when he can take his glider further down the beach, away from the other kids, from the campground, and from the top of the highest sand hill, let it fly on to the beach. When he tires of this, he lies among the sand hills and watches the big black backed sea gulls gliding on up draughts, as they circle above him. How he wishes he could join them. His glider, which he has to admit isn't really a glider because it has a propeller, can't glide very far when the propeller stops turning.

A visit to his underground hut causes him concern. There are signs on the ground near where the entrance that someone, or something has been there recently. He scrapes the pine needles away from the piece of corrugated iron that covers the entrance and lifts it. Inside is dark and his eyes take a little while to adjust. The little table he'd made out of driftwood is still there, but it has been shifted to one side. There are scuff marks in the floor that hadn't been there before.

Suddenly, his hideaway is no longer safe. What if the intruder has been watching him enter and comes and closes the opening, trapping him inside? Panic overcomes him, as he turns to get out as quickly as he can. Then the thought occurred to him that the stranger with a heavy stick might be waiting for him to appear and hit him on his head. He takes a deep breath, raises his head above ground and looks about him. There is no one to be seen. Perhaps, he was being watched from behind one of the tree trunks nearby. He pulls himself out of the hut and replaces the piece of corrugated iron over the opening, and spreads pine needles and dirt over it. If anyone has been watching him, they didn't appear.

Another trap sprung and nothing in it. Bert is sure that someone is setting off his rabbit traps on purpose. Could be that Nathan lad. He'd heard him shrieking and making those strong noises in the forest a moment or two ago. No, he wouldn't be strong enough to set the trap off. Then again, it could be some nut, who hates to see God's creatures caught in a trap. Well below him. A trap is better than shooting the beast, what with bullets flying about the place and killing someone. He pushes aside the dried lupin that he had hid his last trap under, and there, success at last. He unsprung the trap, and taking the dead rabbit out, puts it in his knapsack, which he flung over his shoulder. A moment among the pine trees catches his attention. Someone, possibly the same person who had been sending his traps off. He hides behind the trunk of the nearest pine tree where he can't be seen by the intruder. Whoever it is, comes out in the open. He is stuffing his shirt tail in his trousers and doing up his belt. His jacket is on the ground beside him. When he lifts his head, Bert recognises him. It's that queer church fellow who has been going around the houses in the village offering help to the occupants and preaching to them about joining his church. He must have been caught short and done his business behind one of those trees. For Christ's sake why couldn't he use the perfectly good toilets in the playground. Or maybe, he is one of those nuts who like to sunbathe in the nude. He wouldn't put that pass him either. It's not the first time he'd seen this Len Hales fellow in the forest. He leaves his car outside the shop and walks over the bridge and enters the forest for long walks. He must have seen that Nathan in there sometimes, and probably scared the life out of him by the shrieks and noises that lad makes. He probably thinks that Len Hales is after him or something. Bert waits until Len has left the forest and is walking along the road towards the bridge before he returns to his place.

Bert Saunders slits the belly of the rabbit with his knife and lets its innards slip out to fall in the shallow hole he'd dug. He brushes away with his hand the flies from his face, wriggles his bottom on his stool and picks up his knife before making a cut around the rabbit's leg, just above the paws. Fascinated, Jack watches as Bert begins to skin the rabbit, which was once a fawn furry body, now metamorphosed to become a sleek, shiny one. He puts it on side and taking the skin he stretches it over a wire frame. Fascinated, Jack watches closely every move that Bert does.

"Waste nothing. Everything has its value. This skin, along with the other one I've got hanging on the fence will fetch a bob or two," he says. "And this rabbit what with an onion or two, some carrots, some gravy and a touch of cream enough for a banquet if you ask me."

Bert's short stubby fingers with long hairs growing on their tops works quickly and skilfully. The shirt sleeves unbuttoned flop about his wrist. He wears a blue faded pair of overalls over his thick tartan patterned shirt, and on his head a floppy Panama hat, the brim of which is rather tattered, with loose stands falling down over his eyes. Much of his high cheek boned face is covered in speckled stubble. His slight body crouches over, while he works his thin legs thrust out in front of him. In Jack's eyes he is a very old man, wise in his ways, and to be respected while others might regard him as a comic, sly figure and not as old as he makes out.

"How's your uncle coming on these days, Jack. I see he is getting about a little now and then. See you all go off with that chap, in what looks like your uncle's car every Sunday."

"We go to church. It helps Uncle get well." Len says.

"I suppose we all have our ways, but church isn't one of mine. That Len Hales joker came to my place the other day, offering to chop wood, or pick up anything I might need at the shop or in town. Then he starts preaching me. Not my sort. I wouldn't trust him at all. He's been going around all the houses I hear. See him talking the other day over the fence, talking to Tom Feilding."

"Mr Fielding and his old mother go to our church, and Mrs White and Mrs Collings go in the back seat of his car too," says Jack.

"Well, he must be having some success, I suppose. See those folks staying at 'The Willows' are still there. I wonder how long they will stay. Gone before the Summer is out, I'd say. See those two women a lot over this way now and then, walking, holding hands and chatting away. At least, the older one, that Mrs Golding, she does much of the chatter while the younger woman, Vera you say she is called, that long skinny one, she looks sad and is always sniffing. That Mrs Golding puts her arm around her and seems to be comforting her all the time. Maybe she has lost a close friend like a boyfriend or something. What do you think, Jack me lad?"

Jack shrugs his shoulders. "I don't know. Daphne thinks she is wet, and she doesn't like her. I've seen Daphne being cruel to her, making faces at her and following close behind her, mimicking her and laughing at her. Vera doesn't like it and she gets angry at times. Daphne says Vera is supposed to be looking after her and Nathan, but she doesn't like Nathan, and is cruel to him at times, just because he is a bit crazy sometimes."

"That Len Hales who drives your uncle's car. I see him now and then. He parks the car at the end of the road, or by the shop and goes on long walks in the pine plantation. Queer fellow if you ask me. And that Mr Golding, I've seen him get a bit cosy with that Vera at times. Come across them in the sand dunes. I wouldn't say he was comforting her. But there, Jack my boy, I shouldn't be saying all this to you, seeing you get on with that Daphne girl, but that family seem a strange one to me. Let's forget what I said, put it down to me being too crotchety and let's get on with a man's work, hunting and fishing and the like. That's all that matters when it comes to it, doesn't it? Here, you have a go at skinning this next rabbit."

Sunday morning. The low-lying fog of early morning is drifting away, leaving wet glistening grass paddocks and sparkling gorse hedges in the sun light. This was one Sunday morning that Jack looks forward to with excitement. It is his turn with John Straw to work the bellows for the organ. Since the congregation moved to the new premises in an old church in the countryside, a roster had been drawn up for the boys to work the bellows for Miss Wade to play the organ for the hymns in the service, and today for the first time was Jack's turn.

Instead of having to sit in the hard pews in the church, listening to the rantings of the preacher he and John Straw go to the side door where the bellows are kept, and on a signal from the preacher, they were to pump the bellows as hard as they could. John Straw was an older boy who is to be in charge of the operation. Above them, they hear the preacher's voice at times rising to a shout and then dropping to almost a whisper in an attempt to keep the congregation's attention. There would be some time before they will hear the preacher's thump on the floorboards above them, to alert them to start the bellows.

John Straw pulls a packet of cigarettes out of his pocket, withdraws one and lights it. He leans against the wall and puts it to his lips and draws in. Jack watches fascinated, as the smoke starts to fill the small room. They'll smell it up there," he says.

John smirks and holds the cigarette out offering it to Jack. "You're just a goody, goody kid, aren't you? Here have a puff."

Jack knows that if he is to be accepted by the bigger kids like John Shaw there is an initiation to go through and smoking was obviously one of the most important. He accepts the cigarette and is about to have a drag when they hear the unmistakable thump of the preacher's foot above them. John grabs the fag back and puts it between his lips.

"Come on pump." he says. The sound of the organ now full of air is deafening in the boy's narrow bellows room. John smokes as the boys pump the bellows as hard as they can unaware that the organ has stopped playing and there is the unmistakable shuffle of feet as the congregation leave their pews, followed by what sounds to the boys like a quick vacation of the church.

The door of the bellows room is flung open, and Len comes in waving his arms about to disperse the smoke in the bellows room.

"Get out boys the place is on fire," he shouts and then he sees the cigarette that John drops on the floor and tries to stamp it out under his foot.

"My God, you sinful devils. You will be punished for this. You have emptied the whole church and interrupted God's word. How dare you mock him like this." He grabs both boys by the arm and drags them outside where they face the silent and threatening faces of the congregation.

For the rest of the service the boys sit on the floor in front of the preacher who preaches about the sins of smoking and disobedience and the punishment that would follow. There is still a faint smell of smoke in the church. There is no hymn singing that morning.

On the way home in the car Len and Aunty ignore him until they reach home when Len says,

"Now Jack, you have disappointed us, and you must face judgement. John Straw is to get a hiding from his father and you too must get your just deserts. Your uncle in his state is unable to thrash you and I wouldn't ask your aunty to do it so I'll, on their behalf, carry out the punishment.

You will come back with me to my home now."

He clutches Jack's arm and pulls him to the car and pushes him in the front passenger seat. It's a glum and contrite Jack who says nothing all the way to Len's house. Jack meekly follows Len Hales to the bedroom at the back of the house and then suddenly makes a dash to the door in an effort to escape. But Len is too quick for him. He catches Jack before he gets as far as the door, pins him against the wall and then putting his hand under jack's chin he pushes his head back.

"Try to make a break for it would you. That will be an extra few lashes my lad for you," he says. He pushes Jack on his face on the bed, takes off his suit coat and places it on the chair beside the bed.

"Get up you sinner," he says. "And drop your pants and your underpants as well." Jack remains lying on the bed. He can't believe what he'd been told to do.

"Get them off boy or I'll do it for you."

Jack undoes his belt and the fly buttons on his shorts and lets his shorts fall on the ground, but he makes no effort to remove his under pants. The shame and the horror of being naked in front of Len and being whipped on his bare bottom over comes him. He grips his underpants and pulls them up as hard as he can.

It happens so quickly that he has no chance to protect himself. He is pushed on his face on the bed, his underpants wrenched from his grip and pulled off and then Len is on top of him, touching him on his bottom and groin with his big hands, his legs are pulled apart and the full weight of Len pins him to the bed as Len pumps up and down on him. An unbearable searing pain shoots up inside him making him cry out and scream. A hot, huge hand clamps over his mouth. He bites it as hard as he can and he tastes blood in his mouth. Len curses and rolls off him. Jack finds it difficult to breath with his face buried in the bed cover. He is too mesmerised to be able to move and will suffocate if he can't move his head. He is roughly pushed on his side by Len who is doing up his fly on his trousers. His face is flushed as he sucks his wrist where Jack had bitten him. He pulls Jack from the bed and bends him over the back of a chair and with his other hand he holds a cane in his hand which he brings down forcibly on Jack's bare bottom.

"You despicable little brat, I'll beat the devil out of you," he hisses between his teeth as he continues to beat Jack with the cane. As if red wheals were not enough to stop the beating, he waits until his last stroke draws blood on Jack's buttocks before he stops.

"Get dressed," he demands. "You are staying here with me tonight. You have brought shame enough without bringing more on your aunty."

Try as he might not to cry hot tears flow as Jack tries to pull his underpants and shorts up without them rubbing against the burning sensation on his back side. It was too painful to sit and walking was difficult without pain which he now feels not only across his buttocks, but deep inside between them as well. He collapses on his face on the bed and sobs.

Len doesn't come back to the bedroom although Jack hears him moving in the room next door. Jack closes his eyes and wishes sleep will come and relieve him of his pain, but it wouldn't come even when the room grew dark. How long he lay there he doesn't know, but it must have been for a long time for he finds he can move a little on the bed without the searing pain he'd had earlier. Using his hands, he pushes himself off the bed and walking stiffly and slowly he goes to the window and tries to force it up to open. Len hears the noise of the window opening as Jack tries to raise it. He comes in the room and pushes Jack away cuffing him on his ear as he shoves him on the bed. Jack cried out in pain.

Len leaves the room, returning later with a hammer and nails. Jack is hardly aware that Len is hammering nails in the window frame to lock it. Although in pain, which he feels no matter which way he lies on the bed, he must have passed out some time during the night and he doesn't waken until he opens his eyes to see Len leaning over him.

"Come on lazy boy," he said. "The sun's up long ago. Time to take you home."

Aunty Kate showed no sympathy for him when he returns. She thanks Len profusely and gives him a cup tea. They talk in low voices at the table out of Jack's hearing, glancing at him where he stands by the door. He leaves and forces himself to walk as best he can to Uncle's room, where he breaks out in tears. His uncle is surprised when Jack appears.

"Come on lad it can't be as bad as that. Wipe away those crocodile tears there's a good fellow. Hear you have been up to no good your aunty says. Emptied the church, put the fear of God into them no doubt." He chuckles and then tries to put on a stern face. "Smoking eh. Well what boy hasn't had a try at that. Hardly a sin in my book, but a definite one according to the church. Got a hiding on your back side by the looks of it. Finding it hard to sit. Must have been something of a bashing I'd say. No doubt deserved. We all have a cross to bear my boy. Looks like yours is on your bare backside."

Aunty Kate comes in the bathroom when Jack who has his back to her is in the bath. The red wheals across his bottom, some still oozing blood were plainly visible to her. She says nothing but backs out of the bathroom before Jack notices her.

During the week Aunty, although she doesn't ask him how he is feeling doesn't insist that he sits at the table to eat his dinner. At breakfast on Sunday Aunty asks him for the first time how he was feeling.

"I'm still sore Aunty and I can't sit for long. He hit me too hard and there are still red marks on my bottom." When he realised what he had said he expected a cuff across the ear for mentioning the word 'bottom', but Aunt although she reddens a bit does nothing.

"It will pass no doubt Boy. You can't misbehave and not expect punishment for your sins. But maybe you are slow to heal. How about taking a cushion to church to sit on today? Mind it is only for this once you hear me."

Jack feels a warmth towards his aunt. Maybe she does care for him a little after all. He keeps the cushion under his arm when he enters church hoping that it will not be noticed. He puts it down on his pew seat and is about to sit when he the cushion is pulled away.

"Can't have that. No cousins allowed in here," Jack winces when Len touches him on his shoulder.

"Aunty said I could use it."

"Nonsense you sneaked it in I saw you. Another sin Jack. You have much to answer for before you have redemption."

When Jack tells Uncle Ernie about the incident in church, he said that Aunty was just being kind, but she understood Len's action. If he allowed one cushion to be used in church, there could be many next Sunday and he couldn't allow that.

Over the next week members of the church called and brought cakes, a shepherd's pie, and flowers which they put in empty jam jars that Aunty kept in the kitchen cupboard.

On Sundays sitting on a pew in church was too painful for Jack no matter how he wriggled to make himself comfortable. Instead of sitting he kneeled on the floor and stayed there trying to ignore the stares from others.

The early morning sky still a washed out yellow grows brighter before the sun appears over the horizon out to sea. A few seagulls stalk along the beach pecking at anything that might have been washed up on the night's tide are the only signs of life on the dark sanded beach that stretches for ever towards the faint outline of the Port hills that defiantly jut out to sea.

It is under a lone pine tree nearer the river mouth that Jack finds Daphne and Nathan. They sit hunched up with their back towards him and don't notice him as he creeps up silently. It isn't until he gets close to them that he sees what they are doing. Nathan has caught a blow fly and has pulled off one of its wings. The two of them are watching it, as in an effort to fly, it is buzzing madly as it spins around on the sand at their feet. "What are you doing?"

Neither brother nor sister stop what they are doing.

"Disgusting isn't it," Daphne says. "He gets pleasure of doing this to flies and anything else he catches."

"You look as if you enjoy it though."

"Keeps him amused and out of my hair. What are you doing up so early anyhow?"

"It's church day and I thought I'd get out a bit before church."

"Er, church. Who wants to go to church?" She spits on the sand. "Only good goodies go to church."

"And those like me who are dragged along against our will. We don't have a say."

"Come on bunk it for once. Let's go bird nesting and get some more eggs to blow. I need more blackbird eggs for my collection."

The thrill of bird nesting, climbing the trees, watching for the skylark as it runs along the ground dragging one wing to give the impression that it can't fly because of a broken wing and then watching it fly almost vertically in the sky singing its shrill continuous song while he searches the ground nearby for the nest is for a moment is almost too much to ignore.

"Gosh I'd like that, but I daren't. Aunty would skin me alive."

"Cowardly custard. You always do what your aunty wants don't you."

"Don't you do the same for your mother."

"Mothers. You haven't got one, so you don't know what it's like to have a Mother."

Daphne pulls a face of disgust. "You don't know how lucky you have only got a fussy old Aunt. I hate my mother. She is all over Nathan. Spoils him proper. He can't do any wrong. She doesn't know that he is daft and a little mad. And she and that tart Vera, they get their heads together and whisper about Dad, poor old Dad who wouldn't hurt a fly. You can have my mother if you like."

"I'd like that. You can have my aunt and her church as well if you like."

'I'd rather run away. I hate adults, don't you?"

"I'll come too if you will have me, but I don't know where to go and I haven't any money."

"You are too scared, aren't you? Cowardly custard. Come on, let's do it now, this morning. Forget about your old church and break out." It was what Jack wants more than anything to be free of church and Len Hales. The fear and the shame of what Len has done to him weighs heavily on his mind, and if it hadn't been for Uncle's sake, he would have dearly loved to go with Daphne.

"Not this morning," he says meekly. "Another time though, I'll come."

Jack hates the look of disgust and contempt that he sees on Daphne's face. Then her expression changes, and she smiles.

"Alright then. Tomorrow we are going on a picnic. I'll ask Dad if you can come too," she said. "We can plan to run away from there. We are going to some place miles away down the beach. The farmer who owns the land said there was a track through his land that nearly reached the beach where no one else can go and that's what Dad wants is a place like that with no other people about."

"What about Vera and your mother, do they want to go?"

"Of course, Mother will go wherever Dad goes and as for that old tart, Vera, she can go and hang herself for all I care."

Jack hasn't got a wristwatch but he knows that the sun has been up for some time and he mustn't be late for church. He has to wash and change to his best clothes.

"See you," he says as leaves to go home. Before he reaches the village, he climbs the highest of the sand dunes that will give him a view of where the other two are still in the shade of the pine tree. They are still there but soon Daphne starts to walk away leaving Nathan behind. She hasn't gone far before she meets Vera coming the other way towards her. They are facing each other, Daphne with her hands on her hips shouting as if she is defying Vera who suddenly takes hold of Daphne's arm and starts to pull her towards her. Daphne struggles and kicks Vera's shin which makes her let go of her hold on Daphne. He hears Vera call her a little hussy and how dare she kick her like that. She threatens to tell Mr Golding about her. Daphne stamps her foot, throws back her head and in a loud voice calls out,

" See if I care. You don't own us," she yells out loudly as she runs away leaving Vera who by her stance is obviously very angry.

Jack is about to go on his way but hesitates when he sees Vera go over to Nathan who is still on his knees playing with a grasshopper after he'd pulled one of its legs off and is watching it trying to hop. The morning sea breeze that has sprung up carries away what she is saying although by her tone she is very angry. She grabs Nathan by the hair and pulls him to his feet. He writhes and screams when he is pushed flat on his face in the sand. Before he can recovery Vera plants her foot on his back and holds him down and then with her hand on the back of his neck, she holds his head down in the sand. His muffled screams alarm Jack. He races down the slope of the sand dune and runs towards them. By the time reaches them Vera has let go of her hold on Nathan who is coughing and spluttering and rubbing his eyes. Vera looks displeased to see Jack.

"Well, what do you want. He is a very disobedient boy and wouldn't come when I asked him to."

"But there was no need to push his face in the sand. He could have chocked."

"Nonsense. He did that to himself in defiance to me. You are a cheeky little devil and a bad influence on these children. You just keep away in future."

In the meantime, Nathan has got to his feet and starts to run towards Daphne who on hearing the racket returns and takes Nathan in her arms.

"How dare you hurt him," she shouts. "You're a cruel old hag and I hate you."

"Look who's talking. Don't think for a minute that I haven't seen you being nasty to him, pinching him and giving him Chinese burns and horrible things like that to him missy." Vera snaps.

By her aggressive posture Daphne is finding it hard to restrain herself from lunging at Vera and hitting her with all her strength. Jack steps between them, expecting at any moment to be struck by one or the other, or pushed aside a least, but the two antagonists hold their ground glaring at each other, their half open mouths showing their teeth, their noses wrinkled up and their cold stare of hatred in their half-closed eyes. Daphne breaks the silence between them.

"And I've seen you hit him before and be nasty to him. Anyhow he's my brother and we do things to each other, but I'll stand up for him when others outside our family hurt him and that includes you. You are so much older than us and you are supposed to be looking out for us. That's what Father pays you for and not to be nasty to us." When Daphne with her arm around Nathan leaves, Vera who makes no move to stop them as they turn their backs on her and move along the track towards 'The Willows'.

At church that day Jack's mind is full of what had happened in the morning. He was surprised that Daphne had stood up to Vera like that and had called her those names. He wonders what would come of it. He'd always thought that it was a happy family and how could it be otherwise with a mother like Mrs Golding. How he wishes she was his mother. Daphne was likely to be punished and the picnic might not happen. Even if it did Vera would make sure he wasn't invited. His thoughts are interrupted when the congregation stands, and Aunty drags him to his feet. He looks around bewildered. He hasn't heard a word of what the preacher had said. A hymn book is thrust in his hands and the organ starts playing. He mimics the words of the hymn as those around him sing with vigour. He finds himself shaking uncontrollably when Len stands by his pew and passes to him the blue cloth bag used for donations. He fumbles for the sixpence in his pocket that Aunty has given him to donate. It slips from his fingers and drops on the floor by Len's feet. His aunty digs him in the ribs and whispers for him to pick it up but somehow, he cannot do that. The sixpence has come to rest on its side against one of Len Hale's shoes. It looks so bright and shiny as if mocking him to retrieve it. He can't bear to pick it up it for fear of touching that large black shoe of his tormentor. He feels everyone's eyes on him and senses their displeasure, but he cannot control his shaking. When Len reaches out and touches him on his shoulder he cries out and ducking under his arm he runs down the aisle towards the door. One of the men in the congregation bar his way at the door. "You can't leave yet," he says.

"Toilet please, I must go." His desperate look was enough for the man to let him pass. Later after he'd been to the toilet Jack waited until Len Hales had moved back to his own pew before he returned to sit by his aunty.

As if nothing had happened with Vera on Sunday morning by the river before church Daphne meets Jack next morning and asks him if he still wants to go on the picnic her parents are having the following day. Her eyebrows rise in surprise when he asks if it really was still on after her argument with Vera.

"What that. That's nothing. She won't tell because she knows Mum would be upset about how she hurt Nathan and I won't say anything. That's the way things work in our family. Have a real blow up and let the wind blow the whole thing away and no hard feelings. Dad would be disappointed if the picnic didn't go ahead. Be ready and we will pick you up by the bridge. Bring your togs and a hat."

On the day of the picnic, the dark clouds on the horizon block the early morning sun worries Jack when he leaves the bach to walk to wait by the bridge for the Golding's motor car.

The morning bus to town hasn't left, nor has the morning commuters in their cars to work elsewhere. A cat walks casually, across the road by the community hall, stops halfway across, sniffs at something squashed on the middle of the road, a dead bird or a hedgehog that has been run over recently, regards Jack as he lounges against the bridge's railing and then crosses over to the other side of the road disappearing among the tall grasses at the roads edge. Jack picks up a stone and throws it in the direction where the cat has disappeared.

He smiles when the tall grasses are disturbed marking the cat's hasty retreat.

Jack becomes anxious when long after the bus and one by one the workers' cars have gone and there is still no sign of the Goldings. Have they already left? Daphne hadn't mentioned any time to wait for them, but surely no one would go on a picnic that early. Then, of course they are an unusual family, even if he has little knowledge of how other families work.

The Goldings might be eccentric, but not to the extent of going on a picnic before seven o'clock in the morning. It's more likely they have seen the dark clouds at the horizon and thought that the weather will be too bad for a picnic, and haven't bothered to let him know. A bright ray of sunshine suddenly lights up the water of the lagoon giving it a bright green colour which he has never seen before. Usually, it was too windy and the water too ruffled to be seen as only being a dark blue surface.

He picks up a stone and throws it across the water where it falls with a plop sound, sending circles on the surface from round the centre where it fell.

There is no mistaking the sound of the Golding's car when it starts up. The exhaust sounds deeper, more powerful, and more purposeful than any other car in the village. There it is on River Road coming towards him. They haven't gone without him after all. They are just late that is all. Felix Golding wearing his motor cap, his goggles and long leather gloves is at the wheel. Why he wears all that Jack doesn't understand for the Bugatti has a windscreen and the cabin is fully enclosed. Fiona Golding with her wide brimmed hat sits in the front passenger seat and between them Nathan sits on a cushion his feet curled up to avoid interfering with the gear lever. Jack climbs in the back seat and squeezes in between Daphne and Vera. Not a word is passed between them on the journey. Nor does anyone else speak above the noise of the engine and the roar of the car's tyres on the coarse tarmac. Occasionally there is a high-pitched yell from Nathan to which no one pays any attention.

Felix drives as if he is in a rally or a race, his foot hard down on the accelerator, passing other vehicles and only just avoiding head on crashes with approaching traffic. Then before Woodend village he slows and pulls in through a farm gate. The track through the farm is uneven causing the car to lurch from side to side alarmingly until Mrs Golding pleads with Felix to slow down. "You are having us airborne, one moment in our seats and the next our heads nearly through the roof," she admonishes him.

He either doesn't or chooses not to hear as the car's speed increases. The farmer comes out of a shed further along the track and watches them approach. Felix pulls up beside him and pushes down his window. The farmer's weather-beaten face appears in the open window. "You sure got some speed up along the track," he says." Some car I'd say. Ted Simons is the name and you must be Felix I take it," he speaks out of the corner of his almost closed mouth. He and Felix converse, shouting above the engine noise. Ted waves his hand along the track to another track that leads off the one they were on.

"The gate is open there," he says. "And go on towards 'The Willows' you see over there. Find a spot wherever you like. I usually keep the gate closed to stop the cows from wandering off to the lake beyond and on to the beach, but I've got them in the home paddock today."

Felix keeps the car in low gear for the rest of the journey avoiding the deep potholes in the track. They drive through between 'the willow's and find themselves beside a small lake. Beyond the lake there are a few more willows and pine trees and tall sand dunes. Felix parks the car on the far side of the lake under the shade of a tall willow.

They unpack the car and spread a large rug on the ground in the shade, carry the picnic hamper with its sandwiches, scones, the cake that Vera had baked the previous day, the bottles of orange fizz and two bottles of wine with glasses to the rug and put it down.

Felix unfolds the two outdoor seats they have brought with them and flops down in one, his short, rather plump legs spread out in front of him. He picks one of the bottles of wine and starts to pull the cork out with his bottle opener. He is still trying to open it when Vera opens the large bottle of orange and pours drinks for the three children and herself.

"Damn it," Felix exclaims when after a long pull the cork comes out suddenly spilling some of the white wine over his shirt. He pours a glass for himself and his wife and sits back in his chair.

"Nothing like fresh air and a glass of wine to celebrate," he says. Fiona takes her glasses off, smiles but doesn't comment. She leans across and closes the lid of the hamper.

"I suppose everyone is hungry, but it's too early for lunch. Be off, you go all of you while we have a rest," she says. "Vera will make certain you don't wander off too far."

The three children don't wait for Vera. They run towards 'The Willows' and pines by the sand dunes and hide under a thick stand of lupins where Vera is not likely to find them, nor was she likely to call them, probably thankful to be away from their company and enjoy the solitude of the deserted beach beyond.

Daphne is first to crawl out from beneath the cover of the lupins, shake the sand from her clothing and saunter off to find a place of her own. Jack unsure of her mood, for it is so unpredictable at times, sometimes wanting him to be around and at other times snubbing him completely or making derogatory comments about him. He watches her waiting for a sign from her one way or the other. He begins to wonder, why he bothers with her, his thoughts sometimes vacillating between having no more to do with her, or he had to admit to himself, wanting to be with her always during the day. She is just his friend after all, although he doesn't want to admit it, she is something more to him than that.

In appearance she is much like him, a little taller with auburn hair, with reddish streaks in the sunshine, cut short like a page boy style overhanging her prominent high domed forehead. Her face is different though, with large blue eyes that seem to see through you and blaze with anger when she is crossed. There is no mistaking her mood with the look she gives him. She has a small, pert shaped nose and thin lips that curl up markedly when she is ruffled or put out in any way. She invariably wears a floppy pair of shorts, a loose blouse that hide her developing body and a pair of sandals. Her skin tanned by the sun doesn't seem to sunburn even during the hottest time of the day.

Nathan follows his sister and Jack tags along hanging back waiting for Daphne to turn and suggest what they should do next. They go out from the sand dunes to the deserted beach which seems to stretch on for ever towards the distant hills of Banks Peninsula. There they dig in the wet sand of the ebbing tide for pipis. The long rows of shellfish clustered close together lie on their edge as if defying them to be removed. They dig a little deeper and pull the pipis from their bed. In no time they have as many as they could carry. Tucking in their shirts at the waist bands on their shorts so the pipis can't fall out, they stuff their shirts full of the shellfish and run back to the picnic spot. Nathan stops on the way back and dumps his load on the sand complaining in no uncertain way that his shirt is wet and full of sand and the pipis are hurting him.

Daphne and Jack take no notice of his protests and leave him behind. When they reach the picnic spot, they pull out their shirts and let the pipis drop in a heap by the picnic rug near where Felix is sitting.

"Dad, can we light a fire, Dad, to cook the pipis? We can put them in pot with the boiled eggs that Mum brought for the picnic and get some sea water too."

Felix, a little put out by having the shellfish dumped close to him, screws up his nose at the briny smell they exude, takes his pipe out to his mouth and groans.

"No dear. Sorry, we can't light fires here. I promised the farmer that we would never light a fire."
Vera returns and looks in disgust at the heap of shellfish beside the picnic rug.

"Ug. Take them away. The smell will put us all off our lunch," she protests. The two children are despondent and make no effort to gather them up. Fiona puts down her book.

"Do as Vera says, that's good children," she says." It's a pity about the pips, but as Felix says we can't light any fires. Pity, for I was looking forward to a good feed of shellfish on this picnic. But there it is. No picnic lunch before the pipis disappear." Rather reluctantly Daphne and Jack take hands full of pips and throw them away. Nathan stands by and makes no effort to help them.

The picnic basket is unpacked, and sandwiches handed around followed by hard-boiled eggs, scones, and Vera's cake.

After lunch Fiona suggests that they all take a rest to let their meal digest. Felix of course doesn't need any prompting. He lights his pipe, leans back in his chair, pulls his hat over his eyes and after finishing his glass of wine closes his eyes. Any suggestion of sleep is anathema to Nathan. He slips away undetected and disappears among 'the willow's growing at the edge of the lake. Daphne sits hugging her knees for a minute or two and then she too leaves and follows Nathan.

Jack is on the edge of following her and then thinks better of it. She is in a touchy mood today and he doesn't want to be the brunt of her bad temper. He stays near Fiona lying on his side supported by his elbow watching her smoke a fat roll-your-own cigarette. She draws in a deep drag and then lets the smoke escape between her glistening red lips. Her fingernails and her toenail are painted a bright red too. She wears a sun dress held up by the straps that are tied together over her shoulders reveal her bare shoulders.

She stubbed out her cigarette, smiles at Jack and lies on her side. Jack feels a warm glow inside him when she smiled at him. Her dress which was not much longer than mid-thigh rose further up her leg revealing her plump thigh and a glimpse of her nickers. Jack diverts his gaze thinking that Felix could be watching him and might embarrass him by accusing him of appreciating a nice view of a lovely leg. That's how adult men would see it, but he couldn't appreciate that idea yet. Maybe when he is older, he could see their point of view. What he longed for more than anything at present is the warmth of a mother' s hug and her love. Soon both Mr and Mrs Golding were sleeping. Felix snoring loudly and Fiona more gently like an idling motor car.

Jack sits up with a sense of loss as if he has been betrayed. The excitement of the moment has gone. She could never be his mother, or even a mother figure. She snorts and turns on her side, no longer in Jack's eyes, what a mother should be like. He leaves them to sleep and goes out to find Daphne. When he glimpses her on a sand dune for a moment before she disappears, he runs to the sand dune where he had a momentary glimpse of her but the time he climbs up the dune there is no sign of her. He calls her name. There is no reply. He calls again louder this time thinking that the wind from the sea might have carried his call away. Again, there is no reply, nor is there any sign of Nathan who usually gives his position away by making weird noises or shouting out loud. Disillusioned and feeling sorry for himself Jack throws himself down on the sand between two sand dunes and closes his eyes. Suddenly the feeling of loneliness sweeps over him with no other sign of life except the few gulls gliding above him on the up draughts of the wind as if he was the only person alive.

Daphne isn't far away on the other side of the sand dune where Jack lies. She wanders aimlessly kicking at the sand as she goes, wishing that Jack would appear, but determined not to go and seek him back at the picnic spot. She stops walking when she hears voices coming from behind the grove of willow trees near the lake. She creeps up until she reaches the trees and pushing aside the low branches in front of her, she peers from between the cover they provide. A few yards from where she is hiding there are two adults standing together embracing each other. She pushes away the few leaves that are obscuring her a clear view and then involuntarily she catches her breath.

Before her in the clearing are her father and Vera embracing each other. Her father's arms hold Vera close to him. Her head is on his shoulder and their lips are close together. He is whispering to her in an endearing way, and she is pressing her body close to his.

She lets the branch go and turns running blindly, tears pouring down her cheeks, her heart thumping wildly. She yells at the top of her voice as she runs, and she doesn't see Jack sitting in the valley between the dunes until she trips over him. She regains her feet and stands open mouthed and her eyes a blaze. Jack, alarmed, tries to get to his feet, but she pushes him down when she sees Vera running towards her.

Daphne undoes the buttons on her blouse and throws herself down on top of Jack pinning him to the ground tugging at his shorts in an endeavour to pull them down. When he grabs her hand to stop her, she kisses him fully on his lips.

Then Vera is upon them. She pulls Daphne away from Jack and drags her away. Jack pulls up his shorts and tries to stand. The two females are facing each other, glaring, and snarling with bared teeth. Daphne ducks under Vera's arm and defiantly walks away doing up her buttons on her blouse as she struts away. Vera still shocked at what she has seen recovers her equanimity to some extent and follows Daphne, who stops walking and holds her ground and shouts at her, accusing her of trying to break the family up and using her witchcraft to bewitch her father. The two of them stood there almost toe to toe abusing each other with Vera threatening to tell Fiona about Daphne's disgusting behaviour with Jack.

Jack mortified and bewildered was on his knees his whole body shaking as he tried to stand. He can't believe it. One moment he was lying on the sand, eyes closed feeling a little sorry for himself and the next moment Daphne, who had avoided him all morning, is on him kissing him shamelessly and trying to pull his shorts down. All of this in front of Vera! He is undecided what to do next. Should he return to the picnic or should he just start running along the beach back to Waireka. If he did the latter, he would not have to face the terrible scene that would follow back at the picnic site. But if he didn't show up, they might think he had gone missing and would start searching for him. They would blame him for everything. What a quandary he was in, but whatever the parents thought, it wasn't his fault. Still, he felt guilty and meekly approached the family who were packing up the picnic and putting things back in the car. He stood back hardly daring to look at any of the family in the face. They ignored him until Fiona came over and took his hand.

"Come on. Let's not all get all moody like those two. Whatever you all got up to I haven't the faintest idea, but Vera and Daphne look as if they could kill each other."

Felix avoids the others complaining that picnics are for fun not bickering and bad feelings.

It was a silent and tense atmosphere in the car during their return to Waireka.

On the Sunday following the picnic there was excitement in the village when a caravan in the camping ground caught fire. Jack was at church when it happened and missed the excitement among the kids in the village with two fire engines attending, a police car and a large gathering of campers wanting to get a close look. He heard later when he returned from church that the caravan belonged to Mr Dab, Glady's father, who was burnt badly. The ambulance had left with him earlier so by the time Jack had changed out of his best clothes there was little for him to see of the disaster. One or two campers stood near the burnt-out caravan, but the crowd had gone. Other campers were going to look after Gladys while her father was in hospital.

He saunters on his way back to the bach undecided what to do with the rest of the afternoon. Since the picnic he hasn't seen either Daphne or Nathan. He is leaning over the railings of the bridge hoping to see if there were a few rockabillies in the stream, when he hears his name called. He turns to find Mrs Golding behind him. She is on her own.

"Hello Jack," she greets him. "Would you like to join us on a walk through the pine forest."

"Yes, we would like a guided tour of your neck of the woods if you don't mind." Mr Felix and Vera have come on to the bridge and join Mrs Golding.

"If you like I could do that." It had occurred to Jack that there might be something going on between Vera and Felix after all and Daphne had every right to be angry. After all they had come together, and Mrs Golding had come on ahead. He felt for Daphne's sake he should keep an eye on what was going on between these two. Poor Mrs Golding, she would be left with only Daphne and Nathan. Maybe she had resigned herself to this and would welcome him to join her and the other two kids to make a new family without unfaithful Felix and nasty Vera.

Mrs Golding walks beside him and the other two keep together. He points out where he lives and where Bert Saunders lives at the end of the road. When they enter the Pine Forest, Felix pretends to be frightened of the dim light under the trees. He goes ahead and makes out he is stalking some wild animal turning now and then to face them and puts his finger to his mouth to indicate they must be quiet. Vera keeps close to Mrs Golding and puts her arm around her as if seeking protection from whatever might be out there.

Felix amused by the reaction laughs.

"Well, if there was any danger here, I'm sure Jack has dealt with it long before, eh, Jack."

Before they leave the forest and go to the beach for the return trip home, they pass the clearing where Jack had built his underground hut. He'd hoped that if he kept to the far side of the clearing, they wouldn't notice anything unusual, but Felix's sharp eye had seen where the ground on the other side looked uneven.

"Hello what's this?" he says. "Looks like some sort of depression in the ground over there." He goes over and starts to poke his walking stick in the ground which sank in a little way until it hits something below the surface that sounds as if it has hit something solid. With his foot he scraps away the pine needles that cover the corrugate iron of the hut's entrance. He bends down and lifts the iron and puts it to one side. "Hello, what have we here. A secret underground tunnel of some sort. Perhaps an underground hut. I wonder who built this. Jack did you know it was here. I bet you did, eh. It's a secret so let's keep it as a secret that only the four of us know about, what say."

Vera and Mrs Golding come over and look down at the entrance.

"Let it be a secret then." Mrs Golding agrees. "We must all swear to that. Let's all spit on this pinecone l picked up, make our pledge, and then face the other way while I throw it over my shoulder into those lupins over there where none of us will know where it lands."

Jack helps Felix to put the corrugated iron back and cover it with earth and pine needles. That done they move on.

"Let's go to the beach before we meet any of the inhabitants of this haunted place," Felix says. They return home by walking back along the beach towards the village. Vera keeps close to Mrs Golding while Jack walks behind with Felix.

Daphne sees a Police car pull up outside the store and two constables get our and enter the shop. She follows them in and pretends to be looking at some magazines near the counter while they spoke to the storekeeper. They must have known she was there and could hear what they had to say, but they didn't seem to mind her presence. When they had said all, they had to say and left the shop the storekeeper says.

"Well big ears you heard what they came for and I bet within a few minutes from now the whole village will know also. So, of you go and spread the word. We will have to keep an eye out if we don't want to be murdered in our own beds."

The first person she sees when she leaves the store is Jack. She hesitates unsure of how he has taken what she did to him at the picnic. Jack has seen the police car leave and comes to see whose house they had been at.

"Did you see the cops' car? I wonder why they came here," he says. Daphne is relieved by his response and joins him.

"There's someone they want, and they think he might be around here somewhere. He could be dangerous, and I have to tell everyone I meet to be careful and report anyone who looks suspicious. "Has he murdered someone?"

"They didn't say, but I don't think so by the way they spoke but anyhow they want to find him. He could be hiding in the Pine Forest or anywhere."

The storekeeper had finished sticking a notice on the door of the store the police had given him. There was a picture of the man wanted on the notice and it said this man was wanted for questioning. There was nothing about what he might have done. It said that for safety in the meantime children must stay within the village and not go beyond the last house over the bridge.

"Like to come with me to tell everyone we see?" Daphne asks. "We'll go and tell Mum first because Nathan has been going on this own recently and not telling me where he goes."

They find Mrs Golding in the kitchen. She listens carefully, didn't comment but leaves the kitchen quickly and hurries to the lounge. Nathan is sitting on the floor playing with his toys. He looks up when she enters oblivious of the anxious look on his mother's face.

"I've seen a strange man in the pines this morning," he says in his guttural way of speaking.

"How do you know he is a strange man?"

"He is a bad man because he ran away."

Later when Felix and Vera come home in the car, Fiona tells them what has happened in the village while they were away. Both Felix and Vera seem unperturbed by the news and Vera puts on the kettle for a cup of tea and puts out the cups on the table.

"I suppose we'll have to keep a watch on Nathan and see he doesn't wander off again," she says as if not particularly concerned.

"Indeed, we will," says Felix. "Fiona it looks like Vera and me will have to go to Rangiora to get Nathan's medicine and other things while you look after Nathan. You seem to be the only one who can keep him calm these days. The last few days have been hell what with his increasing tantrums and the like. Nearly set the place on fire yesterday playing with matches. Keep your matches on your person Fiona and make sure he doesn't get his hands on them again."

Fiona sighs. "Yes, he is a handful alright, but I can manage."

A Police van stops outside 'The Willows' soon after Felix had rung, and he tells them what Nathan had said he had seen. Six Police leave the van and cross the bridge and go in in the pine plantation. Jack sees them pass one has a dog on a lease and he waits for a moment and then follows keeping out of sight. He knows he shouldn't be following them, but curiosity makes him anxious about the fate of his underground hut if they find it. It was enough that there are four now who know about its existence and they had all sworn on the pinecone that Mrs Golding had thrown over her shoulder to keep it a secret. But on his last visit by himself he thought he'd found signs that someone else knew of its existence too. The police have spread out and one of them has a dog on a leash. The dog must have caught a scent that it was following which was leading him towards Jack's hut. Jack creeps closer and hides behind a tree trunk and watches. His heart leaps to his mouth when the policeman who has the dog calls to the others. The dog is scratching away the pine needles and dirt that cover the piece of iron over the entrance. By the time he has reached the corrugated iron cover the other policemen arrive and start pulling away the branches that served as roof rafters at the far end of the hut. One is on his hands and knees looking down the entrance which seems undamaged. The dog disappears inside and then comes out again. "Some kid's hut," he hears one of them say. "No sign of anything else there."

Jack now lying flat behind the tree trunk thinks the dog might find him and give him away if he moves too soon. He waits until the police have moved on before he crawls away. He looks in their direction fearful that the dog might still find him and when he turns back again, he is confronted by a pair of legs blocking his way. Whoever these legs were they certainly weren't those of a Policeman. He hears a chuckle above him and looks up to find Daphne looking down at him. "What are you doing crawling along like a baby. Lost your legs is it," she says. Thought you might have followed them. Have they found him yet?"

When she holds out a hand to help him to his feet, he ignores it and springs up and glances behind him.

"Nay. They have a dog, but he hasn't found any scent to follow. I was watching them, but they have gone further into the plantation. I didn't want the dog to give me away, so I kept down low." He wouldn't tell her about how they found his underground hut. The existence of the hut was now known by the Police now, as well as, the other three, and he didn't want anyone else to know. It was broken but looked all right at the entrance end even though the other end had fallen in a bit. He walks back with Daphne to 'The Willows'. As they approach, they hear upraised voices above Nathan's screaming. Daphne takes his arm and pulls him back.

"Let's not go in there just yet," she says. "Let's sit under the hedge and pretend we can't hear anything."

"But we can. "Everyone can't help hear what's going on in there."

"All right then if you must know. Nathan is getting worse. Even I can't help him like I used to and Vera, well she's hopeless. Dad wants to send Nathan away to a boarding place for kids like him. There is one near Christchurch and apparently, he and Vera have been making enquiries. She wants Nathan out of the way so she can have Dad all to herself that's why. You should have seen what I saw at the picnic that day. She's horrible and wants Dad all to herself. Mum doesn't want Nathan to go. She wants him by her. It looks as if it's her and Nathan and she doesn't seem to know that vixen Vera has her claws on her husband and will take him away from her. I can see it all and I want my dad, so there. "

The village is agog with consternation and speculation, when the news of the wanted man being in the district got around. There were imaginary sightings in the village, on the beach and coming and going out of the pine plantation known as Pine Forest, by the locals. They all proved to be false alarms even the report from two campers of a man seen in the paddocks near the plantation in the twilight one evening. They both told of the furtive way the man moved, stopping now and then, as if to see if he was being followed, before going on again keeping wherever he could close to a gorse fence and the deeper darkness under a tree. From what they could make out he wore hat and clothes that were ragged and looked torn that had seen better days.

When the Police made enquiries at the farm, Tom Fielding said he didn't see anyone that night on his property. He said he was always out in the paddocks about that time of night having finished milking he drove the cows to the paddock by the planation where there was good feed for them. He stopped now and then to check that the gates were closed, and the fence was still in good order. He resented their description of his clothes. Did they expect him to wear his evening clothes on the farm?

The camping grounds main gate is locked at night and the lights on the pole in the camping ground are kept on all night. Those in tents felt most vulnerable and someone in each tent stays awake as long as possible listening for any sound of movement in the grounds. There were nights when the wind was up the trees creaked and groaned like a man in pain and no one could get to sleep. Those in holiday homes and bachs locked their doors and windows and pushed heavy furniture against the outside door. Mrs Tubman said she woke one night and saw someone looking through the window. She screamed, but by the time Mr Tubman had woken from a deep sleep and gone outside to investigate, the intruder, if he did exist, had disappeared.

Mrs Cameron, wife of the storekeeper, complained that she couldn't get to sleep because her husband kept getting out of bed on numerous occasions to check that the doors were locked. And then there was the frightful scream in the middle of the night that lifted many heads from pillows in the village. People sat upright, wide eyed and fearful that some terrible murder had happened near them. Who would be next? No one dare ventured outside and no one slept that night.

When they woke in the morning, they see a Police car parked outside the 'The Willows'. A Policeman is standing on the porch of the lodge talking to Mr Felix and Mrs Fiona Golding who is holding a rug around her shoulders. Whatever was said between them the Policeman must have been satisfied because he shakes Mr Felix's hand and pats that mad boy, Nathan, on his head and goes back to his car and drives away. The residents feel a little shame faced about the incident when they realise the scream is what they had heard coming from 'The Willows' on previous nights long before they heard about a wanted man being in the area. Many of them felt the boy should be taken away and put in a mad house of some sort.

By the end of the week the Police announce that they have found the man they sought. He had been apprehended among the sand dunes at Woodend Beach which was miles along the beach from Waireka. Daphne says you could almost hear the sigh of relief in the village. People are more relaxed, mix with others again and forget to lock their doors and bar their windows. Life is back to normal for a holiday place like Waireka. That is until Nathan went missing three days later.

Nathan who usually follows his sister, Daphne along the beach and among the sand dunes today follows well behind her and Jack. Previously his mother or Vera usually followed him and kept a discrete distance from him. Fiona takes a book, a towel, sunglasses and her broad brimmed hat with her and finds a place with some elevation among the dunes where she settles to read keeping a close eye on Nathan as he amuses himself with sticks or other objects he'd finds on the beach.

When Vera takes over from Fiona, she settles herself among the sand dunes to sunbath with the straps of her togs pulled off her shoulders so that she could get an even tan without the white lines of the togs showing on her shoulders. She closes her eyes listening to the sea and the cries of the sea gulls.

She has seen Daphne and that boy going out along the beach and Nathan wasn't far behind them. They will be keeping an eye on Nathan. Daphne wouldn't let him out of her sight for long. That Daphne is just too much, and she is spending more and more time with her father for Vera's liking. She is beginning to hate seeing those two altogether with Daphne using her early feminine wiles to get around her father and he is too easily taken in. Daphne did it to spite her thinking she can replace her in her father's eyes. Ug, she hated that girl. The more responsibility Daphne had with Nathan the better she reasoned. It will solve two problems that exist. On one hand Daphne will have less time with Felix and on the other hand Fiona will be left in peace without Nathan always under her feet. There must be a solution to this dilemma. If only Nathan disappeared, but he always turns up, sometimes sneaking up behind her and giving her a fright. It would be great if Nathan disappeared for good, but not on her watch but if Daphne takes over looking after Nathan more and he goes missing it wouldn't be on her watch. No one could blame her. She must work on Felix to make arrangements for Nathan to be instituted in that Home he is talking about. If that failed well there could be other ways, she thinks that might work.

Her thoughts are interrupted when she notices that Nathan is no longer following the other two but has wandered off by himself. Vera remembering what those two had got up to at the picnic follows some distance back, but not too far away to lose sight of them, but she is distracted when she sees Nathan hanging back and follows him. She pulls the straps of her custom up on her shoulders and slips her bare feet in her sandals. The bright sun light reflected on the sea blinds her for a moment, and she stumbles in the loose sand almost falling on her knee. She thinks of going on the solid sand below high tide for easier progress but then realises that if Nathan looks back, he would be more likely to see her there. The soft hot sand on the seaweed slopes of the dunes is hard going and she tires quickly. Her long hair is blown across her face by the breeze from the sea and she pushes it back holding her hand on it to try and stop it from blowing back and hindering her sight. She is just in time to see Nathan still a long way off, disappear among the dunes and enter the forest.

Daphne is in one of her moods and barely replies when Jack suggests they go pipi hunting on the beach. "Why should I do what you always want to do?" she says in a sarcastic manner.

"Well, you should. I'm a man and you are a woman and that's the way it works doesn't it."

"A man. You are only a little hopeless kid who doesn't know his right hand from his left," she retorts.

Jack tries to think up a good reply but gives up. There was no use trying to compete with her when she was in such a shitty mood. She forges ahead walking with long determined strides leaving him well behind her. He calls her to wait.

"Why should I. I'm not slowing down. the sand is too hot on my bare feet to stand still for any time. You'll just have to keep up."

When a gust of wind blows sand from the top of a dune in his eyes, he blinks repeatedly hoping to clear it away. He waits until he thinks she can't see him when he runs behind a sand dune out of her sight and goes into the Pine Forest to his underground hut. His eyes still hurt when he blinks, and he is mad with her. Nothing's going right today and its times like this that he likes to be by himself in his hut where he can hide and seek solace. He is so upset that he's forgotten that the hut is now partly broken. He stands before it, looking down on the ruins. Of course, it can be prepared, but too many people know about it now. The only thing to do is to find another site for his hut well away from the village somewhere deep in the Forest. He hears someone coming towards him turns and sees Daphne standing behind him.

"If this is your secret hut why haven't you let me in before on the secret? she says. "What a mess. You can't even build a decent hut. Boys are hopeless."

"It wasn't once until the police found it. Your parents and Vera know about it too, but I couldn't trust a girl to keep a secret."

She picks up a pinecone and throws it at him hitting him on the arm. He picks up the cone and is about to throw it back when she runs away among the tree trunks. He knows he can't catch her, but he is determined to throw the cone at her.

Vera enters the forest where she thinks she saw Nathan disappear. The forest is quiet and rather eerie, but she feels compelled to go in further. Anyone could be in here waiting to spring out on her but still she goes in deeper where the trees grow closer together. She stops and listens. She hears the sound of footsteps ahead of her which stop suddenly. A head of her there is a lupin bush and that's where he has gone to hide form her. She picks up a solid piece of dry branch from the ground and forges ahead. "Got you," she shouts as she dashes forward.

When Fiona returns from town there is no one to greet her. Nathan usually hears her come in and comes out to the car when she arrives. She hears noises like someone sobbing coming from upstairs in Vera's room. She calls out and when she has no reply, she mounts the stairs only to be met by Daphne who looks as if she had seen a ghost. She was wide eyed and her face was deadly pale.

"Where is everyone?" she asks. "Where is Nathan?"

Daphne is looking at her as if she has not heard her mother's questions. Her mouth is opening and closing as if she was trying to speak, but no sound came out. Fiona takes her daughter's arm. "Well, what is it?"

Daphne speaks in a barely audible voice, almost a whisper, "We don't know, Mum. He hasn't come home yet. He went off by himself and no one saw him go."

"And where is Vera and Felix. Are they out looking for him?"

"Dad is, but Vera is in shock. Something happened but she won't tell me what. She just sits on her bed staring in front of her, and her clothes are all dirty and torn."

"Is she ill?"

"Must be and she has been sick all over the floor, Mum."

"My god I'm only gone for an hour or two and the whole family falls apart. Come on girl, let's find your father, and then we will search for Nathan before dark set in."

Vera is unable to join them. She is in the bathroom running a bath and doesn't answer when Fiona asks if she is all right and could she possibly help them to find Nathan. Daphne and her mother find Felix on the beach. Together they search the sand hills and the Forest calling his name. When it is too dark to see where they are going, they give up the search and return home. They sit around the dining room table, tired each lost in their own thoughts before they retire for the night.

Felix is up before anyone else in the morning. He makes a cup of tea and puts the teapot on the table. Vera comes down looking pale and obviously very upset. She drinks her tea in silence.

"Someone must have seen him this morning. Vera, we pay you to keep an eye on him.

What have you to say for yourself?"

Fiona is walking up and down in the kitchen. "Daphne how could you let him out of your sight." She is over wrought and finds it impossible to settle. Obviously, she has had little sleep during the night. Daphne is looking at Vera with astonishment. Last night she had looked terribly sick and wouldn't say anything and here she was this morning looking much better as if nothing had happened to her to make her so ill. Vera was uncomfortable under Daphne's close scrutiny.

"Daphne, I saw you and that boy go off together," she says. "I wanted to keep an eye on you after your disgusting behaviour with him on the picnic."

"What disgusting behaviour was that? No one has told me anything about that. Why am I kept in the dark about what goes on here?" says Fiona.

"It's nothing to tell mother. Ask Vera about it if you must and I will tell you what she is up to," says Daphne.

"Let's not get side-tracked. You can tell me some other time. It's Nathan we are talking about now. Surely one of you must have seen him."

Daphne can see her mother is worried and over anxious. "Well, as usual he did follow us to the beach this morning. He must have gone off somewhere because when I looked for him, he'd disappeared, but Vera, you saw him following us because you said you were watching me and Jack, didn't you? You must have seen where he went."

Vera shifts uneasily in her chair and glares at Daphne. "Yes madam," she says in an accusing way, "I saw Nathan with you. He went with you and that boy in the Pine Forest. He was only a step or two behind you and you spoke to him."

"That's a lie and Jack can prove it. I certainly didn't say anything to Nathan. He didn't come with us."

"Come on Daphne. I heard you say something to him. The boy had already gone into the Forest and you hung back and said something to Nathan that made him cry and run away."

"That's a fib, Mother. Why is she saying this?"

Fiona had regained some of her composure and has flopped in a chair.

"Come on you two. This is not a time for an argument. Nathan's safety is at stake and we want no made-up stories. I want the truth Daphne. Were you with Nathan this morning?" Daphne is incensed. She had been staring at Vera opened mouthed and eyes wide open. Vera's expression remained inscrutable.

She turned to face her mother. "No, Mother. He may have followed us, but I didn't see him, or talk to him. What Vera is saying is wrong."

Fiona turned to Vera. "Are you sure you saw Daphne with Nathan before she went in the forest?" Vera's expression remained enigmatic.

"I was certain what I saw, but maybe I was too far off to hear exactly what Daphne said to Nathan."

Although still agitated Fiona took a deep breath. "Well let's not bother about that. What is important is where did Nathan go after that."

Felix suggests they seek help from the neighbours to search for the missing boy.

They all know him of course and Mr Tubman says, out of the Goldings hearing, "That it will be a piece of cake. The boy is never silent but makes all those hideous noises. All they have to do was to listen for those sounds. After all nothing else makes those strange noises of Nathan Golding."

"He's just fallen asleep somewhere," says Mrs Green, a neighbour, to console Fiona who is by now beside herself with worry. "There, there you just stay at home and make a cup of tea.

The men folk will find him and bring him home. He will hear them calling his name."

Fiona usually such a calm, sweet person, is not to be easily comforted. She refuses to stay home and insists that she leads one of the groups searching the area. One group of searchers goes along the beach and among the sand dunes while the other searches the plantation. By lunch time they return without success thirsty and hungry and thankful to rest from the burning heat of the sun. Mrs Tubman and two other ladies had cut sandwiches and made tea and hand them out among the search party. Fiona white faced and looking stressed is surrounded by a bevy of other women all trying to reassure her that it would only be a matter of time before Nathan would be found. Among the men who had turned down the offer of tea for a bottle of beer to quench their thirst there are suggestions that may be the boy has gone to the river and might have fallen in and been swept out to sea. Perhaps they should think about getting someone with a boat to have a look. Someone else thought he may have gone along the road to the Main Road, and it would be worth while checking this out. Someone might have seen him, Tom Fielding for instance was in his paddocks bringing the cows for the afternoon milking about the time Nathan went missing.

None of these leads proves fruitful and Police are called in next day. The Police sergeant and the two constables question members of the family and Jack about what they had seen of Nathan before he went missing. Neither Felix or Fiona can tell them much because they were away for much of the previous day and Jack and Daphne hadn't seen Nathan that day they said.

Vera seems distracted when the Sergeant asks her if she seen Nathan yesterday. She gives the impression that she hasn't understood the question and the sergeant repeats himself. She appears vacant and listless as if she was far away. The sergeant asks again. She sits up in her chair pushes her hair back from the forehead with a sweep of her hand and without hesitation answers, "Yes," she says. I have been watching Nathan playing on the beach until he followed his sister and Jack Waldron into the Pine Forest."

"How long was it before he came out again?" asks the Sergeant.

"I didn't see him come out again."

"Weren't you concerned about that?"

"Not really. He often went in there and came out by the village just to annoy me knowing I would still be waiting on the beach for him to return to the beach."

"And you haven't seen him since."

"No, but I did see Mr Golding come out of the forest sometime later. He came out slowly looking about him as if he was not wanting to be seen." Her monotone way of speaking and her far off look alarmed Fiona.

"But you went into the forest yourself earlier. That old joker who lives at the end of the road by the pine plantation. Bert Saunders, I think is his name, said he saw you come out of the woods by the end of the road in the morning that Nathan was later reported missing. He said you looked upset, and your clothing was covered in pine needles. How do you explain that?"

Vera doesn't flinch and looks the sergeant in the eye. "Yes, I was upset. Terribly upset, and I still am. I'd gone into the forest with the others who were looking for him, but that was later in the afternoon, not the morning and called Nathan's name and when there was no reply I started looking for him in the lupins and other bushes which I think he often hid in when I called him. I was last out of the forest that day because of me looking under bushes and that. I was in a mess and I was wild with him because he had probably gone home the other way. But Mr Saunders is wrong about what time it was that he saw me come out of the forest. I went in the forest in the late afternoon with the others who had been looking for Nathan, but certainly not in the morning." Fiona is alarmed with what Vera is not only saying, but the manner in which she is talking.

She seems unaware of anything and continues to look in front of her as if she isn't seeing anything. It was so unreal and very unusual of her. What had really happened in that forest she wondered.

Jack is surprised by Daphne's reaction to her brother's disappearance. Brother and sister were always fighting each other with Daphne giving the impression that she enjoyed inflicting pain on Nathan by giving him the Chinese burn or twisting his arm up his back until he cried. He in return endeavoured to take revenge in any way he could, but never with any undue malice. It was if it was a natural thing that happens between siblings. Daphne could be a little more sadistic sometimes while at other times she was more playful in her manner, as if no matter how they hurt each other it was what being brother and sister was all about. Perhaps this was why Daphne is so upset. She genuinely misses her brother. She never teased him about his handicap or made fun of him in front of others. Daphne spends most of the day now looking for him.

"You can come with me if you like," she says to Jack when he offers to help. She didn't join the others who were looking for Nathan.

"They don't know where to look, "she answers when Jack asks why she prefers to go on her own.

"I know where he liked to go and hide away from others and that's where he has gone now. Those other kids laugh at him and bully him because he's different and they hurt his feelings and the way he deals with it is to hide."

Jack has a good idea where these hiding places might be. He has thought his underground hut might have been one such place, but now it has collapsed he wouldn't be there.

They searched the sand dunes, poking in places that offered concealment, under the overhanging branches of the dense lupins, broom, and the tunnels under the gorse and even in the channel in Tom Field's paddock which was sometimes after heavy rain full of water, but unfortunately without success.

They are walking back to the village along the beach, Daphne is slightly ahead of Jack, and she is sobbing quietly, trying to conceal her tears from Jack, when she stops suddenly turns to him and without warning pulls him close to her and kisses him forcibly, prolonging the kiss until taken by surprise he pulls away. She pushes him from her, runs towards the incoming wave as it loses its energy on the beach and kicks the shallow water about her as she walks.

When Jack recovers, he is surprise to see Vera standing on a sand dune, her arms folded on her chest her head thrown back with a definite look of disapproval. Daphne who must have seen her had staged the whole scene. Why did she always have to embarrass him in front of Vera.

Jack is perplexed by Daphne's behaviour. In her more distracted moods, she hardly notices his presence and even when she does give him her attention, she seems preoccupation with something else. She drops off in to one of her silences and vacant gazes. When he breaks in, she stares at him in a strange way and then seems to wake with a start. He recognises that she is upset by Nathan's disappearance and the lack of success she is having in finding him, but she has always treated him the same way long before Nathan was missing. He wonders why he has put up with her for so long. He can't desert her now with the problem of Nathan missing, but there are times when he wants to take her by the shoulders and shake her until she falls to the ground. Walking behind her swaggering figure he stares at her hair as it swings from to side in the minute ponytail, he knows he doesn't want to hurt her in any way. She is just a girl and girls are strange creatures and they behave that way. The other boys in the village think he is stupid to want to play with a girl when there are other boys to play with. He likes her in spite of her unpredictable moods.

She stops running in the surf, stops and waits for Jack to catch up. "Come on slow coach. I suppose you are a little put out by me sometimes when I say nasty things to you."

Jack shakes his head. "It doesn't matter. Sticks and stones will break my bones, but names will never hurt me," he says.

"So, you say, but I see you wince sometimes. It's my hormones, Mother tells me. Whatever they are they are racing all through me making me mad and bad tempered, wanting to hurt others and say horrible things about them. Adolescence is on its way, Mother says, and I can't help it.

Sorry."

This is a little incomprehensible to Jack who smiles and says, "Is it catching like measles?'

She laughs. "Something like that I expect. Watch out you don't catch it, but Mother says you have a few years to go before then."

Jack has troubles of his own. He'd missed church more than once recently and his aunt had sent him to bed without any tea. She said it was the influence of those godless people staying at 'The Willows', that was the trouble. She didn't like Daphne, never had and her opinion of Mrs Golding dismayed Jack.

Jack couldn't tell his aunt the reason he missed church was because he was frightened of Len Hales. Three Sundays ago, he had changed to go to church and was waiting on the road when Len pulled up in Uncle's Riley Kestrel. Before Len got out of the car Jack had run off to the back of the section and hid in the bushes. He heard Aunty calling his name and Len saying he thought he'd seen Jack waiting on the roadside. There was no way Jack was going to go in that car with Len even when Aunty and Uncle were there too. But how could he tell them why he was frightened of Len. They wouldn't believe him, and Aunty would have said that the 'The Willows' heathens had put him up to it.

There was some respite for Jack when Mr and Mrs Hudson who lived in the settlement by the Ashley Bridge on the main road had come to take them to church sometimes. He has no objection to travelling with them. Uncle asked him why he didn't like travelling in the Riley, after all it was still his car, on loan to the church and Len was a good driver. He was less likely to have an accident than Joe Hudson who travelled too fast at times. Jack didn't answer.

"Come on boy answer your uncle. Has the cat got your tongue?" she shook him and glared at him menacingly.

"He'll have his reasons no doubt, stupid as they be," said Uncle Ernie. "He'll tell me in good time won't you boy."

In church on Sunday before the service began, Len Hales who, usually sits on the other side of the aisle, comes over and sits beside Jack. He leans across Jack to speak to his aunt and rests his hand on Jack's thigh and squeezes it gently. Jack stiffens and nausea threatens to overcome him until Len straightens in his pew and takes his hand away. When he turns to speak to someone behind him Jack slips passed him and hurries towards the door. He has no idea where he would go once outside. He hears his name being called by Len and is aware of movement in the pews nearer the door. He starts to run to get outside before anyone could stop him. What he was going to do once he is outside, he has no idea other than he must escape from being near Len Hales. His mind races. He knows there is a side door that opens to a small storage room where he could hide until the service is over. He would tell his aunt he felt sick and had gone outside to sit under the tree by the gate until he felt better.

He looks behind him and ducks behind a tomb stone. Len Hales has followed him outside and luckily is looking the other way for a moment before he goes back inside. Jack finds the door of the storeroom and tries to open it, but it is locked. He tries again to wrench it open. It hasn't been locked before.

"Hardly the place to go for a sick boy, eh, Jack." Len said as he grabs Jack's arm. "Come on. I told your aunty you looked unwell, and I would take you home to look after you until the service is over."

Jack twists and struggles to get away, but the more he struggles the firmer Len holds him.

"Sick boys don't go on like that." Len says, and he puts his arms around Jack and starts to drag him towards where the cars are parked. Jack lashes out with his feet and catches Len a blow on his shins. Len reacts by sliding his arm up under Jack's chin. Jack bites him on the wrist as hard as he can. Len curses and throws Jack on the ground and sucks his wrist where he had been bitten.

"You little beggar, you scoundrel," he mutters but Jack hasn't waited to hear anything more and released from Len's grasp he runs towards the cluster of trees behind the church. He chooses the tallest tree with the thickest cover of densely leafed branches and climbs up as far as he can to hide amongst the thickest branch with the most cover.

There he clings to the thick foliage while lying on his stomach, his face pricked by the sharp pine needles and his hands sticky with the gum that exudes from the branch, a frightened fugitive from those who are now calling his name as they pass below unable to see him. His greatest fear is to be discovered by Len Hales who he thinks would be the last of the searchers to leave. Shivers pass through his body from the cold south west wind which filters through the foliage and chills his hands and then his body. It seems hours before he hears the first car leaving followed by others a little later. The sound of voices below has long faded and now he hears only the wind in the trees. He doesn't dare make a move that might give him away. He convinces himself that Len Hales will be below waiting at the bottom this tree and he would stay there until Jack gives his position away. He is determined not to move even a finger or lift his head to see if all the cars by the church had gone even if he has to stay there all night.

Back in Waireka, the searchers for Nathan return to the community hall cold and dispirited. Mrs Kelly and Mrs Tubman who hadn't been on the search have made tea and baked scones which they hand out to the searchers. It has been a long, cold day and even those who had dressed warmly felt the cold. They gather around the small coke fired stove in the hall, sipping their tea or holding out their hands to the stove. There is little talk amongst them. It has been another long, fruitless search, the sixth in a row now and the numbers who have turned out today are fewer. With sun sets, the bright yellow and red sky fades as darkness creeps over the fields outside when Felix and Vera return. They look glum, cold, and defeated and gratefully accept the hot tea and scones. The others try not to catch their eye and shift awkwardly on the long forms to make room for the Goldings. They mumble their sympathy and make half-hearted comments about perhaps tomorrow will a better day. One by one the others leave until the hall empties except for Felix, Vera, and Mrs Kelly who is drying the last of the cups and tidying up the kitchen at the back. Then she leaves.

Felix and Vera hardly acknowledge her when she wishes them a more successful look next day. He moves closer to Vera and puts his arm around her to comfort her.

"What is it Vera. You are not yourself. Is it your father's bad health that troubles you? You look terrible at times. You mustn't blame yourself Vera. It isn't your fault Nathan ran off."

"It is though. I told him that if he didn't behave you would send him to an orphanage."

"Hardly an orphanage. A special boarding school for boys like him. Fiona had discussed it with me before only she will have nothing to do with that suggestion. Come on cheer up. He'll turn up soon wherever he is. He'll be hungry by now."

He gives Vera a kiss on her cheek as the door opens and Daphne comes in.

"Christ," she utters and storms out leaving the door wide open.

Felix gets up and tries to follow her, but she is too quick for him and he loses sight of her. He listens hoping to hear her footsteps, but the wind has come up. Feeling dejected he returns to 'The Willows' and finds Fiona sitting on the sofa. He puts his arm around her.

"It's still early days," he says. "We haven't given up not by a long way. He must be pretty hungry by now. I wouldn't put it past him to steal in tonight some help himself to whatever is in the kitchen."

Fiona's dead pan expression changes a little as a faint smile creeps across her face. She takes Felix's hand in hers and gives it a gentle squeeze.

Felix hugs her and goes out to make a cup of tea. Fiona has been wrestling with wild conflicting thoughts. What if something terrible has happened to Nathan. No, she mustn't think like that. But if something had happened who would have wanted to hurt him. Vera perhaps. She was having trouble with him and Daphne could be horrible to her, but no, Vera wouldn't have it in her to really hurt Nathan. Daphne. What a stupid thought. Those two kids were close even though they fought each other now and then. Felix, certainly not. Sure, he wanted Nathan to go to the special residential place for boys like him. He thought he was doing the right thing by doing this. He was worried that she could no longer care for him and it was getting her down. A stupid thought. I love that boy so much probably because he is different and needs my protection. Who then, could it be? It's absurd to think anyone would want to… no, she mustn't ever think like that.

Felix has come in with a cup of tea and a glass of brandy for her.

"I think I'll stay up tonight and be here when that young devil makes his move," he says.

"And I will join you Felix. We'll both be here when he returns and make him much welcomed."

They are wakened in the early morning by Vera who has been behaving strangely lately. She is obviously very agitated and is muttering something between gasps and deep breath intakes about her bed hasn't been sleep in.

"What are you talking about?" said Felix as he gently removes Fiona's head that had been lying on his shoulder all night.

"Daphne's been out all night," Vera manages to blurt out between sobs.

Felix struggles to get to his feet. His legs felt numb from the uncomfortable position he had been lying on the sofa. "Are you certain? She must have gone out early to search. That's all surely." he says." She must have been taking food to him since he has been missing and she's taken him his breakfast."

Vera, pale faced with the marks of dry tears on her cheeks, hangs her head. "She's gone.

I have failed you both. I'm so sorry." She turns and runs out of the room.

Fiona remains seated and looks at Felix who is flabbergasted by Vera's departure in that fashion. "I know he is gone, and we may never find him. I know from the bottom of my heart," she says. "But Daphne is another matter. I wonder what made her run off like that. Have you any idea Felix? There is a loud knock on the door. Felix who is looking shamed face, starts as if woken suddenly from a deep sleep and answers the door.

He is confronted by Jack's Aunty Kate who pushes passed him and enters the room much to the astonishment of Fiona who has half risen from her chair.

"Is Daphne with you?" Fiona asks.

Aunty Kate who looks menacing when she comes in the room is dumb founded by the question.

"It's more likely is Jack with you? You are all such a bad influence on him and that girl of yours," she says standing in the centre of the room.

When Felix offers her a chair, she refuses his offer.

"Well, where are they," she demands.

Felix and Fiona exchange glances. "For heaven's sake, Mrs Bennett, two of our children are missing and you have the temerity to come in here and accuse us of holding your boy against his will."

Kate Bennett has regained some composure and flops down in a chair.

"I'm sorry I was so blunt. Jack has gone missing. He ran away while we were at church and hasn't been seen since and of course his uncle is worried."

Vera who had kept in the background comes forward and takes Fiona's hand in hers.

"They were as thick as thieves those children, all three of them. Do you think they are together now hiding from us for some reason?" she says.

"Not likely." Felix answers. "There is nothing missing from our house. They haven't taken any food from here. Perhaps, hunger will bring all three of them back. But Nathan has been missing now for over a week. He couldn't last that long surely."

Earlier in the evening, still in his tree, not daring to move, but now that darkness has set in, Jack knows he must make a move soon. Staying where he is not an option, but if he climbs down, he runs the risk of being caught by Len Hales who he is sure will be waiting for him to make his move. The wind is up, the cold is penetrating his clothes and he can hardly feel his hands now which are numb with the cold. He fears the darkness with its scary spirits that live in these trees. With every movement of the branch beneath him tossing in a sudden strong blast of wind he imagines is caused by one of these bad spirits coming to get him. His heart is throbbing. and he is trembling with fear. He glances about him horrified about what he might see.

He loosens his grasp of the foliage and slowly lowers himself to the branch below aware of how stiff he has become and of the danger of falling. The branches which are moving violently now in the wind threatening to toss him off. He wraps his legs around the branch and grips it with his hands. He is aghast at the perilous task ahead of him of getting down safely from the tree. He no longer thinks about what might await him at the foot of the tree, as he fights to control his panic, moving one foot at a time and not letting his hold of his hands on the branch until he feels his feet have reached a secure position on the branch below. Slowly, branch by branch, Jack descends the tree, his hands now cut by the thick bark and sticky with the gum from the tree. He's lost his stiffness and is moving with ease, and then at last, he swings from the lowest branch and lets go his hold, and falls on the ground, tumbling over as he lands. He stays on his hands and knees, looking about him, hoping that if he stayed still for a moment the bad spirits of the night would not spot him in the darkness. And then, he crawls for a few yards, before he stands and runs as fast as he can out of the trees and towards the church.

He knows that if he can outrun them, he will reach the church which will be his sanctuary for no evil spirits can follow him in there. He reaches the church door and falls into the arms of Len Hales who holds him hard against him. "Whoa there. What's your hurry Jack. Anyone would think the devil himself was after you."

Jack clings to Len, sobbing his body shaking, his head lowered afraid to look up for fear that it was indeed the devil who had hold of him.

"Your aunty and uncle are very anxious for your safety Jack, but it is too late to disturb them now. I'll take you to my place, give some hot soup and warm clothes and tuck you in for the rest of the night and take you home in the morning. What do you say to that?" Jack knew what that would mean, but he is too exhausted to protest.

It is a despondent and physically sore Jack who returns to his home with Len Hales the next morning. His uncle notices that Jack looks depressed and prefers to stand rather than sit while eating his lunch. When his aunt insists that he sits at the table like any other civilised person he puts a cushion on the chair before he rather gingerly sits down.

That the two children missing are both from the same family causes speculation among the residents about what must have gone on in that family. Rumours flourish, accusations about the Goldings being unsuitable as parents, and should never have had kids and then what would you expect from foreigners, even if they did come from England. They let their kids run wild and get into all sorts of trouble and were cheeky to adults. And they had that funny way of speaking all toffee like and frightfully upper class, a stuck-up lot those Goldings. If they don't like the way, we do things they go home back to where they came from.

And that's what the Goldings did, but they only went as far as Wellington eventually. The Police had spread their search wider for Nathan, satisfied that he wasn't to be found locally and it was more likely he had been abducted and taken away. Felix and Fiona, aware of the hostility against them in the village and resigned that their son was not to be found locally, packed their bags, and left.

Jack is there to see them go. He hears the deep throb of the Bugatti's exhaust and runs to the bridge to wave as they pass. Felix is driving. His hat is well down over his forehead and there is a fixed, unsmiling expression on his face. Beside him Fiona sits slumped like a sagging rag doll, her clothes ill fitting, her hair in disarray, and she never once lifts her eyes from the road ahead. In the back seat sits Vera, upright stance, her hair done in a tight bun and with a look of utter disdain. They must have seen Jack standing by the bridge waving as they pass, but they ignore him completely. He stays there long after the Bugatti had passed until he can hear it no longer. He wipes away a tear from his cheek and blows his nose. It was with their going that all the fun and his interest in Waireka has gone with them. It was no longer a beautiful place to be. They have left leaving nothing, but a haunting emptiness and the ceaseless sound of the sea. The sky is heavy with dark grey clouds and the land sulks under its heavy canopy.

Mrs Tubman told Aunty Kate that she had heard from her sister who lived next door to Daphne's Aunt that Daphne had turned up at her auntie place in Christchurch and was staying there. She thought she would be going to Girls High school when the holidays ended.

Apparently, Mr and Mrs Golding were staying in a flat in Christchurch and later will move to Wellington where Mr Golding would start a new branch of his English firm. It would appear because Daphne has estranged from her parents the Goldings have lost both of their children.

That night during tea Jack and his uncle and aunty ate their meal in silence. Jack glances from one to the other hoping to see their reaction, but neither say anything about his not coming home last night. He fidgeted in his seat hoping that his unease would be recognised, but both adults ignored his restlessness. Then he found courage to ask, "Don't you want to know what happened to me last night?"

"We know what happened to you naughty boy. You ran off with that tart Daphne Golding. Mrs Golding as much as told me when I asked her this morning." Aunty Kate says.

"That's not true."

We have had as much as we can take of your lies Jack, when you didn't come home after running out of church on Sunday, I rang Len Hales from the phone box outside the store and he said that you were not with him and although he had gone back to the church in the evening, there was no sign of you. Where else could you have gone, but with that girl. Shame on you and look what shame you have caused us running out like that for no reason and going off with her.

"Disgusting." Aunty is upset and gets up from the table and leaves the room.

Uncle Ernie puts his fork of cabbage down on his plate. "You have gone too far this time upsetting your aunt who has done so much for you Jack."

Tears ran down Jack's cheeks no matter how hard he fought to stop them from flowing. His uncle had never spoken like this to him before. He is on the verge of telling Uncle about what really happened last night and why he is so restless at the table, because he is still sore from what Mr Hales did to him again, but he knows it would upset his uncle too much.

"I wasn't with Daphne, Uncle. God's honour. Why would Mr Hales say that I wasn't with him in his house?"

Uncle frowned. "Why indeed if what you say is true," he says.

"It is Uncle."

"Be that as it may, but let's put it down to some misunderstanding. You look pale and upset tonight and you can't sit still for a moment. I put this down to you, staying out all night. Perhaps, your aunty rang Len before he found you. Now I have some more important news for you. Take a good look around you Jack, because it will be the last time you see these walls again. We're moving Jack, back to town and selling this place in Waireka. I have three houses in Christchurch, all of which I have done up myself over the years and rented out.

Well, the one in Beckenham has become vacant and that's where we will live. I've had it renovated, and the work has now finished."

Aunty who has come back in the kitchen says. "I don't know why your uncle bothers with you, honestly Jack. There are times when I think you would be better off in a home. But there it is I suppose, blood is thicker than water. I expect you will be going to the Beckenham school after the holidays."

The day before they left Waireka, Jack is up early before the sun has risen. He hears snoring coming from Uncle and Aunty's bedroom. He knows that he would not be missed if he got back before breakfast. One last look at all his old favourite haunts. It won't take long.

He takes the track to the beach and stops at the place he first saw the Goldings, having a picnic among the sand hills. He climbs the hill where Daphne made her jump from, to land among the family below. He sees her flying in the air, soaring like a bird before landing, without falling over, and kicking sand up over Vera. He jumps but falls short of where the family had been that day.

There is no sign of exactly where they sat now.

The beach was empty, and no one swam at this time of day. He wanders along the beach and among the sand hills where they had played. How empty it all is now the Goldings have gone. He tries to replicate the things they had done but the place is losing its magic. This is where they had jumped to see who could go the furthest, but it had little meaning now that Daphne had gone. He didn't bother entering the Pine Forest and going to the clearing where he used to hold his wars with the elderberries and the lupin flowers as his troops, or even to take a last look at what had been his underground hut. They had no relevance to her. She rarely came into the Forest. All this excursion to try and relive his time with her is pointless. The places themselves remained indifferent. They had no memories of Daphne for him. They were just places, but the memories were his and he would keep them for ever. Their going was a frost on all the frolic they had once enjoyed together. He hadn't realised before how much he missed her.

# 2

# Verity

Notes from Simon have been slipped under my door all evening asking me to see him as soon as possible on a matter of great urgency. Everything about Simon is of great urgency. He has a habit of crying wolf so often that I have long since learnt to treat his urgency with the disdain it deserves. I have replied explaining that I am otherwise engaged in a matter of even greater urgency and slipped that reply under my door to the hall outside. I am sure he will find it and I will soon expect a reply expressing his despair. He must know when I sign my replies with my name, Jack Waldron, that I am put out by his insistence to have my full attention.

I'm in my second year doing a fine Arts Degree at Canterbury. Uncle is supporting me, much to Aunty's disgust.

Earlier this evening, Gladys Dab came to my door with Deepti. One look at their faces was sufficient for me to realise I was in for a highly dramatic evening. They stood in my doorway of my flat in Gloucester Street with their arms around each other. Why, oh why, do I attract such people with their difficult, emotional troubles. Being a student, myself brought about enough difficulties, financial and emotional, for me without having to be a sounding board for others with even more extreme problems.

"Jack, do you mind if we come in?" Gladys asked. I ushered them inside and offered them to sit on my one and only sofa, which apart from a small desk, a chair, and my bed, was the only piece of furniture in the room. They sat on the edge of the sofa, their hands clasped and looked up at me, Gladys with strands of her straw-coloured hair falling over her face and down to her shoulders, her small round face pale, wide eyed and lips parted.

Deepti in contrast, with dark, short hair neatly arranged and her copper-coloured face showed little emotion. They fidgeted, clasped, and then unclasped their hands in unison and then flopped back against the back of the sofa like deflated balloons. I knew better than to show concern or expect an immediate explanation of their behaviour. I'd seen it all before from Deepti, but not with Gladys.

Gladys since our childhood days in Waireka was a follower, someone who found it difficult to stand on her own two feet but relied on others for support. She had attached herself to me even though we attended different High Schools and now again she leans on me as a fellow Arts Student at Varsity. Her lack of confidence I understood was probably a result for the time she had spent as a child in the Cust Commune. It had made her dependent on others and destroyed her confidence. I was thankful that she was two years behind me at University for to be in the same class as her would have been unbearable. Even so she sought me out when she could and asked for my opinion about her artwork and how she could improve. I told her that I too was a student and although I was only too pleased to help where I could, the opinion of our tutors was what mattered at Art School.

Deepti and Gladys were as unlike as chalk and cheese. Where Gladys was withdrawn and shy, Deepti was the opposite, vivacious, good fun and confident. Her genial manner, her laughter, and her love of a good time were contagious. She was in the same year as me at   Varsity and was regarded as a model student, with great potential as an Artist. Her enthusiasm and her creativity were admired by everyone. Then without warning she left Varsity a year ago and moved to Auckland. I was surprised to see her now and with Gladys of all people.

I listened to the garbled tale they had to tell of dismay. Gladys guessing her version while Deepti said nothing until Gladys, realising she was doing all the talking about something that concerned Deepti more than herself, stopped and turned to Deepti.

Deepti straightened her back, ran her hands from her knees along her thighs and held her head high. She had regained her composure. There was little of the Deepti I knew of old, in the way she spoke which was now a little detached, precise, and controlled. She spoke of her early days in Auckland where she met two compatriots, one a man the other a woman from Mumbai at an Art Exhibition in which two of her paintings were on display.

"The woman had a calm spiritual manner that impressed me. She said the meeting had been predetermined and that I was no stranger to her. She invited me to visit them at their home.

There was something compelling about the couple that attracted me, and I accepted."

Deepti, who had come out from India when she was eight years old and had lived with her parents in our Western culture, said she was fascinated by the home of the couple with its Indian decor and furnishings.

"We sat on cushions in a room full of large carved sideboards crowded with bright coloured materials, brass objects and flowers. The atmosphere of the place was new to me. We drank tea and talked, but because I was used to being the centre of attraction in a group, I felt out of place, yet I was strangely affected by the atmosphere. The woman called herself the Guardian and said that she and her partner were reincarnations of a Hindu religious leader. They had been selected by guardians of an energy force and that it was spoken that I too would become part of this force. At first, I was sceptical," said Deepti. "and came away determined not to become involved in any such cult. It was the very antithesis of myself."

She went on to explain that when away from the place and in the loneliness of her flat, for she had not yet formed many friendships in Auckland, she would give it a go. She attended hour long classes and became intrigued. Then followed three-day residential retreats where she met others who had signed up. In exchange they had to make what was called energy exchanges which cost a fee of up to $700. She began to have serious doubts about the guardian's agenda when it was made obvious to her that all decisions were to be made by them and that any member who lapsed in any way was to be 'quarantined' to stop any contamination of others. These lapses could be anything from using too much toilet paper or copying the pose of the Guardian by stretching their neck like she did. "They deprived us of some of the creature comforts such as no bed to sleep in and being consigned to sleep in an open garage.

I couldn't stand it anymore and they asked me to leave. With no money I slept rough in a carpark and in alleyways. They gave me sheets of paper which stated I was a traitor and that the power of the Supreme Grace that saved the Cosmic Fusion from destruction from me. Friends lent me some money and I returned to Christchurch and here I am."

Deepti sat still with her head lowered, avoiding my look of compassion for her misery while Gladys stared at me as if expecting me to come up with some solution. When I offered my consolation, I felt how hollow it sounded and how insincere it must have sounded. To try and cover my embarrassment I offered them a cup of tea and the last of my wine biscuits. Deepti didn't reply and Gladys managed a mitigating smile.

"Let's get some fresh air." I said to cover my rebuff. They agreed and together we left my room and walked down Gloucester Street towards Christ College School, Gladys with her arm around Deepti's shoulder and me a pace or two behind them. We turned up Rolleston Avenue and over the St Asaph Street bridge into Hagley Park. A ground mist was rising from the large green fields of the park as the light of the day faded. The tall trees along the path, devoid of their summer leaves stood like gaunt, silent guardians of the park. Not a word had been spoken between us. I shuddered in the cool of the evening wishing I had put on my jersey before leaving.

The girls seemed indifferent to the cold even like me they were lightly clad.

Slowly at funeral pace we crossed over the foot bridge to the Botanic Gardens. The tea rooms were closed at this hour and the paths were deserted. We moved on in this dreamlike atmosphere as if we were the only ones in the gardens. Then a man with a small dog on a lease came towards us and passed us as if he was completely unaware of our presence.

"Let's see if the cafe is open in the Arts Centre." I ventured in an effort to break the heavy silence amongst us. Neither girl was in a mood to be mollified and neither replied.

"Silly suggestion. It's bound to be shut at this time." I said.

Again, neither replied. I was beginning to be fed up the whole situation. Inwardly I was appalled by their gullibility by being sucked in by this cult and was doing my best not to show my impatience. After all it wasn't Glady's decision to become a member of the Cust cult. It was her parents. Her mother was still a member and her father was living in Linwood.

Simon was waiting for me when I returned. He was in the lounge pretending to be reading, but on the sound of my footsteps out in the hall he was out the door and confronting me with a hug and a sloppy kiss on my cheek.

"I have been so anxious I thought you may have gone out for the night. I can't pretend what I have been through waiting for your return. I have a huge decision to make, and I want your opinion."

I could guess what this decision was. It was the same at this time of the year for the last three years. I groaned inwardly when he asked my opinion on this matter.

"It's come around again." I said. "Choice time. Always a difficult time."

"I sweat blood every time," he said. "Come along to my room. I've laid them all on my bed and I can't finally decide which one to submit."

Simon had been submitting his paintings for admission to the Canterbury Society of Arts for the last four years without success. I braced myself for this soul searching that he went on each year. He railed on against the conservatism of the selection committee.

"Covered with the thick dust of yesteryear. When will they shake the dust off and see what modern art is producing and come to realise its real worth?" I nodded in agreement.

"Which of these two do you think I should submit?" he asked as he pointed to the two paintings he'd finalised.

I pretended to ponder long and hard, rub my fingers over my chin and try to look as if I was about to be serious about the task. I'd done it all before.

I held up one of the paintings and propped it up against the pillow. I stood back, nodding my head while he looked on expectantly. I wasn't going to fall in his trap this year. On previous locations i had given my opinion, freely extolling the merits of the brush strokes, the use of colour and the wonderful composition only to have to put up with his sulks and accusation when it failed to impress the judges.

"You make the final choice this year," I said. "If still in doubt turn the paintings on their back and shuffle them like a pack of cards and pick one to submit. They are all good Simon. Why stress yourself by delaying your choice. Whatever you pick I'll agree to it being this year's choice."

To me the paintings were very much alike in subject and execution, lacking in interest and rather drab. I could not hurt his feelings by telling him this.

"I've made my decision," he said holding up one of the paintings. You see I could not make up my mind without you being here. You're a gem. You give me confidence and stir my heart when I'm with you. We're meant for each other. Neither of us can function properly without the other."

"Go on with you Simon. You're an old sentimentalist," I said with a nervous laugh.

Simon had cottoned on to me at Art School. He'd been there for over four years and still hadn't graduated. He was good fun, light-hearted and good company at parties. Nothing bothers Simon others had said. Always in good spirits although a bit over the top at times. Because we both lived in the same boarding house I had seen Simon when his spirits were low. Because I spent time with him and tried to jolly him out of the dumps, he and I became very close to each other to the extent that he had no doubts about the possibility of our relationship becoming intimate. I on my part have held back, unsure of my feelings and not wanting to form a close relationship, whether it be male or female. Simon appeared not to be offended when I didn't return my affections with the same exuberance that he displayed.

It is of course generally expected that any close relationship I form should be with the opposite sex. I don't necessarily agree with this. I am now nearly nineteen and I have spent much of my time with other males. At high school, I attended Boys High School although since I have been at Varsity, I have met some interesting and pleasant females. I realised that I might easily form a closer relationship with them in a way that was different from that I have always had with other males. Working closely together in the Art School with mixed company has made we aware of this new feeling. I enjoy their ease of communication with others, their genuine interest in you and your work. I enjoy their laughter and the different way they approach problems.

Deepti, to me once was the pivotal image of what a woman should be. Her delightful happy mood and her complimentary remarks about my work, her high spirits at parties and different outings we went on drew me to her. She was the centre of any group I mixed with. Her bright, exciting paintings reflected her personality and were much admired by the other students. Now lately she has become unpredictable and has transferred to studying sculpture under Francis Shurrock, or Shurry from Surrey as we call him.

I joined her with a group of other sculpture students at the beach organised by Shurry. He and his delightful, motherly wife took gramophone, records, baskets of food cooked by Mrs Shurry and other students in their car to New Brighton beach on a Sunday. The rest of us went by tram and meet them where they were preparing to dance old English Folk dancing on the beach.

Because I am not a natural dancer and knew nothing about dancing, except of course shuffle dancing at a party, or in city dance halls and certainly I was completely ignorant of what Folk dancing was all about, I volunteered to keep the gramophone wound up and change the records. The others who had obviously had some knowledge of what they were about to perform prepared for the dance by drooping colourful sashes over their shoulders, tying small bells around their ankles, and putting on colourful hats.

There they were waiting patiently for me to start to wind the gramophone, put on the right record, after two earlier attempts were not the music for the first dance, Florence John, pretty, tall, willowy, adorned in bright, full dress and ribbons, Mac, her partner snappily dressed in flannels and sports coat, Deepti, standing serenely with a warm smile that stirred my heart, her partner, a short red haired, freckle faced student, and the Shurries of course. A small crowd of curious onlookers stood above the high tide mark.

I carefully lowered the needle and on the first note the dancers came alive with dainty steps, flashes of colour and the tingling of the bells as they performed the intricate sets the dance demanded. Some of the couples were having difficulties with the steps required, others like the Shurries flowed effortlessly from set to set, but the one who stood out from the rest was Deepti. She stepped so daintily when required and so effortlessly, dragging her partner with her, her head held back her dark hair streaming behind her and her smile so dazzling that it took all the chill from the onshore breeze and left me with a warmth that I hadn't experienced before. I felt sure that her beaming smile was for me and me alone. Her graceful dancing inspired me to want to take her in my arms and dance on for ever, our hearts beating as one. I'd never felt like this before, but I didn't have the courage or the confidence to get up to dance.

They performed another three dances, before reluctantly, I closed the gramophone lid, put the records back in their sheaves and joined the others in the sand dunes where we had left our baskets of food. My feet seemed to hardly feel the drag of the hot dry sand as light footed, I joined them. The crowd that had watched for a couple of dances had moved on.

I sat close to Deepti while we ate our lunch hoping to make her aware of my feelings towards her, but she paid little attention to me, or exclusively for that matter, to anyone, in particular; chatting away in her bright manner, laughing easily and obviously enjoying being the centre of attention in the party. I tried to emulate her bright spontaneity, by making flippant remarks which I thought were funny, but they were ignored. I felt deflated by the looks on the faces of the others when I thought I'd made a brilliant comment. My heart sank when she avoided me and didn't sit beside me on the tram back to the city, but gave me, along with the others, a brief kiss on our cheeks when we partied.

How could she have jilted me so blatantly when surely, she must have been aware of my feelings towards her. I detected scorn in the laughter and on the faces of the others in our group. How could I, a mere lad of eighteen, have any aspirations towards her. My having been rejected must have been obvious to them and I imagined by their laughter and merriment that they were revelling in my disappointment.

The walk, from the Square where I left the tram to the Boarding House in Gloucester Street, felt longer than usual. There was little traffic at that time of day with only a few cars and cyclists passing through the Square. The picture theatres weren't out yet and the roads leaving the Square looked deserted, their footpaths usually full of shoppers during the week, were empty except for a pedestrian here and there. My feeling of despondency was echoed by this emptiness about me. Every step I took felt ponderous, my legs weary and hardly supporting me as I made that journey that seemed interminable. I stopped on the Gloucester Street Bridge and leaned across the rail to watch the ducks swimming below. Their easy gliding on the water's surface mocked my own heavy going. I stayed for a minute or two admiring the easy unimpeded flow of the water. I pushed myself away from the bridge's railing and dragged my feet along the pavement to the Boarding House.

The front door, which always required an effort to open, didn't budge until I put my shoulder to it. Then it gave way throwing me in the hallway and I might have fallen had I not grabbed at the umbrella stand sending it crashing to the floor. Simon's door to his room flung open and he came out in the hallway. My loud entry had alarmed him.

"For God's sake Jack," he exclaimed. "Do you have to make such a racket on entry. Christ, I thought this was a home invasion by a gang of hobble-de-hoys coming to wreck the place."

"That bloody door," I said.

"You're drunk."

"Never been more sober," I said, and I threw my arms around his neck and we went in his room and closed the door behind us.

We were seated at the only available table in the Stud. Ass, or Students Association, on a Friday evening, Simon and I, eating a dish of shepherds' pie before our last lecture of the week at seven o'clock. Neither of us spoke or even tried to speak above the noise of people coming and going, loud raucous laughter from a large group sitting at a table near us, the scrapping of chairs on the bare floor and the clang of the clash register on the counter behind us.

"Is this place taken?" I hadn't noticed the man carrying a cup in his hand until he stood beside me.

"Not until you take it," I answered. "Be our guest."

"With pleasure," he responded and sat down beside me. He looked too well dressed to be a student, possibly a lecturer or something like that, but not from the Art Apartment. He wore a grey turtle necked jersey and over that a brown cardigan. His grey trousers were well pressed, and his brogues looked new. His dark rimmed glasses gave him a serious look as if smiling was a serious matter and was reserved for those who he thought deserved it and it seemed that neither Simon nor I were in that category. We kept our heads down eating our meal and ignored him until he broke the silent among us.

"A real bun rush at this time of the night," he said. I must have given the impression by the way I looked at him of not hearing his observation.

"Worse that a cat's bloody concert," he said as he leaned towards me.

"Always the same on a Friday. You'd think they are like kids relieved that school is out for the week." I said.

"Well, it is for some, but for others it makes little difference. Still, plenty of swot to be done over the weekend. That is, of course, after a night out on Saturday," he said. "What course are you two doing?"

"Splashing paint around and you?" I queried

"Music. Deafening each other with discordant sounds. Greg, Gregory Moffat is the name."

"I'm Jack and this is Simon."

Simon hadn't taken his eyes off Gregory's face since he had joined us at the table. His intense look would have unnerved most but Gregory didn't seem to notice. I was alarmed at Simon's stare; his mouth half open his eyes wide with a look of wonder at what he was seeing. I gave him a kick on his shin under the table.

"Come on, Simon. Must go," I said as I got out of my chair and took Simon by the elbow. "The paint will be too dry to work if we leave it much longer."

Rather reluctantly Simon allowed me to help him to his feet, his gaze still on Gregory's face until I pushed him towards the door. Before we left Simon turned again to look in Gregory's direction who looked up, gave us a wave and I'm sure for a second or two a faint smile passed over his features.

I saw little, outside of lectures of Simon, after that casual meeting on that Friday night. He had worked beside me at the studio and relied on me for my opinion of how his work was going. Even though this annoyed me at times I suppose I was flattered that it was to me he came to for my advice. Now he set

103

up his easel beside Mary Templeton and ignored me. He seemed to be preoccupied with something which he kept to himself. He no longer waited for me to walk to lectures together, preferring to leave much earlier and take a more circuitous route which took him along Armagh Street where I discovered Gregory had a flat which he shared with other students.

A week later I saw Gregory as he was leaving Varsity, not by the usual way under the clock tower, but going through the Stud. Ass. Intrigued I followed him, wondering why he was taking such a precaution to avoid Simon. He must have seen me following him and waited for me to catch him up.

"Hello there," he said. "You must have seen me sneaking away as if I'd committed some heinous crime and didn't want to be seen."

"You certainly seemed to be taking the long way home," I answered. "Anything to avoid Simon I suppose."

"Just taking the air a bit. Having a little time on my own. Simon, well yes, I don't seem to be able to avoid him these days. He's at my door in the mornings when I leave for Varsity. An interesting chap. I find we have many interests in common, Art, reading and believe it or not, music. We both like hiking over the Port Hills and I enjoy our long discussions, but there are times when a break is needed even from the best of things wouldn't you say."

On a Sunday afternoon, a week later Simon knocked on my door. I was surprised to see him there well-dressed wearing a sports coat, a collar and tie and his best grey trousers.

"All dolled up. Going somewhere posh, is it?" I asked.

"Get on your Groppy Mocker and join me. Gregory has asked you to a musical afternoon at his mother's place on Park Terrace. The music may not be to your taste, but the afternoon tea will be and it's a good chance to see inside one of those posh places on the Terrace."

We were shown into a large drawing room on the second storey of a large house with a marvellous view overlooking the Avon River, the weeping willows on its grassy banks and the vast Hagley Park and beyond. We were introduced to Gregory's mother and took our place among the many other guests. Some were in earnest conversation that at times sounded like heated arguments, or at best disagreement. I heard fragments of the topics they were discussing, concerning the formation of a Christchurch orchestra on one hand and a single choir on the other hand. It appears there were different opinions of how these could be brought about.

Mrs Moffat was clearly agitated as she moved from one group to another offering cakes and cups of tea while her son was endeavouring to place seats and cushions on the floor for the guests who were too engrossed in their arguments to take much notice of his efforts. Then Simon came forward and selected a record from the table by the radiogram and he put it on. He turned up the volume and spreading his hands wide indicated that the guests were to sit. There was a slight hesitation by some, but the majority obeyed by sinking down on the cushions and bean bags about the room. Simon adjusted the volume. These folks were all music lovers and when Mozart was played they all paid homage to him and for the moment forgot their arguments.

I, like many of my contemporaries had little patience for, or indeed any experience of, classical music. Pop music and the latest songs were all a rage for us. I had never listened to much classical music which I considered was music of the past, too staid, and slow for the tempo of modern living. Here I was entrapped in a situation I could not easily avoid. It would be rude to get up and leave and make some pathetic excuse. Instead, I too sank down on a bean cushion and like the others closed my eyes and listened for the first time in my experience to the exquisite music of Mozart. Of course, I had heard of Mozart, top song writer of his time, but that was centuries ago when men wore wigs and dressed in fancy dress and I had long dismissed him as being a serious contender for my most popular song writer.

Maybe it might have been the atmosphere of the place, the silent listeners of all ages lying relaxed on the floor completely mesmerised by the music, and the warm breeze that moved the curtains gracefully by the open windows, or the vista of park land that had such an effect on me. All this was enhanced by the music that touched me as never before, but I found solace, if not the deep satisfaction, that these music lovers in the room must feel.

Simon must have felt this too for he was deeply engrossed, and I noticed his hand slide over Gregory's and stay there for a moment before Gregory rather discreetly pulled his hand away.

I was aware, as one could be, of the possible development of a close relationship between the two. Had anyone else noticed the touching of the hands and the quick withdrawal of Gregory's hand and if they had, did they too suspect a possible illegal liaison between the two men. If they did and took some action the consequences could be disastrous for the two of them. On his part Gregory went out of his way, in public at least, to abstain.

Perhaps I was too sensitive to the possibility of this happening after my experience with Simon's approach to me. Gregory was rather aloof, very discrete, and difficult to get to know whereas Simon was the opposite. Simon made friends easily, lacked discretion and found it difficult to hide his feelings which were often overwhelming causing people to withdraw from him completely. He longed to have a close relationship with a partner, but unfortunately for him it wasn't necessarily with a female. Because I was rather ambiguous about my own relationships, I was only too aware of the interpretations that others might have about my own approach to find a true partner, be it male or female.

All this gave me many sleepless nights of what it meant to me, to be myself, if I was not sure what myself was. My fumbling attempts in my youth to grasp the great world left me bewildered. Perhaps I could be anyone I liked to be, but that would be childish. I wondered how others saw me. They would have an impression of what they would define as being me and I dreaded to think what that might be. The true me is what I kept to myself and I won't reveal that to others, except in the future to my true lover who ever she, or he, might be. I had a lonely childhood without any motherly love and had to fight for myself. That lack of love and the sexual abuse I experienced as a child had left me a sceptic about these matters.

We had a storm that night. It lasted all night and to the mid-morning. I pulled back the curtains and sat in my bed watching it rage outside, enjoying its fury, its blustery wind that rattled the window and hurled sheets of rain over the glass. Flicking light from lightning across the room, followed by deafening thunder that jarred the very walls of my room. My inner turmoil was matched by the tumultuous elements outside making me an apotheosis of some kind. Not a God for I have no belief in Gods, and I had a need of something more earthly than a transfiguration. Then I felt the cold, for I had been sitting up in bed in my pyjamas. I pulled the blankets up to my chin and lay trembling with my arms about me.

I was surprised and intrigued to be invited by Simon to join him and Gregory in what he called a tramp on the tracks on the peninsula. Surprised because I had seen little of Simon in the last few weeks and could not imagine him being much of a tramper, intrigued because I assumed that he and Gregory were an item. Although I had been rather inactive and had not ventured on the hills while at University I had been fit as a boy and had confidence that I could manage

106

anything that Simon proposed. I recall we took the tram to the terminus at the Sign of the Takahe and from there we tramped up the winding track from Victoria Park to the summit at the Sign of the Kiwi. We must have stopped there for some refreshment of some sort, tea, or an ice cream at least. I can't imagine Simon by passing the opportunity for a rest, or for that matter the chance of some sort of refreshment. He wasn't built for long treks and soon tired as we toiled our way up the steep paths to the top. The going down on the other side to Governors Bay was less strenuous although care had to be taken because of the steep and winding road.

Gregory apparently had been staying for over a week in a small cottage on the property of his music Professor who lived in a larger house with his wife who was an artist, and their two children. In exchange for the occupancy of the cottage Gregory baby sat the children when the parents went out. Simon had joined him for a weekend baby sitting and I was soon to find out why he wanted me to accompany him on this excursion. Gregory greeted us with considerable enthusiasm wanting us to go up to the house immediately to meet the two children.

Although, we were tired after such a long tramp Gregory didn't listen to our objections as we followed him up to the house, where we were met by two young kids, who immediately flung themselves at Simon, who unable to keep his balance, fell to be pinned to the ground by the boy sitting on his chest. Gregory, obviously knew what to expect, had held back. Before I knew it, the little girl had wrapped her arms around my legs making it impossible for me to walk any further. The rough and tumble we were subject to by the giggling and excited children would have gone on longer if Gregory, who had gone in the house, came out again and announced that dinner was served. The kids left us on the ground and sprinted inside without any further prompting.

Dishevelled and thoroughly worn-out Simon and I sat on the ground for a minute or two before we followed them inside. Gregory who had served the kids their meal, was drinking a glass of beer.

The two youngsters were eating at an alarming rate and had nearly cleaned their plate of food. To my dismay they suggested that they would be finished and didn't want any more to eat, but instead they couldn't wait to carry on the rough and tumble with us outside. When Gregory didn't object to this idea and didn't offer us a drink Simon flung himself down in a soft chair and announced he was buggered and couldn't play anymore. Gregory sardonically suggested that a beer might restore his energy and make him fit for more tumble and fun with the kids outside.

I got the feeling that I had been invited for the weekend to relieve them of the responsibility of entertaining the children and resented being used in this way. As it turned out that weekend two of us took on that task, either Simon and me or Gregory and me, but never Simon and Gregory together. They were an old combination they explained which the children were tired of but with me, I was a new element in the equation that the kids appreciated. Maybe they did but I remember I certainly did not.

I was to sleep in the spare bedroom next to the kids' bedroom in the house while Simon would sleep in the cottage with Gregory, an arrangement that relieved them of having to deal with any problems with the kids during the night, and I thought, would give them the opportunity of bonding their gay relationship. When the kids were asleep, I joined the other two in the cottage. We sat looking at the log fire in the small fire grate in the cottage, each lost in his own thoughts saying not a word as we sipped the cheap Apple Wine from the flagon we had brought with us from over the hill, Now and then a bit of the burning log would break away and fall among the dying ashes in the grate, sending a shower of minute sparks across the floor to fade before one of us would try to gather it and return it to the fire.

The silence between us was unnerving, a tension we all felt, avoiding each other's eyes and taking longer than was necessary to sip a small mouthful of wine before lowering our glasses, leaving our seats, and pouring more wine which none of us really wanted.

I can recall that evening as if it was only a few days ago rather than many years ago. I had left my seat and gone over to the window and looked out at the scene below us. The moon smeared its faint light on the water of the harbour, flickering on and off as clouds obscured the moon now and then. The silence of the night was oppressive. Gregory had come up and stood beside me.

"Beautiful isn't it from a painter's eye," he said as he moved closer to me.

"It has a beauty of its own, a limited palette maybe, but nevertheless exciting," I said.

"It has a beauty of a different sort to the music composer which one day I hope to be. I hear sounds that probably you don't. You see it as a challenge for the limited palette to convey what you feel about this scene, while my challenge is to interpret those sounds into music which I can write down as music notes. I would try to depict the impression of the light on the water, the contrasting notes of the dominant dark hills and the legato of the moving clouds. We both see the scene before us but respond to it in different ways. We are not that very different. We feel the same, we respond in our own way which brings us together much closer than you think."

"I see what you mean. We both feel the same urge to create which has much in common whether it be by dance, music, art or writing."

"There is of course another more pressing urge that brings us closer together don't you think," he said as he took my hand in his and pressed it gently. Was it the wine that had gone to my head, the sound of his well-modulated voice close to my ear, or the overpowering feeling of being close together and touching each other, for I felt I could let myself go and embrace him and respond if he kissed me. I felt myself slipping as if under his spell. Then he let my hand go and moved away.

"It's cold out here," he said, and he closed the window. "Let's warm up by the fire. His abrupt manner caught me off guard. I stayed by the window for a moment to compose myself before I returned to my seat. Simon sat hunched in his seat unable to look at us and I sensed his deep resentment towards me.

Gregory slapped him on the shoulder. "Cheer up old chap. The wine isn't all that bad, but it can make one feel depressed if indulged in too much. By the way Jack. You will want to meet Annette Manning. She lives over here you know. A great artist and worthwhile talking to about art. Simon here has meet her before and is greatly impressed by her work. How about I take you over there tomorrow first thing. She is up and about early most mornings and is more tractable then. That will mean a change of sleeping arrangements. Simon you sleep up in the house and Jack can stay here with me."

Simon's despondency was evident by the look on his face, but it seemed not to be noticed by Gregory. "How about one more drink before we part," he said.

Simon got up and strode to the door and slammed it shut after him as he left without a saying a word.

Gregory shrugged his shoulders and gestured with his hands spread out that was that and he wasn't surprised by Simon's behaviour. I felt uncomfortable not knowing how to respond. Here I was alone in the cottage with a man who probably expected me to sleep with him. He had made an approach to me and then withdrew it leaving me confused to how I should respond. I didn't really know this man or what his real intentions were. He lit a cigarette, holding out in front of him at an arm's length and regarded me with a faint smile on his lips, his eyes half closed as if weighing up how I would respond to his approach. He walked over to the window again, turned and blew smoke across the room in my direction.

"We were talking about composing weren't we. Well, this evening I'm taking a rest from that subject. Do you swim?"

"Yes." I replied in a manner that made me feel I as if was in the headmaster's office again being interrogated for some misdemeanour.

"Then tomorrow morning, first thing before breakfast we must smite the briny with strong arm and swim to the end of the wharf and back here. A fine way to clear the mind and set all systems at go for the day," he said.

How could I begin to understand his agenda if for one moment, he was making an advance on me and then the next he was impersonal and objective.

We talked late in the night about anything to avoid our feelings towards each other. I tried to make it plain that my interest in him was restricted to Art and Music and whenever there was a pause in the conversation, and he was looking intently at me giving me messages what his intentions were as he moved closer to my side where we sat on the edge of the bed I got up and went to the window.

"Look," I said "The moon has gone, and all is dark out there."

In exasperation he answered rather curtly, "It couldn't be any darker than it is in here." He threw his wine glass in the fire grate where it shattered, and pieces of glass spread out over the floor.

I started to pick up some of the larger pieces of glass.

"Forget it," he said in an authoritative manner. "Just take care where you walk." The door flung open and there stood Simon looking distraught and agitated.

"It's Bella, the youngest. She woke up and is crying. There's nothing I can do to calm her," he said.

Gregory put his arm around Simon's shoulder.

"I understand," he said. "You are not cut out to deal with such an emergency. Now Jack here I am sure can deal with it better than you."

He looked at me and smiled that faint, rather sardonic smile of his.

"Jack, old man you wouldn't mind going up and comforting the child. May as well sleep up at the house. Simon can stay with me for the rest of the night. We'll forget about the swim unfortunately. Children are so unpredictable. The best laid plans of mice and men. I'll call in the morning and we will go and see Annette Manning."

It was Simon who turned up next morning to take me to meet Annette. Gregory had some pressing matter he had to attend to but promised to come up and look after the children while we were away. Simon was in a more buoyant mood much like his old self, talkative, darting from one subject to another while we walked around the bay. We sat on a small rather decrepit seat above the beach at Sandy Bay and watched the scene before us. It was a pleasant morning with the sun dancing lightly and daintily on the water's surface. Pied oyster catchers plied the shore as the tide receded and gulls swooped lazily overhead landing and squabbling among themselves over tit pits found on the beach. The breeze was light and refreshing, rarely stirring the branches of the Ngaio trees that grew on either side of the track we had taken.

"Annette may or may not receive us. She is so unpredictable, often unwell, moody and can be difficult, but it is worth while putting up with all these fads of hers to see and talk art with her if she is in the right mood." Simon said. He was looking across the water and didn't face me when he next spoke.

"How are you getting on with Gregory?"

"I find him a very interesting chap, reserved and discrete. He doesn't give much away about himself. Could be difficult to get close to him." I said.

"Did you?" He turned to face me watching my expression as she spoke.

"Not in the way I think you mean. Look Simon if there is something between you two well good luck to you both. There is no jealousy on my part. I'm not infatuated by him which I think you are by the way. Rest assured that I will keep that to myself. I know Gregory well enough now for him not to openly show his feelings towards you, or anyone else. You Simon must be careful also. It is too risky at present to admit to love between two men. Hopefully there will come a time when you can be open about these relationships."

"Thank you, Jack. I know what you mean. Gregory does come across rather as a cool customer, but underneath he is very sensitive, probably unreliable when it comes to being close to him, but I love him Jack."

I felt a little uncomfortable at this revelation and suggested we should be getting along. The path, or more likely the track up the hill, to Annette's home was rough and overgrown. In places it had subsided leaving only a narrow path to negotiate. Tall stands of gorse grew on either side in places, and it looked as if the path would lead us to utter wilderness until at last, set among the gorse where it as more open, we had a glimpse of a cottage. There was a smell of dampness and decay about the place. The roof was rusty and the down pipe on one corner hung precariously from the guttering that had slumped in places. Where the paint had peeled from the weather boards of the house green moss grew giving the air of a long-neglected place. The windows hadn't been cleaned for some time and large cobwebs hung from the window frames and sills.

A tall woman carrying a bucket came from behind the house. She put the bucket down and straightened her back.

"Well, what do you want. This is private property I'll have you know," she said as she placed her hands on her hips in an aggressive manner.

"It's me Annette, Simon. I have brought a fellow Art student to see your work if that is all right with you."

She regarded me with a look of hostility. "Art Student. Two a penny. I've got nothing to show them Simon, you should know that."

Simon edged closer towards her. "I've got a loaf of bread, some butter and a tin or two of fruit and beans in this bag that Gregory asked me to drop in to you."

She was a tall woman with long, blond hair swept back to fall on her shoulders. Her features were well defined, long sharp nose, high cheek bones and a small mouth and deep-set brown eyes. She took the offered bag of food almost snatching it from Simon's hands and mounted the steps to the door of the house.

"Thank him from me Simon. I'm grateful. You can't come in today. I haven't had time to tidy the place and I'm not well enough to entertain visitors," she said before she entered the house and closed the door behind her.

Professor Wells and his wife, Grace returned that afternoon and we were relieved of our duties as childminders. Gregory and Simon united again as a couple, left soon after to return to Christchurch.

After the disappointment of not having any time with Annette I was delighted to except Grace's invitation to stay until the morrow and see her work and talk about Art with her.

I sat at an outdoor table set in a small clearing among the tall trees that grew on their property and looked out to the Lyttelton Harbour heads. Grace moved slowly, serenely, flowing like a gentle stream as she walked, her smile reassuring, warm and welcoming as she set a tray of cups, teapot and hot scones made that afternoon on the table before me. She had left me for a few moments to prepare the tea and I had fallen under the spell of the sheer tranquillity of the place. It was different from the beach at Waireka which was still fresh in my memory. Here at the Bay being surrounded on three sides by the steep hills of the peninsula, densely treed in places and bare tussock land on many of the slopes, with the calmer waters of the deep inlet of the harbour, there was a calmness that was different from the beach. Among the trees bell birds and other native birds sang their songs of praise. Here I felt transported into another world, where time moved differently, if it moved at all as if I was here, but not there really here, a revenant hovering between both worlds.

I had not noticed that Grace had returned with the tea and sat down unobtrusively in the chair beside me. She must have sat there for some time, her hands clasped together in her lap, not wanting to disturb me until a sparrow landed on the table in front of me and disturbed my reverie.

"I see the place has worked its spell on you as it does with many sensitive souls," she said.

"My husband brings many of his students including Gregory and Simon, over here to baby sit.

They too take away with them the calming influence of this place."

"I know what you mean. It certainly has that influence on Gregory and Simon. They looked so happy when they left this morning." I said.

She put her hand gently on mine. "We know about them and I am pleased for them, but we don't talk about it. Talk on that subject can be too dangerous. I would hate to see them suffer if it ever got out. Gregory keeps his own counsel, but Simon, I fear by his very exuberant nature, finds it difficult to conceal. Gregory, you know had a brief affair with Annette but that is now over. He remains a good friend to her, giving her food and helping to promote her work. We all fear for her, as she slides further into poverty."

Poverty, was that the lot for us who relied on being an Artist for a livelihood even though we might not be eccentric and mentally unstable as Annette. That night, in my room after everyone had retired for the night, I sat on my bed and thought about my future. This, I had thought would resolve itself, something that would happen depending on what opportunities came my way. I had long given up the childish notion of growing up to be an engine driver, a pilot, or a sea captain. I had no precise and definite expectations. I had simply drifted into Art School because I had a talent that way and Uncle Ernest had offered to pay my way at University. Aunty Kate had different ideas. She saw me as a builder, or a plumber, or something worthwhile like that. An artist, what a crazy idea she had said and because of her opinion, to spite her, I'd taken up Uncle's offer. Now I wondered if Aunty might have been right. I envied older men, who seemed so sure of themselves, dressed in smart suits, showing a little grey in their hair, married, owning their house, and not wanting for anything.

Then there was the life of adventure to be considered, of travel, taking up new opportunities, perhaps not as secure of course, but not as dull as the life of the older men, I thought, I envied. Perhaps all these thoughts were premature. Life at present for me was enjoying being young, parties, taking risks and drinking of course. This other stuff can be kept for later. I would sleep on it and maybe the morning it would bring resolution. Who cares!

There were nights when I slept fitfully, waking suddenly wondering what had wakened me. My breathing was short and rather alarming, my face hot and sweaty, and I lay long on my back, before I dropped off again. I know I should clear this mess of memorabilia off my bed before I go down, but this fit of nostalgia is still with me. I start to put some of them away in the suitcase, but hesitate when I find the preliminary sketch I had drawn of Verity, before I painted her portrait in my old digs in the Gloucester boarding house. It is a loose, quick sketch but I had certainly caught some likeness of her. I take the sketch to the window where the light is better and study it closer. I had caught that barely perceptible glint in her eye and that enigmatic smile the very essence of her personality. I see her now as I knew her then before we left Varsity. I held the sketch in my hand and sat down on the chair and relived those happy days.

On a wet Friday evening, when streetlights danced on puddles on the streets, the gusty showers beat on the pavements and the streets were deserted that I first came across Verity. I had heard of her of course, who hadn't on campus. I'd been working late in the painting studio at Varsity eager to finish a painting I had been working on for some time and had decided to call it a day. I pulled my scarf tightly about me turned up the collar of my jacket and head down made a dash across the quad when the bright light from the Great Hall suddenly spilled out in front of me as the door swung open and a group of students entered. The Friday night Barn dance in the Great Hall was in full swing. The blast of music from within died with the closing of the door behind the students. Any thought of returning to my cold, uninviting room at the boarding House with its one bar heater was quickly dashed and I followed the others inside.

Surrounded by a group of blokes, standing by the log fire in the large stone fireplace, its flickering light in the dimly lit Hall, was on the face of a lively girl who seemed to be holding court. She was like a freshly sprung, glorious tulip among a bed of weeds, each of which moved aside to make room for it to grow. I first saw her in action at that dance hall surrounded by adoring males competing for her attention and hanging on her very words as if mesmerised in her company. What struck me at the time was that there were no other girls in that group by the fire. They either sat on the forms on the opposite side of the hall or danced with each other, or with the few chaps who had given up trying to impress the fire goddess, Verity. I heard her name frequently among her admirers. I didn't try to join them, but stood by the door with two other guys, who like me, lacked the courage to ask one of the other girls to dance and instead watched Verity's performance. She was a teaser, urging the blokes on with her response to their advances as they tried to outdo one another. There was no place for me among those extroverts with their exaggerated behaviour.

I remember returning to my digs, thinking what fools those chaps were, to be captivated by a girl whose obvious agenda was to court popularity. Then over a cup of tea, I had other thoughts which stayed with me when I got in to bed. She was a looker, had personality and was playing with those gullible blokes. They ate out of her hand. I'd heard stories before about this ravishing blond, long haired girl who swept across the campus conquering all before her. Well, I determined I would not be one of her victims. Better to concentrate on my degree than get all tangled up in those long tresses. Before I fell asleep that wet Friday night, I had to concur that I too, if rather reluctantly, I was intrigued with her.

I asked about her on campus. "Verity. Oh, everyone knows Verity about here. There was no fun without Verity. She lights up a party with her vitality and her gorgeous smile which melts the heart of the most cynical males amongst us. She was cool and possibly shaggable. She was Verity."

"There is no one like Verity if you want some fun," was what I was told.

I followed her around the campus, but always at a discrete distance, but near enough to hear much of the talk among them as she and her infatuated males swept across the quad. She told them what they wanted to hear, about how she would rather be with men than women whom she said were bitchy and emotional. She'd rather drink beer and go to rugby games than go out with other girls.

What she said made sense to me at the time for I was vulnerable then, eager for someone to steer me in what I thought was the right direction. Because of my indecision about my sexuality, I was sensitive to any ideas that conformed with my own. I spent as much times as I dared following her around and she must have noticed me hanging back which, she told me later, that I must be an ardent acolyte, but obviously too shy to push myself forward.

I can still feel the moment of prophetic revelation that thrilled through me when late one afternoon I rounded the corner of the building and nearly collided with her. Instead of stepping aside to avoid me she blocked my way and she smiled at me. It was a dazzling smile that I will never forget. She said she had seen me following the herd, as she called it, and wondered why I didn't join them. She must have looked upon me as an outcaste and why I bothered to hang around with them. On the spur of the moment not knowing what to say I told her I was doing Fine Arts and I would like to paint her portrait. She seemed amused and asked why would I want to paint her. She was nevertheless flattered when I gave my reason that she would make a great subject and after a short deliberation she accepted my offer. We made arrangements for her to come to my digs next day. I had done few portraits at the time and didn't think they were particularly good. What prompted me to offer was not that I could make a good job, but that I would have her to myself in my room during the sittings that it would need. To think that I had the temerity to not only make the offer, but to go ahead with it amazed me for I knew I would run the risk of being ridiculed by the jealous herd. God what was I doing?

The first sitting was to be at two o'clock that afternoon. Had I been too presumptuous. Just look at the state of my room, bed unmade, dirty washing in piles on the floor which I hadn't swept for some time, a pile of books sprawled across the floor in the corner of the room, all of which was acceptable to me, but it wasn't me I had to impress. It was a sitter, no other than the goddess, Verity, herself. This was a real make or break situation, but I was determined to go ahead with it. I pushed the clutter on the floor under the bed, gave a cursory sweep of the floor with the common broom, which was kept outside in the hall, pulled up the bed and stood back to admire my effort. At best it was slapdash, but I hoped presentable.

These were not only the preliminary problems I had to consider before Verity arrived in an hour's time. What about the light and how would I pose her? Would she want to lie on my rather unattractive and probably dirty bed spread, or if considered a head and shoulders portrait was my one and only chair suitable. God, the light in this room was dingy even when I pulled back the torn, old curtain from the window. And did I have a suitable canvas and what medium would I use? A quick search through my box of paints solved that problem. It had to be oils and even then, I was out of ochre and I would surely need to use that.

I panicked and knocked on Simon's door. We had seen little of each other recently. He listened to my predicament with folded arms and with a wry expression told me I was out of my depth and If I had to get infatuated with a female, I couldn't have made a worse choice. She'll eat you and then spit you out was his conclusion. He could see that I was in a fix and the whole thing would be a disaster and I would end up never to be able to show my face about campus again without being ridiculed. He stood there, arms folded and a smirk across his face.

"You are a fool to have fallen for that vixen," he said. "Well out of your class and I would think of the wrong sex wouldn't you say." He thrust his face closer to mine as if tempting me to hit him.

I could have struck him as I clenched my hands. I took hold of myself and became aware that the tension between us was slowly diminishing. He watched me closely as I relaxed and unclenched my hands. Cress fallen and feeling rather stupid I was about to leave when he spoke again.

"Still, you have got yourself in to this mess and I will, rather reluctantly, help you to get out of it as best I can," he said. "Leave the canvass and the oils and brushes to me and if you can't make your room more presentable you can use my room for the sitting as you know I keep it in tip top condition always."

I accepted his first offer but declined the use of his room. The thought that I would have him in the room while I worked was out of the question.

I recall that first session with Verity. She seemed a little bemused as she looked around her.

"What no drink," she said. "Or are you the sort who uses drugs to get your way with me?" I reassured her that I was too poor to provide booze and drugs were not my thing.

Obviously, she remained sceptical. "Well, it is the first time any guy has used the excuse of wanting to paint my portrait to get me to come to his room. You would be surprised what other strategy they use."

When she saw that I did, indeed, have a canvass on the easel and brushes I think she really thought I might be genuine. She had arrived late dressed in a brightly coloured floral dress and excessive make up on her face. All the spontaneity of her personality was repressed, and she presented a faded image of the person I wanted to paint. Not wanting to hurt her feelings I made a few

117

charcoal and pencil sketches of her as she sat in the chair with light from the window on one side of her face. Even these drawings were of a staid, serious girl lacking completely any of her outgoing personality. As tactfully as I could I suggested that next time she came dressed in what she wore on campus and with less, or better still, no make-up.

During the sittings that followed she put me at my ease, and we got to know each other better than before. Later I went with her to dances, jazz concerts featuring rather obscure bands, drank cheap plonk until we were either sick and vomited, or were too drunk to find our way home.

Gradually, we went out less often preferring to stay in my digs, but I could not make love with her. Something, that I didn't recognise then was holding me back. Given her reputation I began to wonder how long this would last until she finds another partner to party with. Alone with her I saw another side of her which she had kept to herself, one that I had not anticipated. I began to see her as a different girl from the one she had displayed to us gullible males.

From a girl who said she adored rugby, dirty jokes, which she could go one better than those that were told to her, burping and playing poker for cash, liked beer, hot dogs, hamburgers, or in short, anything her boyfriend likes, to someone who during our time together, became a thoughtful, intelligent even argumentative girl with all the characteristics I admired in Daphne when I knew her during our early teen years.

I admired her for the different roles she could play when in new company, the immature teen age girl successfully being popular with the boys, the mock serious one she adopted when in the company of older people and the silly giggling one used to impress other girls of her age.

Which one of these, if any, was the true Verity I was determined to discover.

By the time she had left university she had dropped many of her old roles and to me showed glimpses of her own true personality. Her work as a reporter for the Press with the grim reality of some of the scenes she witnessed in the courts and the wider community tempered her outlook somewhat without dulling her spontaneous vivacity. We still partied, enjoying the company of each other. She no longer tried consciously to be the centre of attention. It just came naturally even when she got involved in heated arguments, she had a way of making light of a tense situation which often resulted in laughter and an agreement to differ in good faith.

I thought of myself, then, as a serious conventional sort of a person. I didn't have the security that a good upbringing gives, nor did I have confidence of being absolutely sure of my sexuality with what had happened to me when I was eleven. I wondered what it was that made Verity happy with my company. I'd often wondered why Daphne also bothered with me when we were kids together. Both girls had qualities that I admired, but also envied, their liveliness, their confidence, and their faithfulness. Maybe, it had a lot to do with my feeling of inferiority because of lack of family life and the effect of what had happened to me when I was eleven. I just couldn't tell anyone about that.

We were sitting at a small table in a milk bar in New Regent Street drinking one of Murray's special milk shakes. She was stirring her milk shake with the straw when said rather casually, "I don't expect you to be interested, but My Pop wants me to attend the debutante ball of my old school next week. I'm not that keen, but it is the thing that has to be done and for Pop's sake I feel I must oblige. The thing is, I must have a partner, before Pop presents me and I was wondering if you might be that partner?"

This was out of the blue. I'd been at ease with her social life so far with parties and get together with others, but this was something well out of my league. I understood that this Ball would be a snobbish affair, but I understood that because she was an old girl of a Girls' private school, she felt obliged to attend. For me to mix in such circles was well beyond my experience and I had no notion of what it might involve. I certainly didn't have a suit or bow tie and didn't have the money to hire one. I hesitated before I answered. "Thank you very much I said. I am honoured to be asked but I will have to think about it."

"Not for too long Jack. I have to know before Friday. I've put you on the spot, haven't I. Not your thing and you wouldn't have the gear or be at ease with all those stuck-up types you'd meet there. Forget it. I'm sorry. I mentioned it really."

I could see the Ball meant a lot to her and her father. She was reverting to her own upbringing and mixing more with the people she moved amongst before she went to Varsity. And these people were remote from me living a life far removed from mine.

"When did you say the Ball was to be held?" I asked.

She wasn't looking at me when she answered, "Next week on Saturday night."

"Oh God! I can't." I said. "That is the weekend that I have promised Aunty Kate that I would drive Uncle Ernie to Dunedin for specialist treatment. I'm sorry." She put her hand over mine on the table.

"So am I Jack, but it can't be helped. I'll find someone else at short notice. There are plenty who will jump at the chance I suppose."

I think it must have been three weeks later before I saw Verity again. I heard that she was going around with the bloke who was her partner at the ball and was probably sleeping with him. I was spending as much time as I could with my studies and was annoyed one afternoon when there was a knock on my door. I didn't answer hoping the caller would go away, but there was an even louder knock which demanded an answer. I swung the door open and much to my surprise and delight there stood Verity. She had come to invite me to meet her father who was very impressed with the portrait I had painted of her. I was rather non plussed while she was her usual vivacious self, full of confidence as if there had never been a rift between us.

Verity lived with her father in a swanky house in Fendalton. We rode our bicycles across Hagley Park and along Fendalton Road to her place in Waiwetu Street. Verity rang the doorbell. "Damn it," she said." I forgot my door key. We will have to wait ages before old Mavis answers the door."

She rang again keeping her finger on the bell button for some time. Eventually we heard someone on the other side of the door probably withdrawing the bolts, but still we waited.

Verity became agitated.

"God, I hate it when I forget my key. It's the same every time. The door is bolted on the other side and now old Mavis has gone to find her key, that's if she can remember where she left it. Come on follow me. It's the bathroom window for us. That's never shut."

We went round the side of the house and I bent over supporting my hands on my knees while   Verity climbed on my back, pulled open the bathroom window, wide enough for her to climb through. A moment later, she appeared from around the back of the house. "Come on I opened the back door," she said.

Inside in the hallway we came face to face with a hunch-backed old woman. She seemed unaware of our presence until she was almost on us. She shrieked and put out her arms as if to ward us off.

"It's alright Mavis it's me, Verity. We came in through the back door."

The old lady came closer and peered closely at Verity's face putting out her hands to touch Verity's face for confirmation. A door in front of us in the hallway was flung open to reveal a short, rather plump man with receding hair, a prominent nose and wide almost protruding eyes that gave him a look of surprised disbelief. "What's this," he demanded. Verity ran forward and flung her arms around his neck.

"It's me Pop. Sorry we gave Mavis a shock, but I left my key back in my flat. Silly of me." He was eyeing me suspiciously. "And who is this?" he asked.

"Oh! this is Jack," Verity said.

"Jack Waldron," I said. "Pleased to meet you, Mr Wilson."

"Waldron. Do I know a Waldron? Can't say I do. Foreign lot or something are you?" he asked.

"No Pop. You remember, I showed you the portrait of me he painted," said Verity.

"Paintings, I won't have a painting in the house. Took them all down when Mary died. Just cluttered up the place."

"I have my portrait hanging in my room," said Verity.

"How would I know. I never go in your room. Artist or something, then are you?" he asked me. "I have no time for that sort. I hope you don't think you can marry into this family. Verity brings blokes like you into the house much like my dog used to bring in dead rabbits and dropped them all over the floor. Disguising habit so, don't bring any of your damn paintings in here, or they will go the same way as those dead rabbits."

Verity ushered us to the lounge and offered me a seat. Mr Wilson stood in front of the fireplace glaring at me as if he thoroughly distrusted me. During the time I was there he never stayed still for a moment, always fidgeting with something, which reminded me of Nathan, or going in and out of the room as if he had forgotten something and had gone to find it.

When Verity left the room to help Mavis prepare afternoon tea his conversation with me was brief, and impersonal, something he had to get through in hurry and move on to some other more pressing matter. He didn't mention the portrait of his daughter again which I assumed he had had forgotten about already. During my stay Verity said little and offered no further explanation about me. I was certain she left the impression with her father that I was just a casual friend, one of many she knew at Varsity. I was relieved when Verity said that we had to leave to swot for our exams due in the next fortnight.

121

"You don't know what I saved you from Jack. Afternoon tea that's what. Poor old Mavis burns everything, the scones, the cake and if it was possible the water for the tea. That's if she could find any tea bags to make tea. Pop doesn't seem to notice, but I can't live there anymore," she said.

A fortnight before exams everyone had their nose to the grindstone and we saw little of each other. And then when the exams were over, we all went our separate way and soon lost touch with each other. Perhaps that's what happened between Verity and me. I did once go around to her father's place and make enquiries, but he had forgotten ever meeting me.

"So nice of you to drop by." he said. Have you come far? Verity, she had a life of her own. Only comes around for cash when her till is empty. Gone off to London or some such place to a drama school I think."

"Do you have her address?" I asked.

"What address? She has had so many. "By the way," he asked me, "Are you the cricket chap? 1 seem to remember a chap of your name as being a cricketer who Verity brought around here a lot.

She was always bringing chaps in here much like my cat used to bring in dead rats."

"Rabbits, sir. Your dog brought in dead rabbits."

He gave me a disdainful look. "Dog! what are you talking about I never had a dog." He said.

If he ever knew Verity's phone number or where she was living, he has forgotten it. Likewise, Verity must have forgotten to contact me again and leave her address and phone number. Forgetfulness and eccentricity must be part of the Wilson make up. Or perhaps, there is method in their madness.

I thought that we loved each other, prepared to give a little of us to each other wherever that might lead. Perhaps, I was mistaken. Our affair was only a temporary one which we both accepted and temporary affairs are often more pleasurable.

While at University, I visited Uncle whenever I thought Aunty would not be at home. He had never talked about the war, at least not to me as far as I can remember. Whenever the topic was brought up and he had a few draughts', as he called them, he would say.

"I have given some thought to it from time to time, but not much thought before time and even less after time. The whole business of thought is a very tiring thing and is to be avoided at all costs. After all, when they call 'Time-up' at the pub one is expected to leave but somehow, I find my legs desert me, and I am unusually unsteady on my legs and that's how I ended up with this damn accident that's crippled me. It just goes to show that you can never tell what time really means or how much thought one ought to give it and what consequences it can have when time is called."

As a child, I was confused about what he was talking about. Nevertheless, I enjoyed hearing him talking such nonsense which he only indulged in when Aunty was nowhere to be seen or heard.

After his accident, he became more serious and rarely talked like that often. He now relied on others for their support and, in particular, on my nemesis, Len Hales. He had once looked upon him as his deliverer, but towards the end of his life he was beginning to have doubts. He realised that he was converted when he was particularly vulnerable. "Got me when I was low," he explained to me one day." There are folk who go through life looking for victims. Perhaps Len was one of them folks. Picked me up a bit when I was down in the spirits, I suppose."

But towards the end of his days, he told me that he was having serious doubts about all that religious stuff. I wasn't to say a word about this to my aunty he insisted, not a word.

"She thinks of Len Hales as being a true saint, and it would break her heart if she knew what I really think about Len now."

Perhaps, this was the time for me to tell him about what Len Hales had done to me when I was a child. I had plenty of opportunities do so when I visited him when Aunty was out, but somehow, although I was on the verge of divulging everything, I hesitated and changed the subject. He was aware that I was holding something back and asked me why as a child l had a thing about Len Hales, something you haven't told us he had said. On numerous occasions when I visited him towards the end of his life, I had resolved to tell him all, but because of the shame and guilt l had felt about the incident, I couldn't cross that threshold.

He liked to talk about time, how it never stayed still, the present too soon becomes the past he insisted.

"My time is nearly up," he said one evening. "I only have the past to look back on now. Too many memories too many losses, too many lost opportunities. Grab time by the balls my boy and get on with life as best you can. Don't look back like me and regret how much time I've waisted over the years."

It was on that same evening visit for the first time he mentioned the war.

"Too many of us blamed the war, and what it did to us, as an excuse for not getting on in life. Well, boy," he said as he looks me in the eye, "It did put the brakes on things for me and many others like me. I suppose, I was a real bastard when I came home from the war with bits of German metal still in me. Christ, I'm ashamed about the way I behaved then, and if it hadn't been for Aunty, I'd would have been a real cot case. She put up with me and helped me to settle down again."

He'd looked at me and smiled which I hadn't seen him do for weeks and put his hands on my arm.

I recall his words still.

"Son, I know you and your aunt don't get on all that well. You probably find her too dictatorial and set in her ways, but she has been very patient with me, and I thank her with the bottom of my heart that she agreed to take you on as a child when my sister, your mother died."

Simon, Doug, Greg and myself left our digs early and pooled our cash to see how far it would go. It never went far in those days although, there was usually enough for us to buy six and sometimes a dozen bottles of beer. We never considered anything other than that because our money went further with beer than with any fancy drink, like spirits. We meet under the clock tower at Varsity and planned our night. First the beer which had to be bought after hours of course, then it was to the Latimer hop and who knows what might come next.

"Your turn Jack to go around the back. We will be right behind you to help you carry the grog.

Don't worry," said Greg.

I waited until the coast was clear and keeping to the side of the pub to avoid detection I went to the back door. I could hear muffled voices and now and then hearty laugher coming from inside the pub. I looked behind me to see if the others had followed me before l knocked heavily once on the back door. The sound of voices from within ceased followed by a deep silence and then the sound of running feet, chairs being knocked over and windows being opened.

The window beside me opened and a figure appeared halfway out of the window until he saw me.

He slammed the window shut and disappeared somewhere inside. Later they told he had thought I was a cop because one loud knock on the back door was a signal from a very understanding constable that a raid was about to take place.

Realising what I had done I ran after my friends who had taken to their heels the moment that I had knocked on the door. Unfortunately, for Simon instead of following the others he had run to the footpath and into the arms of the Police who had arrived outside the pub in a van. They grabbed him, handcuffed him, and put him in the van along with two others who they had caught leaving the pub through one of the windows.

I was out of wind, by the time I caught up with Greg and Doug.

"Hoist, over here for God's sake and get down." Greg called to me from out of the shadows behind a high wooden fence. "We don't want the cops coming this way. They seem to have caught a few and seem satisfied, but if you make as much noise as you made back there, they'll be up here in a jiff."

"I think they have grabbed Simon, poor bastard," said Doug. "Jesus, I thought you knew the right knock. It's three times and then a lull before you knock again."

"It looks like we have not only lost Simon, but we have no beer. I can't go to a hop without being tanked up a little. God, it's hard enough to ask a dame to dance even when you have had a few, but running on empty that's beyond a joke," said Doug.

"We'll give it a minute or two before we move out of here. Come over to my place and we can drown our sorrows with a few songs. They say the necessities life are wine, women and song. Well Jack has stuffed up the wine part and as for the woman I agree with Doug. We can do without them, but at least we can have the song part of the equation," said Greg.

I felt I had let them down badly and spoilt their night, but I doubted that Greg and probably Doug too, were not too put out by missing out on the women part of the necessities of life.

We drank cold tea and gathered around the piano in Greg's digs singing the few songs that Doug and I knew while Greg, oblivious to our lack of interest, played Mozart and other classical composers' music until I made the excuse that I wasn't feeling well and left. Doug stayed for what reason I could guess, and it wasn't to listen to more music.

On Monday morning, the three of us took a seat in the public area in the magistrate court.

Simon was to come before the beak on what charges we were not sure.

Simon was called last of the three men arrested on Saturday. The first two were charged with drinking after hours in the pub and were found guilty and, then it was Simon's turn to appear in the dock. He looked defiant and resolute at first, and after looking for us in the public gallery he smiled weakly, and he dropped his head to look at the floor at his feet giving us the impression that he had given in.

The Prosecutor laid a charge against Simon of attempting to procure sexual relations with another male. He didn't appear to be convinced as he read out the charge and often hesitated as he set out the evidence he had. My heart sank. My action on Saturday night seemed bad enough to deny us any beer over the weekend, but this charge was a serious one which was treated with severity in the courts.

The defence lawyer on duty didn't ask to question the constable who had made the arrest until a note was passed to him by a clerk of the court. He took some time to read it. "Yes, I do indeed have a question to ask the constable," he said. He got to his feet and holding the note he had been given in his hand in front of him he asked. "Did you actually see the man charged here make a proposition of a sexual nature to another male?"

The constable looked uncomfortable and muttered something that was inaudible.

"Speak up. Did you actually see this approach by the defendant," the lawyer said.

"Well, he was outside the hotel and was with a number of other men two of whom we later arrested for being in the hotel after hours. He was acting suspiciously," the Police witness replied. "Suspiciously and is that why you arrested him?"

"Not exactly."

"But you didn't see him approach anyone with a proposal to have sexual connection with him."

"No, we got him before he made his move. It was preventative really. I could see he was the sort of person who would fancy his chance with drunken men like those on the footpath who had come from the bar after hours."

"But you haven't charged him for being on the premises after hours."

"No. We have no evidence that he was on the premises."

"And I put it to you that you have no evidence that this man is guilty with the charge you have made against him," said the lawyer.

The Prosecutor who was looking rather shame faced approached the bench. After a minute or two of conversation between him and the magistrate the case against Simon was dismissed by the Magistrate and Simon was free to go.

That night we celebrated Simon's release at Max Sadler's place in Latimer Square. Max was studying to become a lawyer and was a member of a respected old Canterbury family. He had written the note that had saved Simon. He had written that he had Simon for tea and after had offered to drive him home. Simon had accepted his offer and asked to be dropped in the Square saying he would walk home from there as it was a fine night. The hotel where Simon had been arrested while passing by on the footpath was on his way home.

We regarded Max as being more mature and sagacious than us. He said the police would be smarting over the court decision and might go out of their way to get Simon in the future. He advocated discretion. Simon must be more careful in the future and not be seen hanging around Public toilets or go walking on his own after dark in Hagley Park. Simon was a marked man and could be watched by undercover Policemen in the future.

All this was rather frightening, and I had serious misgivings of my own proclivity in matters like this.

For a few weeks after Verity moved out of my life, I made no attempt to find someone to take her place. I still enjoyed girl's company at university and appreciated their looks and the way they dressed, but kept my distance, choosing to have the company of other blokes for my relaxation. I knew this couldn't last and I felt the longing to have a girlfriend again.

Because neither Greg nor Simon seemed not to have this same longing I started to drift away from their company and went back to the Latimer Dance hall on Saturdays. I often offered to take a girl I fancied home after the dance without considering how I would manage to do so when I didn't own a car. Sometimes I had an arrangement with a friend who did have a car and off we would go with a girl each usually, or at times I was the only one with a girl and he would try to win my partner over by trying to impress her with his cheap wit.

That I had a number of these short, often a one night stands sometimes without the reward of a kiss or a cuddle didn't bother me. I had not thought of a long-term relationship while at University.

In my last year at University, I started going to the Varsity Barn dance in the Great Hall on Fridays. These were often rather staid affairs, a chance to relax after a week's lectures and not in the same league for finding partners as the Latimer.

There were few at the dance on the night I meet Barbara. She was a docile, sweet little lass, diminutive in stature with large blue eyes and long blond hair. She sat on the opposite side of the hall from me with another girl, her sister, I found out later. I stood with my back to the fire, hands behind my back, feet apart and surveyed the talent on the other side. Barbara, and her sister Gwen, had danced once together, but had spent the evening so far sitting out any further dances. Two men had approached them and probably offered them to dance and had been refused.

As the suitors returned to my side of the hall feeling snubbed, thinking all eyes were on them and wishing for the floor to swallow them the two girls exchanged glances and giggled gleefully.

I was outraged by this and before I could give it another thought I, holding my head up high chin thrust out, strode across the hall with great purpose. I was hardly aware of the looks from the girls as I neared them. I bowed and gave a wide sweeping gesture with my arm and in a loud voice demanded that one of them should not languish in obscurity by denying the assembled guests their grace and beauty on the dance floor. I must admit that I had had more drink than I usually had on occasions like this. If they denied me, I was determined to make quite a scene of the whole thing, which I was certain I would be cheered on by the males on the other side of the hall who had already been refused by the girls.

How prim and proper they seemed to me as I got closer to them. Their giggling expressions had changed to a look of surprise with a hint of interest on Barbara's face compared to Gwen's disdainful look.

As if propelled from her seat, Barbara was on her feet and in my arms, or should I say really, at almost an arm's length from me. I swept her off her feet onto the dance floor. She danced gracefully and daintily her long blond hair flowing out behind her. Her head was turned to one side, refusing to look at me, and when I pressed my arm against her back to draw her closer to me, she stiffened and bent her back away from me.

"You dance with great grace your feet hardly touching the floor." I said. She didn't reply, dropping her head and keeping as far away from me as she could and still be my partner.

"Ah." I said. "Such grace, such breeding." Was this me saying this or had someone else taken me over.

"You say such things you flatterer," she said as we swept around the hall avoiding other couples as we went. "I mustn't stay long. Gwen will be feeling a little put out, me going off like this."

"Tweddle Dum and Tweedle Dee," I said. "Such loyalty. I am impressed. One more round and I will return you to your place beside your dear sister. Will you have another dance with me?"

"Oh dear. I'm not sure. I don't like leaving Gwen for long. We are close and have never parted before."

"Until tonight, is that it?"

"Of course not. But I can't let her down."

"But it is only another dance with you that I ask."

We returned to where Gwen was sitting. She almost rose from her seat as if to claim Barbara back. Her look of disapproval not lost on either Barbara or me. I couldn't help but countered. "Could I see you home tonight do you think?" I asked in a defiant tone of voice.

My request met with a sullen silence, and then Barbara looked up at me and met my gaze. "If you like, but you will have to see both of us home of course. How noble of you," she said with a smile. I heard the withdrawn breath of Gwen and felt the cold of the frosty look on her face.

We caught the last tram to their house in Riccarton Road. They sat together whispering and every now and again looking over their shoulders at me where I sat behind them. I got off the tram at their stop and we stood together on the footpath.

"I hope this is not where our paths branch." I said.

"It is tonight," said Barbara, "But we would like to meet you again soon." Gwen stood a little apart from us and didn't comment. Again, 1 felt the urge to meet her hostility to me face on. "Good." I said. "How about a trip to Sumner on the weekend." We agreed to meet on Sunday in the Square at ten o'clock.

"Come on Barbara. Father will be worried about us being so late home." Gwen said.

I had a long walk home to my digs in Gloucester Street. By the time I reached my boarding home I had convinced myself that I would not be going to Sumner on Sunday and that I was indeed stupid to get involved with the sisters.

Saturday was catch up day with washing, cleaning the room and then getting down to a few hours of swotting. By three o'clock I had enough of studying and closed my books and lay on my bed thinking what I would do for the rest of the weekend. Why had I got myself involved with those two sisters who apparently were under the strict control of their father, probably a grouchy old geyser who wouldn't let his daughters go. Then again Barbara might be able to be wooed away with a bit of strategic planning.

On Sunday I was there in the Square at ten o'clock and boarded the team to Sumner with the two sisters. They of course sat together with me behind them. They were rather conventionally dressed for a day at the sea side, with large brimmed sun hats, long dresses with hems well below the knee and lace up shoes. How old fashion! it occurred to me.

Before we went for a stroll along the length of the beach at Sumner I bought ice creams and we joined the other strollers on the beach. I carried under my arm my swimming togs rolled up in my bathing towel.

"Keen for a swim later?" I asked. "We haven't brought our swimming costumes with us," said Barbara.

"Father would never allow us to go swimming at a public beach without him being with us," said Gwen.

"He would be upset if he thought that we had disobeyed him," said Barbara.

"Come on you two. You are having me on. This is mid 1970s not mid-1870s." I said.

"I know what you mean," said Barbara. "We are big girls now. I work in town in an office and Gwen stays at home looking after Father. We can and do make our own decisions at times, but never any that would upset Father."

"No, we could never forgive ourselves if we did anything to upset him even now," said Gwen.

"Have you asked him if you could go out today with a young man?" I asked.

The two girls exchanged glances and started to lick their ice creams.

Barbara stopped walking and looked out to sea. "Not directly, but we did ask before we left today," she said.

"And what did he say?"

"Nothing really, but we know that he would not have tried to stop us now. That is, if, we return early and not keep him waiting," Gwen said.

"I suppose he is resting, and will want you home in time to get his tea." I said in a rather sardonic manner.

Gwen spoke quietly almost reverently when she replied, "He doesn't want any tea now. We have put him to rest, and he will rest in peace forever if, we do not disturb him by disobeying him." The two sisters stopped walking and held hands. Barbara's voice broke when she said. "Father has passed over three weeks ago now, but he is always with us."

The two sisters looked out to sea to avoid me seeing the tears in their eyes. I stood aghast at this revelation.

A little further on we sat on the dry sand nearer the road. Both girls were embarrassed and wouldn't meet my eyes when I expressed my sorrow. For a minute or two we sat in silence listening to the sea, as its waves tumbled as if, in dispute with the beach, but caressed it gently before retreating. We watched a small group of children making a sandcastle. They at first worked together taking turns to dig more wet sand and piling it on the heap that they had dug earlier. Then came the shaping of the castle and that's where the cooperative work was marred by individuals wanting to shape it in their particular way. A squabble broke out followed by throwing sand at each other and smashing each other's' efforts until a mother intervened and quietened things down.

Gwen was first to break our silence. "I suppose all this sounds rather morbid to you, but it doesn't to us," she said. "You probably think we are downtrodden by Father's influence on us and in a way I suppose we are. Father rather ruled the roost and we had got into the habit of obeying his wishes until we became unable to make our own decisions."

"I wouldn't put it quite like that," said Barbara. "We have tried to break out before."

"And look where that got us," Gwen replied. "In real hot water."

"But you must think you can do it again now your father is dead."

I felt them both stiffen and by the look on their faces I knew I had offended them by using the word dead. That was too strong a word for them to accept.

"That's it," said Gwen. "We can't accept that he is no longer with us. We have made a few efforts since he passed over like going to the dance the other night."

"And coming out with you today. Father would never let us go out with a young man without his approval."

"And we still feel guilty by breaking his code of behaviour for young women," said Barbara.

"We are afraid, and that's why we decided to come here with you today and talk to you. You seem such a nice young man. The sort that Father would approve of surely. We don't know what to do." Gwen said as she put her hand over mine.

What is it about me that people come to me about their problems. Well at least they do, which is more than I have been able to do to approach others with my own hang ups.

"I don't know if, I'm the one to tell you what you should do except to get out more. Make a list of what you want to do and just do it, I suppose." I replied.

"It sounds easy, but somehow we can't," said Gwen. "It took a lot of courage to go to his room after he passed over, and when we did neither of us wanted to be the one who opened the door. We just stood there shaking with shock to be in his room when he wasn't there." Barbara put her arm around Gwen.

"But we felt he was there. We opened his draws and there were his socks, shirts and under clothing. We just couldn't touch them, and then we looked in his wardrobe and it was as if, he was still there among his suits and coats. It was awful. We ran out of the room and locked the door. And We haven't been back in there again. We can't." said Barbara.

"You must try." I said and then realised what a trite thing to say. Neither girl replied, and I felt as a confessor in their eyes. I had let them down. A small dog nose down following a scent, I suppose, looked surprised to see us sitting there, paused with one of his front legs lifted and then continued on his way.

Gwen got to her feet and dusted the sand from her dress. "We should be going. It is getting late."

Barbara and I remained sitting. "You can please yourself now your father is no longer with you." I said.

Gwen gave me a withering look. "That's it. He is still there in spirit in that house, and his influence over us is still there too."

Barbara remained sitting. "And that's why, after talking to you, Jack today, I think we need to shut up the house and go on a long holiday in the North Island as far away as possible," she said. "I'd like to see you Jack, when we return. Promise me you will call on us."

They stayed up North longer than they had thought, and a fortnight later I received a letter from Barbara telling me of the good time they were having and how the time away was proving beneficial for them both. They now thought they could face coming back to their father's house in Christchurch. I do wish to see you again Jack, as soon as we return, she wrote, and I was surprised to find a lock of her hair in the envelope. I am ashamed to say that I made no effort to call on them again after they returned. I saw her and Gwen once in the street outside Woolworths one day but didn't cross the road to speak to them.

"What is it with you Jack?" Max asked during one of our long conversations when we were lying on the grass under a large Oak tree in the Gardens. "None of us is prepared to come and admit he is a homosexual because of the danger that brings with it but at least we accept it ourselves and keep quiet about it, but you Jack you are on a swing that never stops swinging going from being one of us to behaving like a straight guy? You could be a fifth columnist and we can't tolerate that in our ranks. Make up your mind."

"That's it Max. I like your company, your companionship but I have a longing to be with a girl. Yet somehow, I cannot bring myself to let myself fall in love with one." I said.

"Sad state of affairs Jack. You will need to sort it out."

I made an attempt to sort it out as he said during my next trip to New Brighton. On the tram I sat next to a girl whose two friends were in the seat in front of us. I made myself known to my companion who was called Judy and we talked amiably. When we arrived at new Brighton l was introduced to the other two girls who volunteered to buy the ice creams which they were going to pay for leaving Judy and me alone among the sand dunes.

We were sitting close together looking out to see when I took her in my arms and kissed her for the first time. The spark of that kiss when our lips met erupted into a raging fire, as she refused to disengage our lips, and pushed me over on my back, and continued to kiss me with great passion. Excited and aroused I responded by thrusting my hands under her blouse and caressing her prominent soft breasts. But even aroused as she was, she maintained a certain degree of decorum and withdrew hastily when my hand slid up her thigh under her skirt. She jumped to her feet and stood over me adopting a stance of defiance, feet apart and head thrown back, red faced and panting while she smoothed her skirt down.

How clumsy was my approach, but it was born out of my suppressed passion, but I hadn't expected her defiant response. She strode off and when she met the other two coming over the road she must have told them about what I had done to her. All three of them stood there looking at me when I stood up and waved to them. For a moment, I thought they were going to come over to me, but instead they walked away, back towards the shops.

I never thought I would see Judy again, but I was mistaken. I must have awakened something in her for when I ran into her again a few days later on campus she came over to me.

"Hi," I said. Good to see you again. I must apologise for my behaviour the other day. I don't know what got into me."

"And so you should Jack. The others were disguised. They thought you went too far. Even a nice chap like you can't be trusted."

"I suppose I'm no more to be trusted than any other guy with a lovely lass like you Judy."

"Go on with you. But I have forgiven you and I would like to go out with you soon."

Then we met again and started to go out together to dances, films and on Sundays to the beach. Her persistence started to worry me, and I started to make excuses for not going out with her as often she wanted. One night when we were in my room Judy respond to my advances with more enthusiasm than she had shown before. There were no restrictions this time when I went beyond the kissing and breast stroking to removing her panties. I became excited when she not only didn't protest, but unzipped my fly encouraging me to go the whole hog with her. Our actions of disrobing were clumsy as we tumbled about on the bed. Until then, I had remained highly excited, but suddenly for no reason I could think of, I lost my erection, and a feeling of some unexplainable guilt came over me, and I rolled away from her.

Judy was first to regain her composure. She slipped from the bed without saying a word and she started to dress. I was utterly embarrassed and could not look at her and turned on my side away from her.

"That's right don't dare face me. You disgust me," she said. "Leading me on as if you meant it, and then switching off like that. Are you a man or a mouse?"

Those words of condemnation stayed with me for ages. To hear them said with such loathing, and from a person like Judy was shattering. I lost confidence entirely and resolved not to be in that situation again as long as I lived. My affairs of the heart and sex in general were over. I stopped going to dances and parties and lived the life of hermit to protect my over sensitive feelings.

Then much against my will I accepted an invitation to attend a small party put on by my friend Max in his Latimer Square flat. It was to be a small affair he said with just a few friends some of whom I would know. The evening was a quiet one with no music. Glasses of wine were passed around as we sat in the comfortable lounge chairs of Max's rather posh flat. I felt relaxed and was being to enjoy myself when suddenly the door to the lounge was flung open and in came Judy. She didn't look at me at first, but apparently rather tipsy, climbed on the dining table near me and started to dance lifting her skirt to reveal her rather shapely legs. She stopped in front of me her face contorted, her eyes blazing and started to pull down her panties.

"I'll show you something you never saw, you loser," she said in a very sarcastic way.

"Others have. Oh yes, I've had a few since I met you. Would you like to try again if you are up to it." Max was not surprised by her appearance but seemed to be by her performance. He took her arm and helped her from the table. She was shaking and tossing her head about and stamped her foot. Max escorted her out of the room. When he returned, he offered no explanation and I had the impression that the whole scene had been staged with his knowledge but not to that extreme that we had seen that evening.

"It's a despicable thing to led on a girl like that. You have broken her heart and what might that lead to?" Max said. "It is better if you don't see her again. The damage has been done."

"I had no idea that she took our relationship so seriously."

"You don't believe that she had had many lovers after you, do you? You were the only one and she told me she couldn't live without you."

"I'm sorry, but I don't feel the same about her." I said.

Later that evening, back in my room on reflection I couldn't help but be reminded of that day of the picnic when I was eleven when Daphne had thrown herself at me. I was to find out later, she had done that to get back at Vera when she thought she saw her embracing her father Felix Golding. It turned out later that he had been comforting Vera who had received a letter informing her that her mother had died back in England. Judy's performance at Max's flat was to get back at me for avoiding her.

I graduated that year and lost touch with Judy. Even if she was seeking me, I think she would have drawn a blank. I had left my flat in Gloucester Street land, was living back with Aunty Kate and Uncle Ernie in their renovated house in Beckenham suburb. They owned two other houses which they rented out. Uncle's health had deteriorated since moving to Christchurch. Aunty had mellowed since joining the church, and she remained devout while Uncle was having a few late doubts possibly because he could no longer attend church.

I hadn't expected Uncle to be at my graduation nor did I think for a moment that Aunty would be among the crowd in the town hall to see me capped. Those students around me in the front rows who knew their parents would be there chatted among themselves, excited at the prospect, looking forward to being photographed with them, going out in family groups for dinner later and generally being the centre of attention for at least for one day. Those of us who knew we would not have such filial support sat glumly with our mortar boards in our laps knowing that at that moment we had all been looking forward to for years when our names were called to be capped, there was no one out there to share that moment.

I was surprised that by what I expected to be only the usual polite, restrained clapping when my name was called, there was loud clapping from the right-hand side of the audience. There standing up from his seat was Uncle Ernie holding his large hands out in front of him clapping with great enthusiasm and sitting beside him Aunty Kate was clapping more politely.

After, outside on the footpath, Uncle embraced me while Aunty smiled and patted my arm, and congratulated me. They didn't stay as Uncle had not been well all week and had made a big effort to be there at all. Aunty insisted that they should go home, and Uncle must get his rest. She told me he had made a big sacrifice to attend. Uncle on his behalf made a half-hearted effort to deny that he needed to rest, but I could see that he wasn't well.

I saw them to a waiting taxi and opened the door for them. Before she got in Aunty turned to me.

"Now it's your turn to earn some money and pay back some of the hard-earned cash that your uncle invested in you," she said Any thought I might have had of Aunty changing, now she lived in town, was dashed when I next visited them in the Beckenham house that I had lived in after leaving Waireka, and before I attended university. She greeted me at the doorstep, arms folded, imperious, demanding subjugation if I as much as put a foot on the doorstep. I followed her meekly to the kitchen for I was now on her territory on her terms.

"You can't see your uncle now. He's asleep and his health is not good," she said. I sat on the high stool by the kitchen table while she stood on the other side of the table facing me.

"You needn't think you can come back here to live. I'm much too busy looking after Earnest to see for you. You don't know how much sacrifice he's made to send you to University. What for, I ask myself and I've tried to reason with him too, but he is stubborn like all of his family, the Waldrons. Just look at that mother of yours, his sister, too stubborn for her own good. Couldn't see anything in that father of yours, even when we tried to convince her, no good would come from marrying a hopeless, godless cur like him."

I hadn't come to hear one of her tirades about my near non-existent family. I rose and would have left the room if she hadn't moved quicker than me and blocked the doorway.

"Not so fast. It's time you heard how things are. We took you in because there was no one else who would, or could, look after you. You're a fully grown man now and must look after yourself. If you want my opinion, you have wasted enough time going to that university and what has it done to help you earn a living? If you think painting pictures will keep the wolf from the door well think again. I know Ernest thinks he's done the right thing for the sake of his sister, but he's too sick to tell you what I have just said. Get out there, stop trying to paint pictures that no one wants and get a proper job."

There may have been much truth in what she said, but I resented the manner in which she had said it. This was nothing new to me. For some time, I had been looking at what prospects I might have after I'd graduated. I had joined a number of young artist who having failed to be recognised by the Arts Society had held our own Group exhibitions without much success. We were modern abstract painters, not accepted by the traditional members of the Canterbury Art Society. She was right in saying we needed income from other sources. I left in a huff and angry that I hadn't been allowed to even look in at Uncle while he slept in his room. I had been banished and I resented her dominance over him.

During my three years at University, I had taken a number of part time diverse jobs, from cleaning big stores in town to being a shed hand at a back-country sheep station, none of which I had contemplated as being my future full-time job.

I was shocked by Uncle's appearance when I finally got to see him again. I'd timed my visit to correspond with Aunty's absence from the house when she was visiting an old friend of hers. Timing was the essence of my visit. I'd waited in the park across the road until she left the house before I made my move. The visit could only be of a short duration before she returned after having afternoon tea with her friend. Because Aunt was punctual, I knew exactly how much time I'd have with Uncle. He was out of bed sitting in his chair and after exchanging niceties on this visit with him I made a cup of tea and buttered one of Aunty's date scones to take to him to give me the courage I needed to tell him about me leaving the church which I thought had become the cornerstone of his life.

137

I brought the afternoon tea to the sitting room and poured the tea. He had closed his eyes while I was away and until he became aware that l had returned, I had time to look at him more closely. How old he had become. Deep lines on his face, brow and the finer, but very apparent thin lines at the corner of his eyes and mouth, had aged him. When he spoke his lips barely parted, and his words were slurred and at times incoherent. A few strands of grey hair brushed back to cover what else would have been a balding head gave him the appearance of someone much older than he was.

We drank our tea in silence, neither of us wanting to talk about what I was doing now varsity was over. When I brought the subject up about the church and how he was managing to attend he told me that Aunty had a car, and on some Sundays, he felt well enough to attend church, but not as much as he thought he should. The journey out to the country church was very tiring for him.

I dreaded what was to come up next and prepared myself to tell him that I no longer went to church. I softened it as much as I could saying I knew how much it meant to him and how it had helped him to recover from his accident, but it didn't have the same influence on me.

He looked at me scanning my face with his eyes looking for a hidden meaning in my words.

"Did Len Hales have anything to do with you not believing any longer?" he asked.

Taken aback by his direct question l hesitated to answer. I couldn't bring myself to tell him outright what Len Hales had done to me on a number of occasions when I was eleven years old. I think it would break him. He thought so much of Len and he would have been in the predicament of choosing which of us, Len or me, to believe. His eyes had lost their spark, his mouth had turned down at the corners and his face was a grey pallor. I could see he was wrestling with the problem, and I was glad l hadn't told him the truth about Len Hales. It would kill him for sure.

I saw as much as I could of Uncle, timing my irregular visits between the times and days that I knew Aunty wouldn't be there and when I wasn't at work. I had a position then with Whitcomb Tombs design and printing department which was bringing in a regular income.

Uncle's health for a while looked as if it had reached a plateau, until four months before his death when it deteriorated suddenly. Aunty, who must have been told by him of my previous visits when she was not around, tolerated my more frequent visits now when she was at home, for she must have realised he was not long for this world.

Although apparently, he lingered for a week before he died, Aunty made no effort to let me know that the end must be near. On my last visit he was hardly conscious and was probably unaware that I was there, but I would have liked to have been by his bed side before he drew this last breath.

His death notice was in the paper, but there was no mention of where, or when, the funeral would take place. It wasn't until I rang Mrs Kelly who was our next-door neighbour at Waireka, that I found out about the funeral.

The night before the funeral we had a storm which lasted all night with a force that I hadn't experienced before. I sat up in my bed, the sky dark and threatening, the flickering light in my room and the roar of rain on the roof of my flat. At last, I thought, Uncle was not going with a whimper, but like Thor astride the thundering clouds he was hurling his lightning bolts to earth, triumphant on his last ride, defiant and now an apotheosis of some kind of climactic experience.

He's going not with a whisper, but with a decent shout.

Next morning the sky had cleared as if Uncle had taken the storm with him, leaving its aftermath of wet roads, overflowing water races, ditches, and large dripping drops of moisture from trees.

There were a number of cars outside the church in which he had spent his last years as a member of the congregation. The faithful, of whom I had once been a member, filled the pews. I saw the coffin with a bunch of flowers on its lid, the pastor standing beside it and Aunty Kate alone in the front pew before Len Hales stepped out in front of me barring my entrance. Hatred I had thought was not part of my makeup until I felt it overcoming me as I stood toe to toe with him at the church door. He stood with folded arms, a smirk on his face, his head thrown back to try and gaze over my head, but instead I meet his beady eyes and with triumph I saw him drop his gaze and shift uncomfortably on his feet. For a moment I thought I had won and only had to push passed him to enter the church, until he regained his composure and said in a voice that all could hear.

"The church is full. There is no place for unbelievers here. Please leave." The whole congregation, except Aunty Kate swivelled in their pews to face me, their hostility towards me evident in their expressions.

I left the church, but determined to be there when they buried Uncle Ernie, I stood by his newly dug, damp grave. I stood my ground and held my place when his coffin was brought out followed by the congregation. Len Hales this time stood away from me on the other side of the grave his eyes down caste. Perhaps, he thought I might expose him for the criminal he was, if he tried to have me removed. I stood alone for none of the other mourners would stand near me as if I was in some way contaminated. When the pastor had said his last words, I followed Aunty to throw a handful of earth on his coffin as it lay in the grave. I moved over to her and stood by her with my hand on her arm to support her as the others left.

# 3

# Helen

I wondered what Helen really thought about Aunty. To sit immobile for an hour in one of Aunty's uncomfortable lounge chairs with a cup of tea on a saucer in her hand, and a plate with a buttered date scone, or a rock biscuit on her knee, was too much for Helen to bear during our visits to Aunty, after Uncle died. Aunty sat opposite her boasting of how well she had handled herself in the difficult circumstances. During those interminable Saturday afternoons, Aunty hardly said a word to Helen.

Helen made excuses for not attending after the first three visits, but I, thinking it was my duty, kept Saturday afternoons for Aunty, staying for as short a time as possible. Aunty, after Uncle died, sat in her chair staring into space as if I wasn't in the room with her. Our talk was usually restricted to domestic affairs and the weather, but in other times there was a long silence between us. When I thanked her for the tea and offered to take the tea things to the kitchen she accepted the offer in good grace. She never once enquired about Helen and our newly born daughter, Alice, or about how I was doing with my business. She seemed to have shut down since Uncle's death, much like what had been once a powerful geyser ready to blow at any time, was now only a hardly discernible dribble.

We took her to the Botanic Gardens one fine spring morning, Helen, and me with Alice in her pram. We walked slowly admiring the new spring flowers and the blossoms. Because the journey over the bridge to walk among the fields of daffodils under the trees was too trying for Aunty, we had tea in the cafe near the bridge near the car park.

"Who is this woman?" she hissed at me when Helen went to order the tea.

Somewhat surprised I answered, "Helen is her name. She is my wife."

"Don't be stupid, wife indeed. Next you will be telling me that brat in the pram is yours too. Don't you remember Aunty. You came to our wedding and later to Alice's baptism. Surely you haven't forgotten."

She gave one of her dismissive shrugs. She had a way of showing her disapproval by the way she sat, straight backed, skewed sideways in her chair, her withering look enough to leave no doubt about her disapproval.

Helen came back with an iced cake and tea things on a tray. She handed the cake to Aunty who looked scornful.

"What is this," she demanded. "I didn't ask for this. You must know by now that I never eat cakes like this, and that tea is bound to be cold by now. I can't abide cold tea."

Helen and I exchanged glances. "I'll take it back if you like," she said in a way that showed me she was struggling to remain civil.

"No need for that." Aunty said.

"I'll eat it." I said.

"That's typical of you, isn't it? Take anything you can get your hands on. Waiting no doubt for me to die, so you can get your hands on my money. Well, I have news for you young fellow, you'll not get a cent. It's all going to the church. You know you killed your uncle after all he did for you. When he paid for your education you threw that back in his face, but what really killed him was when you told him you had left the church. It broke his heart."

I recall after all these years that afternoon and what was said. The hurt is still with me.

Aunty was true to her word I never got a cent from her when she died. When she died, she had been sitting in a garden seat by the river feeding the ducks which were still fighting for the crusts she had thrown in the river A mother with a baby in a pram sat down beside her and was alarmed when Aunty fell against her spilling the last of her bread crusts on the ground at her feet.

Years later we sat in the doctor's waiting room, Helen and I flicking through the pages of magazines without consciously taking anything in. We were the only two there in that larger room with its rows of empty chairs against the walls and the table in the middle with piles of magazines, mostly women magazines, although amongst them there was one about motor cars and another on fishing, both of which could be of interest to women as well as men, I supposed. The glass partition of the reception desk was closed which gave the impression that work for the day was done. Had they forgotten us? The corridor outside was empty. The sound of passing feet had long passed.

I looked at Helen and shrugged my shoulders.

"Maybe we have come on the wrong day, or maybe your problem is too trivial for them to be concerned about, I said. Helen smiled. "No this is the right day and the right time," she replied as if resigned to whatever her fate might be.

I went to the window and looked out on small, enclosed courtyard below. A woman dressed in a smart suit and wearing high heeled shoes walked quickly across the courtyard and I fancied I could hear the clicking of her steps on the stone court slabs below. I waited until she disappeared through a swinging doorway before I returned to my seat. Unable to settle I walked over to the free water dispenser and tried to pull down a paper cup only to end up with three or four cups stuck together, and in my attempt to separate them, all but one fell on the floor. Operating the water tap proved to be just as frustrating. The first tank was empty and the other tank which was probably full had a stiff tap which wouldn't turn no matter how much effort I made. Thwarted, but convincing myself that I didn't really want a drink of water I threw the cup towards the bin. It fell short and skidded across the floor in front of a receptionist who had at that moment come through the door.

She gave me a censorious look, bent, and picked up the cup and put it in the waste paper basket and turned to Helen.

"Mrs Helen Waldron. Doctor Hart will see you now," she said.

Although, she hadn't invited me to come, I followed Helen and the receptionist out of the door along the corridor to a door at the far end. The receptionist opened the door and we entered.

Doctor Hart sat behind his desk at the far side of the room. He looked up and invited us to take a chair and then went on writing as if he had dismissed us. I declined his offer to take a seat and instead went over to the window and looked out. The scene below was less prepossessing than the one from the window in the waiting room. There was nothing to see except a blank concrete wall on the opposite side of a narrow pathway between the two buildings. Then I suppose surgeons are not interested in views except those of the insides of their patients.

I looked back at the surgeon. His hair was turning grey and brushed back sternly from his forehead to form a long thick style at the back of his neck. He wore a dark blue suit and an open necked shirt. He looked up, smiled, and leaving his chair he shook Helen's hand first and then moving over to me he shook mine.

His grip was firm, but not crushing as if he was demonstrating to me his controlled strength and sureness of touch which I suppose l would expect from a surgeon.

Helen sat forward in her chair her hands clasped in her lap. I could see she was anxious although by her manner she was trying not to show it. She cleared her throat and shifted in her chair.

"Well doctor what have you found out about me after all those tests I've been through.

Have I got a clean bill of health?"

I was surprised by her manner, her voice a little louder than usual as if trying to veil her true feelings. The surgeon looked at her his eyebrows rising halfway up his forehead as if surprised by her forwardness. His smile showed his big protruding teeth.

"Not quite. I am afraid we must have a closer look at that lump on your breast. It may be benign, and if it is, there is nothing to worry about."

Helen sat upright and crossed her legs, her hands held higher. "And if it is not, what then?" The surgeon impressed with her forth rightness, hesitated before he answered, and then launched into an explanation of the possible action that might be necessary, and the treatment and medicines now available. Helen seemed detached, as if not listening any longer, her expression blank.

"We will need to have you in here, when we will take a biopsy, and we will go from there. You will receive a letter notifying you when that will be."

He rose from his chair and we followed him to the door. There he shook hands with us again giving me a man to man smile and put his hand on my back gently.

We sat in the car on the way home saying nothing, both with our own thoughts not wanting to express them to each other. The uncertainty of the outcome of a further examination weighed heavily making us strangers to each other. We stayed in the car when we arrived home, loathing to face the unknown they lay before us. Helen turned from me and looked out across the bay where the boats on their moorings swung to face the incoming tide.

"Let's not get down about something we don't know about." I said to break the impasse.

"It's the not knowing that I find hard to deal with," she had replied.

At last, we went inside having no reason to stay in the car any longer. She stood in the middle of the sitting room without taking off her coat or her gloves looking around her as if to memorise everything there, the wood burner, the lounge suite, the pottery on the shelf and our paintings on the wall. Bright light from the sun still above the crest of the hills near us flooded in from the conservatory. I took her coat and gloves and threw them over the back of a chair. She smiled and threw herself down on the sofa.

"Let's have a gin to celebrate," she said. "Time will tell and after whatever the outcome we'll be celebrating with a double gin then."

While I poured the drinks, I looked at her as she lay sprawled on the sofa. She was still attractive, with her high cheek bones, her full naturally red lips, smooth skin, and her slightly upturned nose.

"Do you know what it is. It's a bugger. I had hoped to find out that there was nothing to worry about and we could go on what we have always done, enjoy life without any dark clouds to dampen our enthusiasm."

"Of course, we can. Let's not eat our fish before we catch them." I replied.

The letter for her admittance to hospital came sooner than we expected. Helen hadn't opened it when I came home from work. It lay with the other letters on the table. I picked up the letters and looked at them and then casually asked had she noticed the one from the hospital. She just as casually answered that she hadn't bother to look through the mail that day and she had almost forgotten about any letter from the hospital ever coming. I handed it to her, and she opened it, put on her glasses, and read it aloud. She was to be admitted to the hospital next Monday.

There was an air of resignation about Helen when she packed her bag, carefully selecting what to take with her to hospital, not wanting to take too much as if she expected a long stay, or just a few items for a much shorter stay. The uncertainty of the outcome of what she had to face challenged her usual cordial, outward demeanour.

A waiting room again for me half filled with other people, with anxious looks, others trying to look detached by thumbing through magazines, or with heads pressed low over hand-held cell phones, remote from each other.

Helen had been whisked away down long interminable corridors to places unknown by the rest of us in the waiting room. One by one those waiting left to follow nurses along other long corridors to disappear behind different doors until I was the only one left in the waiting room. I became more anxious as time passed even though I had been assured that the procedure wouldn't take long although there could be some delay before the analysis can be determined. I am an impatient man at the best of times, but this was far from that. I imagined that the operation had not gone well, and complications had set in. I dreaded the visit that I was sooner or later to have informing me that it had gone wrong. I tried to convince myself that such fears were unfounded after all the procedure in removing the lump from Helen's breast would be simple enough and the delay was probably due to it being a busy day in the laboratory.

I wasn't prepared when a young man still wearing the light blue uniform and hat of the operating theatre staff came in, introduced himself, a name I promptly forgot, and asked me to come with him. We entered a small typical surgery room with a high bed along one wall, a desk computer and two chairs. He sat at the desk and asked me to take the other seat. He smiled and turned to face me but avoided my eyes.

He looked down when he spoke in a quiet, solicitous tone, still avoiding looking at me directly. He told me that Helen said she was uncertain how long she had the lump in her breast, but unfortunately it had proved to be cancerous and because it was likely that the cancer might spread, they have had to remove her left breast. And then before I could take this in fully, he asked me if I needed counselling, to deal with this, and that there would be after treatment for her condition, and could I cope with the situation as he put it. He was genuinely concerned and gave me the impression that he was more concerned about how I would take this, and how this could affect Helen and my relationship from now on. I assured him that our relationship was set in concrete, and nothing like the loss of one part of the anatomy would shatter it.

He seemed relieved and took me to see Helen where she lay in her bed in a ward. Her head on the pillow was turned towards the wall and I took her hand in mine. she squeezed it lightly in response and turned to look up at me. The colour in her face and the light in her eyes had dimmed and her smile flicked, but briefly.

"They have taken part of me away," she said. "Looks like I'll be a little lopsided from now on. Can you get used to that?"

When Helen was discharged from the hospital, I was not ready for the change in our life from now on. It wasn't as if she was bed ridden or had to have a special diet that worried me, as much as how our relationship would adjust. From now on I would have to face things as they are, not as I imagined them to be, for our life has changed. We were embarrassed at times by not knowing what to say to each other and a feeling we had of having some sort of resentment.

Seeing her coming home from her regular visits to the hospital for treatment, her lack lustre appearance and her need for assistance in walking from the car made me realise what she was going through. Then there were the days of rest, lack of appetite and disinterest of what was going on around her. Then unexpectedly she would be back to her old self, bright, full of talk, interested in what was happening and ringing friends for long chats, wanting to go out for the evening and seeing as many folk as she could, only to deflate suddenly like a blown-out tyre collapse just as dramatically and take to her bed for a day or two.

Betty was our first live in-home help. She came to us with a good recommendation of being a reliable and hard-working girl. She gave the impression of a rather crest fallen girl, extremely shy with little to say for herself, as if she had little sense of self-worth. She hung her head when speaking to us, refusing to meet our gaze, although giving little indication that she had understood our instructions, she carried out her work in the house diligently and expertly. She was particularly shy with me, not wanting to stay in my presence for long, hurrying away as if she had forgotten to turn the gas off on the stove. She gradually gained confidence with Helen, who showed great patience, made few demands, and praised her for her work. Her gentle handling of Betty, broke down a number of barriers that led to Helen being able to have long conversations and finding out a little more about Betty.

A week after she had been with us, I found Betty wandering along the hallway in her nightie long after she had gone to bed for the night. I had come out of the lounge door and meet her face to face. I apologised and stepped to one side to let her pass. She didn't seem to notice me and walked on. Her vacant look alarmed me, and I called her name. She continued on, as if she hadn't heard me, towards our bedroom and then stopped suddenly and crumbled to the floor sobbing and holding her hands on either side of her head.

"What is it Betty. What is wrong?" I said. When I put my hand on her shoulder to support her before she fell to the floor she shrieked loudly and started to crawl along the hallway before collapsing in a heap against the wall her hands clutched together on her face.

"Don't hit, don't hit me," she pleaded in a timid voice.

Helen appeared in the bedroom doorway and bent to support Betty, who as if slowly coming out of a trance, got to her feet, and flattened herself against the wall. Her look of bewilderment as if she had seen a ghost surprised us. Without apologising or saying anything to excuse herself she pushed passed me and ran back to her own room and slammed the door behind her. I swear that had there been a lock she would have locked herself in.

There were other strange incidents that made us wonder about her sanity, strange little habits she had in the house, her insistence of scrubbing the kitchen floor and bench at least twice a day. Then there were the nights when we heard her screaming followed by loud thumps. When I rushed to her room half expecting to find an intruder with her, I found her sitting up in bed staring before her, wide eyed, her face inflamed with sweat running down her cheeks and her night dress wet with perspiration. Her nightmares became more often and more extreme.

Helen later sat down with Betty one afternoon and had a long conversation with her. I was in the next room and heard the conversation clearly. Betty did most of the talking after being prompted by Helen to tell what frightened her since she had come to us.

"They said I was wicked because my mother was wicked by having me born," she said.

"Who said you were wicked Betty?"

"The Nuns at the orphanage. I was an orphan there since I was born. Some of them whipped me with their belts, cane or rosaries or anything they could reach. They said I had to have my wickedness beaten out of me."

She pulled up her blouse to show her back to Helen. "Look at all those marks on my back."

Helen grimaced when she saw the unmistakable marks of her having been thrashed severely. "You poor soul. That's terrible," she said.

"That's nothing now. They don't hurt any more. It's what they did to me that is what is wrong with me. It makes me have nightmares and horrible fits. I can't get it out of my mind. I tried to be a good girl, worked hard and did everything I was asked to do, but those other things they did to me."

When Helen put her arm over Betty's shoulders for support she winced and tried to pull away as if physical touching was something she couldn't stand.

"What do you mean other things, Betty?"

"I don't like to say. It makes me feel horrible, but they touched me, some Nuns and the older girls, in places they shouldn't have touched me and then and then I was raped by a priest when I was sent to Timaru to look after a Mrs Murphy for a fortnight, but no one believed me, said I was a wicked girl to make things up like that, but I know, don't I?"

"Did you see a doctor?"

Betty looked at Helen as if bewildered by such a question. "Doctor. There was no doctor. I told the Nuns, but they held me down and whipped me harder than ever. They thought the devil was in me tempting me to make such an accusation. They thrashed me until I was nineteen when I left Nazareth for good."

No wonder she had nightmares and sleep-walked and woke screaming. We were appalled and devastated to hear her story which we had no reason to doubt. Apparently, later her case has been put to the Catholic Church who wished to mediate but would not accept any blame on their behalf.

What was pertinent to us was how long could we put up with Betty's extremely disturbed behaviour. She was already receiving help from a counsellor, but how were we to deal with her in the house. Helen was adamant that she could put up with the nightly disturbances at present although it was very trying for her when she came home after treatment. I argued that of course Betty needed the help that she was getting from us, but it needed to be long term help that was beyond us to provide. I had to put Helen's health first. Not only was she drained of energy after treatment, but she was spending more time in bed or lying on the couch between treatments.

Helen of course wanted to help Betty and although I thought I was taking a hard line I suggested that Betty should go. This upset Helen who for a long time refused to discuss the matter any further. Betty's nightmares continued often waking us from sleep late in the night. I could see Helen's condition was worsening. She looked drawn and lethargic not wanting to go out or be sociable any longer. At first, when her friends came to visit, she was more like her old sociable self, but tired quickly and retired to her room. They passed it off as being only to be expected for someone who had not long been home from hospital, in fact they said she was remarkable, overlooking the obvious signs of her being no longer able to socialise like she used to, her very obvious loss of weight and her gaunt appearance. They tried to reassure me that the treatment she was undergoing took a long time before there was much improvement.

Nights for Helen were worse, not necessary caused of the almost nightly disturbance of Betty's nightmares, for she slept, but little most nights, lying awake for long periods thinking about what was happening to her. I could almost feel her fear throbbing away inside her wondering why this should be happening to her, now only early middle aged when she had so much time to live. She would move in the bed turning from side to side as if trying to get more comfortable. Betty's nightmares were of no consequence to her. They didn't wake her. She was awake already before Betty's screams shattered the night.

There were nights when Helen's wakefulness and constant turning from side to side in the bed which pulled the bed clothes from me and made it impossible for me to sleep. I would then drag the mattress from the bed in the spare room and put it on the floor by our bed and there I would try to get to sleep. In the morning I put the mattress back in the spare room before Helen woke.

She wasn't giving up for her body had cured lesser maladies before and there was no reason that with extra help from the treatment it would do the same again. She would curl up on her side away from me breathing heavily. She was not in any pain, but said it was the uncertainty of not knowing how she would ride this one out. On those long sleepless nights lying side by side on our backs we talked of our past together, reminding each other and sometimes correcting the memories of trips we had been on, the different houses we had lived in, the numerous parties we had been at too many to remember all of them, our first date and the many happy memories we had.

She turned on her side away from me breathing regularly as if going to sleep. I lay on my back my mind still full of memories that we shared over the years. It was at a party that we had met. She was the centre of attraction surrounded by other girls who looked up to her, laughing and enjoying turning down offers to dance or go to another room in the house with some gorm of a bloke. She had picked me from all those other blokes who sought her company and we had danced the night away.

We reminisced about my visit to her father in their home in Merivale.

Henry, her father, liked to give the impression that he was a fellow well met, welcoming and genial to newcomers, although by nature, he was cautious and suspicious of any one he didn't know. He greeted me with open arms, smiling and offering me a drink which he served and then sat regarding me closely. No doubt he had been introduced by his daughter to many young men and I was just the latest to be made to feel welcome in his household. By his small talk and his rather flippant attitude towards me he left no doubt that I too would go the way of my predecessors to be amused and then summary dismissed. I can still conjure up his surprised expression when it finally occurred to him that I was here to stay to win the hand of his daughter. His wife, Helen's mother, had died when Helen was fifteen. Since then, father and daughter had grown close, and I suspected that Henry's attitude to me was that I was only someone who would pass by like all the others.

There were frequent parties with numerous guests, loud music and champagne flowing like water from a tap. I came to many of these parties and marvelled how easily both Helen and Henry mixed with ease among the guests. There was much hilarity, high jinks and possibly the start of new affairs between the guests for all I knew or cared. I stayed with Helen as we mingled and enjoyed the light-hearted talk and the exaggerated efforts some made to be noticed.

Helen was very much the attraction, laughing off attempts, mock or otherwise, by the older men to become her lover. I, still being young then and inexperienced, was jealous of the temerity of their approach to her. I admired her skill as she dealt with these approaches without offending those middle-aged men.

Then one evening Helen and I slipped away from the party and went for a long walk among the trees of Little Hagley Park. It was a warm evening, calm, and cloudless. We held hands while we walked pleased to be away from the party atmosphere. On our way back even before we turned into the street, we heard the sound of tipsy revelry from the house. Helen stopped and pulled me back. We stood together on the footpath her hand in mine, and for a moment I thought she might want to go back to the park as far away from what was going on in that house. Instead, she looked up at me her face close to mine and said, "How about we marry just like that."

At first, I thought she was joking and perhaps flirting with me as she did with other men at these parties, but she was serious, and kissing me on the lips threw her arms around me holding me tightly to her. I responded with equal ardour and we were reluctant to break our embrace even when there were loud whistles from passengers in passing cars. All that summer I had been like a chained dog wanting to break the chain and take her away from this artificial life of parties and social occasions with people older than our selves. Helen had freed me from the chain, and we were free to follow our own whims, or was I to be drawn even deeper in that hedonistic life, which she and her father had revelled in since her mother died.

Our wedding breakfast was held in a large marquee erected on the spacious back lawn of Henry's house. It was late summer when the heat of the day still lingered for a while in the evening. Throughout the afternoon cars pulled up on the road depositing guests, many of whom I recognised from the evening parties of the past, some well-dressed ladies and girls wearing large brimmed hats, white lipstick and knee higher boots, young men students in sports jackets, short back and side haircuts and Henry's business associates, dressed in well-cut suits, shirts with different coloured collars and shiny well-polished shoes.

I don't recall the speeches, the raucous laughter from the corny jokes usually at my expense, or the hilarity when a dumpy older women very drunk fell on the floor during a dance and lay there shrieking her head off until someone helped her up and took her outside.

As the light faded and the dark shadow of the house next door fell over the garden and the marquee and the last couples were still dancing on the make shift wooden floor in the marquee, their eyes shut and the women's heads on their partners shoulder their arms entwining each other, Helen and I, left to ourselves for the first time that day, stood close together our arms around each other as a flock of birds returning to roost in the trees at the back of the section flew over and settled among the branches chattering exuberantly.

The last ray of light caught Helen's long tresses high lighting them as they fell away from her forehead down her back. Her hair was indeed a striking feature of Helens, a lustrous golden shade that even now as she approached middle age had little, or no, grey hair.

I turned in the bed and snuggled against her. Next morning, we were returning for another of her treatment session at the hospital when Helen said that in a month or so she would be as bald as a coot. I asked her why should she say that.

"There's another woman, Jane is her name, who is having the same treatment as me who is was quite bald and thought she would warn me that it could happen to me too so it wouldn't come as such a shock when it happened.

I will be, like father's old friend lascivious Larry, as bald as a coot, who would have thought."

All night I lay awake by her bed, my mind refusing to switch off, no matter what conscious effort I made to shut it down. My thoughts took over and I lay helpless as they crowded in and denied sleep.

Helen had come to consciousness at times during the night in the rest home and then drifted back again. She would open her eyes and stare at me wide-eyed in the dull glimmer of the night light by her bed. I didn't know if she knew me. I felt panic come over me and I bent over her hoping she would give some sign of recognising me. Even when a trolley going passed the room, broke the silence when it must have collided with something out in the corridor, she did not flinch. She still stared at me, as if surprised that I was there, almost suspicious of me. She moved slightly in the bed and stretched out her hand and gripped my wrist firmly. I feel that grip yet. I looked at her closely, willing her to stay her with me. She was breathing softly but regularly. I spoke her name, but she didn't respond. She let go of my wrist and let her arm lie on the counterpane, her fingers twitching briefly. Then she closed her eyes, and her breathing was more regular. I stroked her hair and murmured endearing phrases which I cannot now recall.

She opened her eyes and turned her head on the damp pillow and whispered in a low voice. "They are going now. The clock is slowing. the world is slowing." A faint hardly perceivable smile and a slight nodding of her head gave me hope.

"We will rewind the clocks together." I said.

As she slept my thoughts returned to those early days when I first saw her talking to two other girls at a party. There was something about her that took my attention and quickened my heartbeat. It might have been the way she was standing her head held to one side her chin almost touching her neck, her relaxed stance, and the way she curled a lock of her long tresses in her finger as she talked, intrigued me. She was wearing a flared skirt like a party dress with a leather belt which emphasised her narrow waist and a light blue blouse with the collar turned up at the back of her neck. When she turned away from her friends and went to the table, I took the bottle of wine and offered to refill her glass. Her radiant smile which lit up her whole face seared through me like a fiery dart. We chatted and I offered to see her home and although she refused at first, I could see she was interested and finally consented. It was the beginning of our relationship which developed slowly over the next few weeks and me meeting the father and the parties that followed before we married.

I like to think she was different from any other girl I had, but on reflection that was not necessary so, probably it had more to do with my approach to her. Previously, I had been a bit of a dilettante with women, trying to impress them with a sometimes-brash approach, brought on to some extent by having had too much to drink, but never wanting a serious relationship with them. They on their part soon tired of my foolish behaviour and cooled their interests in me, but with Helen this was different. I'd never been serious about wanting to settle down, always wanting to be the eternal student, wine, women and drink and little else. Now I had meet someone who I felt something deeper than words could not express, someone who I thought I could really love. Our love for each other was rather like a pavane piece of music unfolding slowly. We felt something really deep about each other but dared not to talk about it. We liked being close touching and cuddling, kissing, and stroking each other's hair but not going any further than the undoing of the top few buttons of her blouse for me to stroke her wonderful soft breasts which I could reach without undoing the bra strap. I took the lead and she followed never restricting my caressing, but somehow there was a problem. My problem, not hers. I ached for her to lie with me both of us naked and make love even before we married, but there was something that stopped me going any further than these preliminary caressing while we were fully dressed. She didn't complain, responding with her sweet, gentle smile. She loved me in spite of my reticence.

I look back on our wedding night when having eaten little since the wedding breakfast, I toyed with a cherry on my plate, speared it and offered it to Helen. She received it graciously, smiling, her blue eyes bright with passion. I poured another glass of wine and offered one to her which she refused. I tried not to look at our unused bed behind us, talking rather loudly to cover my dread of what was to happen, hoping to delay the obvious, knowing I couldn't delay it much longer. Helen seemed unperturbed, smiling up at me. How desirable she appeared to me. I told she looked ravishing and was the most beautiful of all women. She looked puzzled by my reluctance to go to bed and sensing my ruse she started to undress in front of me.

This was it. My excitement mounted as I watched her disrobe until completely naked, she went over to the bed climbed on it and lay on her back. I turned my back on her and tore off my clothes as I fought to hold an erection. Could I keep it up long enough for us to make love. I threw myself on the bed beside her and threw my arm over her and rolled on top of her. I sensed her stiffening, and felt her arms pushing me up from her. This is not what she expected, but I knew that I could not spend any time with the necessary foreplay. Already I knew my erection had soften. I felt her relax as I thrust hopelessly between her thighs now spread wide apart but without success. In complete frustration l tried again and again until Helen pushed me off her and l lay beside her exhausted by my futile efforts. We lay side by side in silence until l jumped from the bed and went over to the curtained window.

I remember standing there with my back to her, feeling miserable, utterly frustrated, and inadequate. I know now that there was a wall that keeps something out and something in and I unwittingly I had built such a wall between us. On the outside is the facade I'd hidden behind to impress others all the time only too aware of my insincerity with my relationships with others. I'd indulged in what I now know was a fantasy of being happy, well met and over friendly flirting about like a demented butterfly, but never settling avoiding capture. And now I had done the same to my wife Helen and left her in distress and confusion.

Then on the other side of the wall striving to get free was my other self, the hollow man without any true feelings for others, unloved in childhood and unable to love others and feeling sorry for myself because of being sexually assaulted when I was a boy. Had these things caste a frost on my frolic which was unable to thaw even on my wedding night!

I dared not look back at Helen. Not yet. I needed time, but would she give me that time to try again, but how and when would I start. I felt her arm about me and the pressure of her head on my shoulder.

"Don't worry dear. I've heard it is often difficult on wedding nights. We must be patient and try again later until we have success," she said.

"I'm so sorry dear. I don't know what came over me. It's the excitement and the tension of the day. It will be better next time."

I had dreaded the thought of going to bed in the evenings making excuses that I had a lot of business paperwork to catch up and perhaps it would be better for her to go to bed and not wait up for me. Often, when I did go to bed, she would be awake and snuggle up to me. I'd make the excuse that i was too tired and would turn in the bed with my back to her.

There were other nights when I'd go to the pub with some of my mates. We'd make jokes of a sexual nature and denigrate women in general maintaining that their place was in the home looking after the kids while we were the providers and if desire got the better of us, there was always the possibility of a little on the side, or if really desperate, a prostitute would fit the bill.

I soon realised how shallow these thoughts were and how insecure we blokes were, and I began to envy those at work who went home regularly and only occasionally joined us in the pub.

I think they pitied us and left early preferring to go home to their wives and kids.

I recall those nights when we lay on our backs after another futile effort to make love and although there were no words spoken between us, we held hands. I lay there willing myself to open up to her and tell her something I'd never spoken to anyone before. I seemed to always be in a cold sweat as I made an effort to break through the wall that was separating us. I supposed in my effort to speak I'd be squeezing her hand too tightly and she would look at me in alarm. I would manage to tell her how I loved her and that it wasn't her fault that we hadn't consummated our marriage yet. It's just there was something that was holding me back making me think that what we are trying to do is dirty and shameful and that I would only hurt her, and I couldn't bear to do that.

She knew it was something more than that, when I told her that I had this great feeling of guilt and I couldn't tell anyone about it not even Uncle, when he was alive. She had asked if I couldn't tell her then, there was someone who I could possibly try.

She made an appointment with Mary Hunt a psychologist which I didn't keep. When I rang to apologise, she had said it was no big deal only she'd expect me the next day, which was an appointment I was thankful I kept. She put me at ease from the first moment of our acquaintance, talking about anything other than my problem. I think it was on my third appointment that I opened up to her. It suddenly gushed out of me and went on like water from a tap. I told her of my guilt and disgust of what had happened to me as a boy. She had smiled and said that it was better out, I think her words were, and she got up and made me a cup of coffee as if I had just dropped in for a chat and nothing more. She told me that it was something I must face as an adult now not only for my sake, but for Helen as well. She said that we were both in this together and together we would overcome it. It had been a great release and I felt that frost that had fallen on my heart was beginning to thaw. A few weeks later we successfully made love together and after a miscarriage and then later to our great joy Alice was born.

When I reflect on those earlier times when Alice was still a baby, I like to think how happy we were and how I loved her. I deeply regretted that later my work took me away from home sometimes for a fortnight or more at a time and I became a stranger to Alice. I was hurt when after a long absences because of my business Alice came to think of me more as an uncle who brought home new gifts than as her father. During her school years we drifted more and more apart Helen although aware of the gulf that had developed between Alice and me still welcomed me home with open arms and her sweet smile.

Now as I sat with her with my loving memory of her with her bright blue eyes, I kissed her and stoked her hair and I swear she opened her eyes and smiled. Soon after I must have dropped off to sleep.

Helen died before dawn. I woke with a nurse shaking my shoulder and taking my hand from Helen's hand. I must have been holding it though out the night.

# 4

# Daphne

"The Willows." I asked the girl behind the counter at the shop, but she shook her head and said she had never heard of it.

"Jack Waldron is my name. I lived here years ago, and I wondered if 'The Willows' which used to be for rent is still available?"

An older man who had been stocking the shelves with tins of food turned and came to the counter. He scratched his head and ran his hand through his hair and said, "I know most of the places in Waireka, but I'd never heard of 'The Willows'. I'd heard some of the old folks around here talking of some place that had a bad reputation that used to be rented for wild parties and disturbed the peace around here, but that was well before my time. If you are looking for a place to stay, because if you are, there is the Lodge that takes in folk now and again."

He gave me directions and pointed to a notice board nailed to a fence on the other side of the road. It looked as if it had been there for some time, and I could hardly make out the faded words 'Omanga Lodge', with an arrow pointing down River Road.

I left the car parked outside the shop and walked up the road. This was certainly in the direction that 'The Willows' had once existed. After all it was in 1965, fifty-four years now since l was last in the township and I must expect changes. There were certainly more houses on River Road than before and from what I had seen since I arrived the whole place looked more settled with permanent homes than bachs. In those days there were still a few old trams that had been converted to bachs. Now there was even a new road to the left off River Road with modern two storied homes.

Fifty-four years ago 'The Willows' was the only two storied house in the township. Perhaps it had been pulled down and replaced by one of these modern homes. I walked on a little further and there it was standing on a slight promontory above the river. Once it had been the grandest home in Waireka and the only two storied building. Its location making it stand out among the line of bachs on the sand hills on the other side of the playing field. It was no longer called 'The Willows'. Printed in bold letters on a board on the gate was its new name, 'Omanga Lodge'.

I remember there was only a single, caste iron gate which squeaked alarmingly as it swung in the wind. There was now a double gate with an imposing curved driveway leading towards the house. A well-kept lawn and flowerbeds grew on either side of the driveway, where before there was only sand covered here and there with clusters of succulent ice plant with their yellow and orange flowers.

From what I can remember, there wasn't a veranda on the north side of the house, but there is one now. Although, the one in the front, which no one used because it faced the cold Easterly wind from the sea, was still there. From the road, the paint work on the house gave the impression of being new but on closer inspection it had peeled in places and on the windowsills. The front door was painted a deep blue. I could have sworn that it was red in the old days. The drapes in the sitting room seemed old and stained in places. The willow trees that grew near the back of the house have gone, leaving a clear view of the wide riverbed and the gently flowing river as it nears the sea.

An elderly man, who wore a red waist coat and a beret pulled well down on his forehead, sat in a wicker chair on the new veranda. A woman came out of the house carrying a tray with two cups and a tea pot. She put it on the small table by him and pulled up a chair. When she looked up and saw me, I smiled and left.

Back in Christchurch I stopped for a cup of coffee at a cafe. She had come in to the cafe and asked me if I minded her sitting at my table, as all the other tables were full. I felt flattered that a young woman would want to sit with me. We smiled politely and we avoided each other's gaze, sipping our coffee while looking at others in the cafe. Now lying on this bed, I closed my eyes and saw her clearly sitting across the table in the cafe, our eyes met, and we held each other's gaze for a brief, but meaningful moment. I reached across the table and took her hand in mine. She looked startled and then she smiled, her eyes full of meaning. A brief touch which could have been the beginning of something wonderful but for the earthquake.

The horrible jerking movement that sent us both from our chairs, and when we tried to get to our feet, we were knocked down again. The noise, the dust, and collapse of the walls and the falling of debris on us. Her high-pitched scream remains in my head and her limpness when I carried her outside and took cover beside a parked car.

She was taken from my arms and put in an ambulance. I never knew her name and though I tried to find her again, I failed. With no name it was difficult to trace her. I visited the wards of the hospital, put adverts in the paper, made exhausting inquires to no avail and even visited the morgue. Perhaps she never existed and was only a figment of my imagination. I fretted for weeks, walking the streets, asking anyone who would listen to my story until exhausted and resigned to my fate I stayed in my motel waiting for the phone to ring hoping for some news of her. For nearly seven years I waited for that phone call that never came. I finally gave up all hope and rang Miss Myrtle Symington at the 'Omanga Lodge' and moved to the Lodge with my few belongings.

My room does have a view, something I imagine it didn't have when the Goldings lived here in 1965, when the tall willows that grew behind the house were there. I look down across the wide river terraces to the Ashley river as it winds its way to the sea, which is obscured by the tall pines at the end of the village. I like to think that this room was once where Daphne slept, but I have no way of verifying this. There is no trace of the Goldings in the house, not even a forgotten hair pin wedged between the floorboards, a faded photograph that might have fallen off a chest of drawers and lay undetected under the floor mat, or initials carved in the architrave of the doorway, no lingering scent which I remembered Fiona Golding splashed on and about her and no article of lost clothing or shoes to be found in the cupboard under the stairs. To expect to be any sign of the Goldings still in the house was unrealistic. During the fifty-four years that have elapsed since they lived here there must have been many families occupying the place.

Could my room really have once been Daphne's room? Maybe. I am only guessing for in those days I got no further than the bottom of the stairs. That she lived upstairs once I'm certain, but in which room. Since I moved in, I have found there are four bedrooms up here. One would have been her parents' bedroom; another Nathans and I suppose the fourth bedroom was Vera's. Other rooms have been added downstairs to serve as bedrooms since the place became

160

a boarding house. During my childhood days, it had been owned by an absentee landlord who rented it out to families in the summers.

There are two of us sleeping upstairs now. My neighbour occupies a bedroom near the front. I remember him as being the old gentleman who wore a red waist coat who I saw sitting on the veranda when I first returned to the village. He is not very friendly and behaves towards me as if he resented my presence, and barely nods his head when I address him. The Major, as Miss Symington calls him, takes his evening meal in his own room. Miss Symington who runs the place brings his meal up to him on a tray which she places on a small table outside his room, knocks on his door and not waiting for a reply she goes downstairs.

He has his breakfast downstairs, not in the dining room, but at a small table in the corner of the kitchen. There he sits bent over his cup held in one hand, never far from his lips and takes sips now and again. He has his own marmite jar, butter, and marmalade close beside him as if he fears that it might be taken away, if he didn't keep a close watch on it. Lunch, which is often a boiled egg, sandwiches, and a piece of fruit he eats on the veranda. Why he doesn't use the dining room I don't understand. I'm the only one in there. When, or where Miss Symington eats, I don't know.

The other guest is Miss Clements. She is away at present and I have not met her yet.

The Major may have been in his younger days, tall and upright, but now he stoops and shuffles rather than walks with the aid of a carved, heavy looking walking stick. He invariably wears a dark blue refer jacket, well pressed trousers and a tam-o-shanter, pulled down on one side of his head. I suspect he has his red waist coat under his jacket for I'm sure I caught a glimpse of it when for a moment when he heaved himself out of the deck chair on the veranda.

Miss Symington has her own suite of rooms downstairs at the back of the house. There is a door in the hallway leading to her rooms that remains closed and she has made it perfectly clear to me and no doubt, to the old gentleman, that part of the house is private and neither of us is invited to her sanctum. Miss Symington is a spritely, tall woman, who waffs between rooms and down the hallways hardly disturbing the air or disturbing any dust. She wears rather drab coloured long skirts and white blouses done up to her neck even on hot days. Her greying hair is in a bun without a hair out of place and because of her light step I'm not always aware of her presence in the room. Her unsmiling, stern look and her dark deep-set eyes give her an unfriendly appearance. Yet when spoken to,

161

she is pleasant and non-threatening. I'm not sure yet, for she avoids the question when I ask, what her position is in the Lodge, whether she is the owner, the housekeeper, or is acting in another capacity. She prepares and cooks all the meals, does some of the housework and gardens occasions.

There is Mrs Tubman, a large, jolly woman who comes in daily to help in the house and her husband, Willy Tubman who does the heavy work in the grounds and carries out repairs within the house when required.

Mrs Tubman would spend much of her time gossiping if I gave her the opportunity. She lives locally with her husband, Willy, who is the silent one in the house she tells me. I have no difficulty in understanding that. She tells me that straight after the big earthquake the lodge was full, but they have all moved away. I came in at the right time she says. Any earlier and I would not have got in. Oscar Enright, who Miss Symington calls the Major, was the only one who didn't move away. He has been here for years she explained, and he was pleased when the others found places to live and left the Lodge. Miss Clements has only recently arrived to stay.

"He doesn't say much does the Major, a crusty old gent and rude when he wants to be. Can't say I know much about his army days although he says he fought in the wars and was highly decorated. Not that I'm one to pry, but I couldn't help notice that he doesn't have a uniform in his wardrobe and I've never seen any medals and the like," said Mrs Tubman.

I suppose I am lucky to have found a place to stay in the meantime. My house in town is uninhabitable after the earthquake and still is after seven years A week after the earthquake they let me go in for half an hour to remove as many of my belongings as I could carry. The whole building of flats where I moved to after that will be demolished and I have been living in a motel until now. When I rang Miss Symington, she said a room would become available after the weekend and I gratefully accepted it. And as fate would have it here, I am living with all my memories of 1965 when I was ten years old in what I will always call 'The Willows'.

There comes a time in life when everything seems to be going downhill, a loss all the way, not only the loss of hair, or loss of income, of family and relatives, of opportunities that were once so plentiful, but most important of all is the loss of friends. Have I lost all these, or am I just feeling sorry for myself. I still feel deeply the loss of my dear wife, Helen. Her memory is with me for ever. When I think I'm no longer grieving for her, something that reminds me of her brings tears to my eyes. Thank heaven she died before the earthquake and didn't have to go through all that. Then there was much earlier my broken close friendship with Simon. It is too painful to dwell for long on that breakup.

Why I came out here I'm not certain. Perhaps, because of old memories, and once having a feeling of at last being part of a family who cared for me, even if Aunty was sometimes harsh on me.

Then perhaps, I had an inflated idea of once being happy here. I have walked my old haunts of years ago hoping to regain the pleasure of what I once felt as a child for this place, the beach, the steep sand dunes, and the silence of the Pine Forest. How dull and uninspiring it all looked now seen through my adult eyes. How could I have lost the capacity for discovery and self renewal I once had as a child on these long walks. Life experiences away from this place had dulled my senses to appreciate what was around me. Now on these walks the grey sea, the sand dunes no longer the tall mountains of my childhood, and the gloominess of the Forest depressed me. I flopped down on the sand between the dunes and the pine trees and took in the modest and commonplace vista before me. Gone is the glamour I once had for this place which after all is only an unimaginative scene hardly worth a second glance.

Then a slight gust of wind from the sea between the sand dunes sweeps across my view. The tawny patch of long grass bends in unison in agitated motion, sand near the summit of the dunes nearby stirs sending minute grains of sand tumbling down its slopes and the shorter dandelion flowers nod at each other. Pollen dust from the pine under which I am sitting drops faint clouds of pollen on me and the ground about me while the deep gloom of the forest, undisturbed by the slight gust of wind remains still, and I feel a stirring of a long-forgotten inspiration I once had as a child from even the simplest event of what was happening around me and I rejoice.

There are many thoughts and memories that I suppress for different reasons. I will not admit to myself, let alone to others, that some actions and decisions I had made in business had caused hardships to many others nor do I dwell on the part I played in a case of fraudulent dealings which saw others found guilty while I got off scots free. Even now I have retired I still deny their existence. Then there are other events in my life even if painful to me, I know I cannot bury. My Aunty's attitude towards me and my wife have been hard to endure. But even more difficult it is to remember the pain and bravery of Helen as she fought to hang on to life which she had loved.

From a pile of envelopes held together by a rubber band I took out one dated in the late1970's and opened it. A lock of hair fell out of it with three pages written in a neat obviously woman's hand. Who could have sent me a lock of their hair? I had no memory of receiving it before and when I read the letter, I found it was not signed. I was relieved that it couldn't have been from a man because of the handwriting. It must have been from one a number of girlfriends I had during those years at Varsity. When I read the letter again it dawned on me who Gwen was who was mentioned a number of times on those pages. The letter must be from Barbara of course whom I thought of as more of an acquaintance than a girlfriend. How heartless I had been to avoid her later. She was a sweet girl, but the close attention of Gwen at her side dulled any interest I could have had in Barbara. Had I disappointed her? Probably, but I hope it hadn't gone as far as to break her heart.

When I think of those rapturous, carefree days as a student tinged of course with the discipline of having to complete assignments on time, or the slog of serious study for exams, I marvel that somehow some of us graduated eventually. There were those among us some who revelled long into the night for most of the year. They were from some well-off families who were at university for a good time, parties, women, and drink. They didn't have to worry about qualifications knowing they would probably take over the family business later, or failing that be supported by the same business for much of the rest of their life. Then there were those like me from less fortunate families whose parents made sacrifices to keep us at university. We had a different outlook. We were there to take things more seriously for a least for some of the time. I don't think our life was curtailed greatly. We were just better organisers of our time mixing pleasure with work more successfully than the privileged students.

Late teens and early twenties is a time of indulging in experiences which we considered essential. Drink featured foremost among these. Without drink how did one have the confidence to impress those of the fairer sex. But drink was hard to come by with the pubs closing at six o'clock and finances were limited. Saturday night was our night out. My city friends tell me they like to think of me as being in a quasi-retirement position now I'm living in the country. They think if I stay too long, that life could become one of inertia, and withdrawal from their society, and I could run the risk of becoming like Oscar Enright overcome by strict adherence to routine and rigid opinions. Although I scoff at this, I do take care to be more adventurous than Oscar by not following the same route on my daily walks and read a book instead of falling asleep like he does while sitting on the veranda on hot days. I abhor his habits and go out of my way to avoid them. Perhaps if I stay here too long, I might well become like him. God forbid. I must get out more and visit friends and places of interest even if it means I must buy a car again.

With these thoughts on my mind, I go up to my room and instead of lying on my bed as I have been doing more often during the day, I pull out from under the bed the rather tattered leather suitcase with its broken hinges and locks and empty its contents on the bed. Old black and white photographs taken years ago from my Kodak box camera, some coloured taken from the last camera I owned, our wedding photos, letters, cards, and a couple of diaries from the past, all mostly forgotten memorabilia, scatter across the bed spread.

A slip of paper now yellowed with the passing of time fell on the floor. I picked it up and unfolded it and recognised that scrawled hand wiring at once. Simon had written, 'Why are you avoiding me. I must see you now.' Why had I kept it for I have no memory of doing so when I was at varsity in the early seventies. It probably had no more significance than any of the other numerous notes he wrote to me which I threw in the waste paper basket in my room. I must have thrown this one in the open suitcase by mistake. I sat on the edge of the bed and read it again. When I sift through the cars, photos and papers on my bed I find an old programme for a concert from the New Zealand Symphony orchestra featuring music of New Zealand composers. among those included is an old friend Gregory Moffat. I remembered that concert back in 1990. I had half expected to see Simon by Gregory's side, since homosexuality was no longer illegal, when Gregory was surrounded by admirers in the foyer after the concert, but there was no sign of him there. Later when Gregory left, he was accompanied by his mother. I went to the window and watched the river flowing gently towards the sea. The finding of that old concert programme conjured up old memories of when I hung out with Gregory and Simon and was still unsure of my own sexuality. I had to admit that I had once been close to Simon in those days, and I recall all too clearly those days of exploration on my part as if had happened yesterday.

When I think about it, I was ashamed that I had tried to convince myself that I didn't miss him, pleased to be no longer bothered by his constant presence at my door, the sound of his quick footsteps in the hall and his manner of knocking on the door, one short tap followed by two loud thumps that made the door shake as if it was about to come off its hinges. Simon, a nuisance, a bore to be avoided if possible, could not be ignored. In company he tried to dominate, his high-pitched voice, his staccato manner of speaking rising to an even higher pitch in an attempt to dominate the conversation in an effort to make his point, which was often obscure and caused more consternation than clarity.

Did I really miss those poems and entreaties written on old envelopes, or torn sheets of note paper that were forced under my door when I didn't answer his demanding knocking on my door? I'd hear his deep breathing and the shuffling of his feet, as he penned a quick note on whatever piece of paper he had in his pocket, probably holding it against my door as he wrote and then the paper would appear under my door. I never answered his often-garbled notes. Somewhere in the form of verse, others in terms of endearment.

Simon had come out fully to me risking the consequences during the time, 1960's, and 70s that homosexuals were regarded as criminals if caught cohabiting. We had been close as young men often are, but we had not been intimate with each other. He had obviously seen me as a fellow traveller and had made advances to me, which I didn't find obnoxious at first, but as he persisted, I withdrew further from his company. Then he would make a scene of it, trying to belittle me in company, inferring that I had let him down and wasn't to be trusted.

Sometimes these tantrums were outrageous and caused alarm to everyone. Some of our fellow students feared for his mental stability. Then he would calm down suddenly as if he'd thrown a switch, and was all charm and full of solicitudes, as if nothing untoward had happened.

Poor Simon, alas, I know not what became of him in later life. I'd like to think he has found peace and a suitable partner, for there was much that I liked about him during our student days.

When he realised that we were not meant for each other he cast his net wider, treading more carefully, aware of the attitude towards gay people at the time was hostile and could lead to trouble for him. Simon, for all his faults, knew better than to seek a liaisons with another gay person in sordid situations such as public toilets. Instead, he looked further afield than the Art students he mixed with.

I can't find a photo or any reference to Uncle among the mess on my bed. Surely there must be something I must have kept. I search, more thoroughly this time, but without success. Still, I have vivid tangible memories of him that will be with me for ever. How could I ever forget him when he meant so much to me.

I have long cleared the memorabilia on my counterpane and put the letter case back under my bed. I resolved to put aside the nostalgia that I have indulged in for the last week except of course my memories of Helen which I can never forget and look now to my future.

The Major has his own routine which he follows diligently every day. He is an early riser. I hear him in the bathroom whistling to himself probably shaving and then I hear the toilet flush the closing of the door with force and the sound of his footsteps along the corridor and later on the stairs. There is the unmistakable shudder through the building of the front door being slammed shut and he is gone wearing his red waist coat under his blue reefer jacket, his beret on one side of his head and his carved, wooden walking stick in his hand which he swings backwards and forwards as he walks. His walk invariably follows the same course, across the green playing field to the northern end of the village, where he follows the path leading to the beach and along the beach just above the incoming waves which gently swirl on the sands before being sucked back to sea, and then he goes as far as the track between the sand dunes near the camping ground. He lingers there as if waiting for an invitation to breakfast, or perhaps simply to tarry to take in the lovely smell of bacon in a fry pan cooked outside a tent, or is it because he might hope to catch a sight of a young girl changing into her bathing costume. Denied such pleasure he leaves to pick up his newspaper from the store before returning to the Lodge.

It isn't long before the smell of eggs and bacon wafts upstairs. Miss Symington has anticipated his return and is cooking this breakfast which he eats alone at the table in the kitchen. I once intruded on his lone dining and saw that he had a small suitcase in which he keeps his supply of sauces and spreads. These were arranged on his table, around his plate and now and then he'd pour one of the saucers over his breakfast of eggs and bacon. Having eaten he'd retire to the lounge, or if there was little or no wind, and the day is fine, he'd sit on the veranda to read his newspaper. Nothing could disturb him from this task. If I as much, or for that matter Miss Clements, who came down later for her breakfast greeted him he would barely grunt in reply.

Mrs Tubman was in the kitchen when I went to get my breakfast of muesli, an orange and tea.

She must have heard me greet the Major.

"You call him that too I see. No more a Major than my giddy aunt," she said. "My father was in the compulsory Military training camp at Burnham with him in the fifties. He was a major all right according to Dad. A major pain in the backside. He was only a Private like the rest of them. Miss Symington, bless her heart, calls him Major to make him feel he is important. His name is Oscar Enright and that's what I call him. He doesn't half like it though. You should see the look on his face when I call him Oscar. He was a salesman in the menswear department in the D. I. C. Department store in town before it closed.

I couldn't bring myself to start calling him Mr Enright and certainly not Oscar. That would be going too far. I would continue to humour him although I referred to him to others as Mr Oscar.

Miss Clements took her breakfast in her room. From what I once saw on her tray breakfast was confined to tea and a piece of toast with marmite. I never saw her in the dining room at lunch time. At night she merely pecked at her food and sent much of it back. How could she have existed on such a frugal diet. I did discover her secret when I examined the contents of her waste paper basket before tipping it in the rubbish bin. It contained numerous wrappings from chocolates and sweets. I could imagine her sitting upright supported by numerous pillows in her bed taking nibbles of chocolate and now and then feeding her little dog, Fellows I think she calls him, with tit bits of biscuits and sweets. I suppose she is content with her lot in life. Her walks with her dog were sporadic, dictated no doubts by the necessity to allow the dog to relieve himself outside rather than in his box in her room.

I was sitting on the veranda when I heard her dog barking incessantly. Miss Clement came through the gate dishevelled and obviously in distress. She nearly stumbled and fell as she came towards me. I rushed to her aid and offered my arm for support. She looked at me as if I was a stranger, about to assault her; her wild, open-eyed look startled me, and I released my support. "What is it?" I asked.

She struggled to reply. "It's him again. He attacked me and tried to rape me," she gasped. I helped her to the veranda and sat her down on my deck chair. "I'll ring the Police, and then go and see if I can find him." I said.

She lay back in the chair fanning her face with her handkerchief. "Do that."

Mrs Tubman and Miss Symington were standing in the kitchen door when I went into the hall to phone.

"What's it this time. Someone snatched her handbag or tried to kidnap her or some such thing?" asked Mrs Tubman.

I picked up the phone. "No, a man who she says has attacked her before, tried to rape her." I replied.

The two women exchanged meaningful glances. Miss Symington took the phone from my hand and replaced the receiver.

"She's full of fantasies poor soul. I saw her from the kitchen window walking along from the store as sedate as ever with her dog on its lease. Then she must have had one of her turns, and she started screaming and running and looking all flustered. We have seen it all before. I'll make her a cup of tea and a biscuit, a chocolate one of course. She'll soon forget all about it," she said. "We have other things to think about. The builders will be back tomorrow, and they will need feeding. They are building three self-contained units at the back for holiday stays during the summer. We make sandwiches and pies for their lunch. I do hope the noise will not disturb you. The owner of the Lodge thinks it will be worthwhile. They are going to knock out the wall between the TV room and the dining room to make the dining room ready for the influx of dinners next season for evening meals."

"Things will change then. It won't be the same any longer." I said.

"It won't make much difference. This will still be the Lodge for permanents like you. You can have your evening meals earlier or in the kitchen, that's about all."

"The owner of the Lodge you say. I thought you owned this place." I said.

"Good gracious. What made you think that. No, Mrs Marsh owns the Lodge. She owns hotels in Auckland, Queenstown, and Christchurch and Sydney. She comes to visit us now and then."

I began to wonder why such a woman would bother with a Lodge at a small place like Waireka. Perhaps, she was the one who changed the name of the Lodge from 'The Willows' to 'Omanga' a place of refuge for the Major, Miss Clements and now me.

Alice, our daughter rang this morning and is coming out to take me to the cemetery where Helen is buried. She must be in her late twenties now, still not married, attractive with long blond hair falling loosely to her shoulders or sometimes tied in a ponytail that bobbles up and down when she walks. Like her mother she has a winning smile, that shows only some of her upper gums, and has her mother's open, sunny nature.

We have been in the habit of visiting her grave on the anniversary of her burial annually for the first five years, but our visits have been sporadic since then. We stand by the grave in silence each lost in our own thoughts, holding hands with our heads bowed. We tidy the grave, take away the old flowers and arrange the newly cut flowers in their place. We don't linger much after that. Nor do we speak as we make our way back to the car. The feeling of uneasiness in Alice's company that I sometimes have disperses on these occasions. Helen's death has thrown us more together than before and although the feeling of kinship is always present, I can't help but have a guilty feeling about my role as a father. As we approach the car, I recall the words of Ursula Bethell's poem 'Pause': 'When I am very earnestly digging, I lift my head sometimes, and look at the mountains, and muse upon them, muscles relaxing.'

How often when working long hours did I pause, when Alice was young, to lift my head to look at the mountains, my family, or give them much thought. A father in name only too busy with his work to spend much time with his family. Does Alice blame me for my absence from her childhood. I grieve now for the loss of my wife and the loss of sharing Alice's early life. Now I have sold the business and travel overseas no longer does she see me in a different light. If she does, she doesn't mention it. As has been our custom after these visits, we go for a drive and have lunch in a cafe. "Where to now Pop," she says in her light hearted way of speaking. She answers her own question. "Why not to Sumner. There's a lovely cafe at the end of the promenade, serves great coffee. By the way I'm getting married next month."

This announcement, as if it was only a trivial event of little importance, catches me off guard.

"Do I get an invite?" I ask. She gives me that radiant smile that reminds me so much of her mother. "You Pop are to give me away. You haven't met my husband to be. Terry is his name. We have been living together for six months. Thought it would be a good idea to tie the knot. I'll bring him out to see you in the weekend. Must get acquainted."

All this brings home to me how separate our lives were. I know little of her life and she didn't appear to be interested in mine either.

"Pop, do you expect to live at Waireka for long. You can't possibly want to stay any longer than necessary. You'll be bored out there in no time. You don't surf, fish, or hunt. You are a city slicker. You are out of your pond in the country. After the Earthquake when the house was ruined you moved around for a number of years and I expect you won't stay at Waireka for long." She knows more about me since Helen's death than I realised.

"You are right, of course. I'll only stay until the insurance is settled for our house after the earthquake. Then I'll build again or buy a home near the sea, possibly Sumner."

"Why not. You must have been living at Waireka with your uncle and aunty when that body was found somewhere near Waireka."

"Body. Was there one found? Certainly not while I was living there with my uncle and aunt."

It was a still Autumn day, all coppers and golds on the trees and on the road, piles of leaves waiting for the next breeze to send them on their way to pile up against fences and block the drains. Over lunch we talked more freely than I can remember. She told me of their wedding plans, something simple without fuss for which I of course would be only too pleased to pay.

When she took me back to the Lodge, I was beginning to find that we had become closer together, father and daughter than ever before.

Back in my room I thought about what Alice had said about why I had come to stay in the Lodge, of all places, when I could have found accommodation closer to town. Strange how a casual comment can arouse a long trail of thought. I had not asked that question of myself although deep down I think I knew why. There was a vacancy which was more than I could say for motels and other boarding houses, not that I tried very hard to find other places to stay. There was something that drew me there and I wasn't absolutely certain what that was.

There was nothing here for me here except nostalgia for memories of my own short time here as a young boy which must be trivial at least, mostly forgotten yet they had a strong pull on me. As a boy hadn't I longed to see inside of this house and see where they lived, where they ate, slept and spent their evenings. The Goldings why did they have such a fascination for me and here I was in this same house which was very much the same as it had been fifty or more years ago. This very bed I slept on had been slept on by Fiona and Felix and Daphne's room was where the Major Oscar now slept. There were changes downstairs and new units were being built out the back, but essentially much was the same as it had been when the Goldings lived here. Had I come back to try and recreate the past and to find out what had happened to the family. Surely not.

There was no one living in Waireka who would remember them.

I went downstairs and sat in the bay window and watched the sky darken, listening to the pounding of the sea on the beach. My thoughts of my day with Alice faded as memories of Helen flooded in as they always did more often after visiting her grave. Our marriage had been one of love. We had each given part of ourselves to each other which we thought would last forever, but already my memories of her are fading. I wondered now how well we knew each other. Perhaps, I was too self-absorbed to give our relationship the thought it deserved yet it pains me to think it is a matter of blame on my part. Perhaps I expected too much of the whole business. Helen knew more about me than I know about myself.

Now Alice is foremost in my thoughts. She is to marry, and I must rejoice.

The Major is moving about upstairs preparing to dress for dinner and having a short dram or two before he comes down. Miss Clements is already in the dining room with her little dog at her feet.

There is a clattering of pots in the kitchen. Miss Symington and Mrs Tubman will have the dinner on the table soon. I wonder what it will be tonight. Something surprising no doubt like boiled eggs and mashed potatoes with black pudding. Those two women do get their meals mixed up a bit serving a mixture of breakfast food with dinner dishes. Oh well, there is nothing like the unexpected.

Rain had set in by the morning with the easterly blowing grey clouds over the darkened sea speckled here and there with white caps. The driven rain covered the window panes and the floorboards of the veranda to the front door. There would be no morning walks today. Even the Major had restricted his usual stroll and with his umbrella held against the steady wind had gone no further than to the store to get his morning paper. Miss Clement hadn't made any appearance yet. I'd read the two books I had brought with me and there didn't appear to be any other books in the Lodge as far as I could see. I'd asked Miss Symington who shrugged her shoulders as if she had no interest in books and probably couldn't understand why I shouldn't be content, if not knitting like her, then filling my time doing something useful like that instead of wanting to waste time reading books.

Mrs Tubman was in the kitchen when I asked her and like Miss Symington, she seemed surprised that I wanted books to read. I suppose her attitude was much like Miss Symington after all neither Miss Clements nor the Major read books so why should I. She said there might be something in the high cupboard above the sink that might fit the bill. I climbed on one of the wooden chairs in the kitchen to reach the cupboard. There were a few old recipe books, two Australian Women's Weeklies. A newspaper cutting fell out to the floor. I got down from the chair and picked it up. The paper had yellowed and I expected it would be old perhaps about something about Waireka in the past. It must have had something spilt on it years ago which made the printing hard to read. My interest grew when I found it was a Press cutting dated January 1965. I was still there then. "A twelve-year-old boy son of Mr and Mrs Golding who are on holiday in Waireka has been missing for six days. It is thought that he may have left the immediate area and Police have widened their inquiries."

I climbed back on the chair and found two other cuttings taken from the Press on separate dates in 1986 between two pages in a copy of the 'Australian Women's Weekly'. I climbed down again and took the cuttings to my room and sat on my bed to read them. In 1986 I had been working in England and had little news of what was going on in New Zealand. The first clipping from 1965 had aroused my interest immediately. The 1986 cuttings heightened it further. 'The remains of an unidentified boy of about twelve years old has been discovered by a man who was walking his dog in the pine plantation near Waireka. The dog seemed to have discovered something of interest to it and had dug earth away in a slight depression in the ground and uncovered a piece of rusty corrugated iron. The man, Mr Ross Wood, pulled it off and found two rotting planks of wood and a few driftwood logs covering the remains of a body. A police investigation was underway.' The next cutting was a report from the forensic division released by the Police that there were suspicious circumstances surrounding the case. The boy's skull had been crushed in at the right-hand side by what could have been the result of a heavy blow. The Police have opened a murder inquiry.

Rusty corrugated iron, two rotten planks of timber and a few bits of driftwood. These words stirred in me memories that I thought I had long forgotten. My god this could be the underground hut that I had built when I was a boy and that body found there could be that of Nathan, murdered, but by whom?

Apart from me There were only five others who knew of that hut's existence and the Police of course, Felix, Fiona, Vera, and Daphne, and an unknown intruder. It was years ago, but surely it hadn't been forgotten in Waireka. There could be later newspaper cuttings to be found in between the pages of those magazines which might give further information about the murder case. I went back downstairs to the kitchen. Mrs Tubman was washing the evening meal's dishes. My hasty entrance must have surprised her for she dropped a cup on the floor at my feet. I pushed the china fragments away with my foot and pulled up a chair to the cupboard where I had found the Press cuttings.

"Whoa there," she said. "What's your hurry. Look what you have made me do. What are you after now?"

I reached up and opened the cupboard and found it empty. "Mrs Tubman, do you remember what was in this cupboard? I could have sworn there were a few magazines here this afternoon?"

"Possibly, but I can't say for certain. I never opened that cupboard. Too far up for me and Miss Symington didn't like me poking about in those high cupboards anyhow."

"Do you know anything about a murder that took place in Waireka many years ago?" I asked.

"Murder, bless my soul. I know of no murder here in Waireka, but I could tell you a few tit bits about other goings on in this place but murder that's going too far. I never heard anyone around here talking about a murder. You look all in, Mr Waldron, I must say. You look all come over with nerves. Better to take a little drink of the doings before you settle for the night."

I was suitably dismissed and wouldn't get any information from her about the where the magazines might have gone or anything else that concerned me greatly at the moment.

She was right of course. I must have looked agitated, and my impatience annoyed her. I didn't take her advice to have a whisky before I retired for the night. I found it difficult to concentrate on what I was doing, walking up and down in my room, going to the bathroom along the corridor without my toilet bag and then having found it I misplaced my toothbrush. I tried to get a grip on myself but somehow those paper clippings had disturbed me considerably. I went over and over in my mind of who could have been guilty of murdering Nathan, and what part I might have unwittingly aided. Surely, it couldn't be Felix, even though I remembered that he had wanted to put Nathan in a home of some sort, I couldn't think of him as a murderer. Certainly not Fiona for she loved the boy. Anyhow both of them are dead. That leaves Vera. I wonder what has happened to her. Maybe she was the one. Perhaps she is in prison even now. And Daphne she seems to have disappeared also. I couldn't bring myself to believe that she was the killer. Then there was this other person who must have known about my hut. Did they find out who he was and charge him. These thoughts ran through my head causing me more anguish than I realised. I must find those magazines. There could be more clippings between the pages that might solve the problem.

I changed for bed, pulled back the duvet and climbed in bed. As I lay on the pillow my mind in a whirl, I turned on my side hoping to doze off, but sleep didn't come easily.

I must have slept for I was woken with a start by loud banging on my bedroom door. For a moment I was too disorientated to go to the door. Then the banging started again, and l heard Oscar call out.

"Are you all right in there old chap. You were making the devil of a noise. A chap can't get off to sleep with that racket you are making. Whatever it was you were shouting and yelling something I couldn't understand."

I staggered out of bed, my face felt flushed, and my pyjama top was wet with sweat. Cold sweat ran down my back. I stumbled to the door and opened it. Oscar stared at me with a look that left no doubt about his concern. I apologised for disturbing him and then I saw Miss Clements in her dressing gown further down the corridor. "Sorry about that," I said. "Had a bad nightmare.

Must have been something I ate."

Next morning, I found the magazines and the old recipe books stuffed in the rubbish bin by the back door. When I flicked through the pages a cluster of cuttings held together with a pin fell to the floor. I replaced the magazines and took the cuttings to my room to read. On the way upstairs I ran in to Oscar who took avoiding action by flattening himself against the wall. "My, old Man what's the hurry. Some demon or something like that after you. I wouldn't be surprised after that palaver last night kept us all from our beds."

I didn't bother to answer and pushed past him and went to my room and eagerly unpinned the articles and read them. The other articles in 1986 covered the report of the Coroner's court and the case against Felix Golding for the murder of his son. There was insufficient evidence at the time against Golding and he was not charged. Golding who was living in Wellington at the time died from a heart attack and a key witness against him was away in Australia. The case remained open.

Who could have kept these clippings I wondered. Not the Goldings or Vera for they had left before Uncle and Aunty and I moved to Christchurch. Perhaps Mrs Tubman had kept them although she wasn't working at 'The Willows' in 1965. But she could have been working at 'The Willows' in 1986. As for Miss Symington I wasn't sure how long she had been housekeeper here.

A grey dismal day. The rain has not stopped and coats everything outside, trees, river roads, with its own dull mantle. Except for Oscar Enright, who I refuse to call him Major after last night's rude awakening, who has stayed in his own room since after breakfast, we are all in the Lounge each engaged in their own pursuits almost oblivious of each other. The predominant sound in the room was the clicking of knitting needles from Miss Symington and Miss Clements who are preoccupied with their tasks. I have picked up Oscar's newspaper which he must have, uncharacteristically, left on the small table in the lounge. He rarely shared his morning paper with any of us preferring to keep it in his own room.

I hold the paper up in front of me giving me the opportunity to glance over my glasses at Miss Symington as she works. If she as much as senses my scrutiny and lifts her eyes from her knitting I drop my gaze to the paper. There is something familiar about her that I can't make out. If I had known her before, it must have been many years ago. She must be well in her seventies now I surmised by her the deep wrinkles on her face and her prominent veined hands. At times the light from the window when it fell on her face made me think of someone I knew long ago with a fuller more rounded face and a harassed expression of permanent uncertainty. Could she be, certainly not. I had seen an envelope on the kitchen table addressed to Miss V. Symington. Could the V stand for Vera or perhaps Veronica. If she is Vera, I had never known her surname. I lowered my newspaper and looked at her. Our eyes meet and she held my gaze.

"You remember then, who I am. You certainly took your time. Have l changed that much. l must say apart from your loss of hair and the filling out of your torso you haven't changed all that much after all these years," she said.

"You are Vera, of course," I said. "I knew there was something about you that I thought I recognised, but it was such a long time ago. When I left here, I lost touch with you all. I remember after Nathan disappeared, Daphne went to stay with her aunty in town, and you and Mr and Mrs Golding left to go to wherever you went. You must tell me what happened to you after that."

She gave me a pitying look when she replied." It was a sad time for us all. Felix was such a kind man. He comforted me many times whenever I heard sad news from my family in England. He hugged me and held me close and kissed my cheeks, but that was all there was in it. He did the same to others when he felt sorry for them. That was Felix all over, kind and generous. Daphne of course got the wrong end of the stick and took it out on me, but she was young and didn't understand. It wasn't Felix I loved. It was Fiona I loved more than anyone."

"What happened to you after Felix died?" I must have looked rather contrite as if I was still an eleven-year-old delinquent boy, who had been put in his place. I was aware that Miss Clement was looking at me, and Oscar had come in the room at that moment. They were both regarding me with distaste.

"I'd rather leave it like that. I have nothing more to say." Vera said.

"Don't harass the lady, old boy," Oscar said. "You heard clearly enough what she said." I returned to my newspaper and the tension between us in the room slowly dispersed.

What a day of enlightenment it turned out to be in spite of me being put firmly in my place and the dull weather outside.

Mrs Tubman was to be the source of my enlightenment. Feeling a little put out by the treatment I had received in the lounge I sought refuge in the kitchen where Mrs Tubman was preparing vegetables for the night meal.

"Big occasion here on Friday," she said. "It's the annual visit from Mrs Marsh, the owner of the Lodge. It's a big occasion for us all especially for Miss Symington. She and I will be busy all week cleaning and cooking for that visit. You lot will have to keep out of our way and make do with what we can manage for meals for the rest of the week."

"I thought that Miss Vera Symington owned the Lodge. Who is this Mrs Marsh anyway?"

"She's some lady who, owns hotels all over in Auckland, Wellington, Christchurch until the earthquake, and she has hotels in Queenstown and in Australia. Been married three times and if you ask me, she has done pretty well from all of them."

"Why then would she want to own a Lodge like 'The Willows', I mean the 'Omanga' of course, in a little village like Waireka. I wonder. Have you met her before?" I asked.

"Lots of times now. She and Miss Symington are very pally. Knew each other years ago it seems. Their friendship has something to do with this place I think, but what I can't imagine." Vera had come in the kitchen. "Has Mrs Tubman been telling you about our visitor on Friday?" she said. "Mrs Marsh, the owner is coming to see the progress on the new units being built and she wishes to discuss with me the alterations that will be carried out to the Lodge. I have asked The Major to take you in his car to Rangiora to see a film or to do some shopping which ever you wish while Mrs Marsh is here. I'm sure you understand that Mrs Marsh is a busy woman and she will not stay long."

On Friday, there was the hum of expectancy about the place. Breakfast was earlier than usual, and we were told the table would be cleared by 8.30 and preparations were to start for the arrival of Mrs Marsh who had come to see the builders and to have afternoon tea in the lounge after. Oscar, the Major, was wearing his blue reefer jacket, tie to match and his newly pressed grey trousers. Miss Clement had outdone us all, dressed as she was in close fitting bright pink trousers, a slightly less pink blouse, and a snow-white shawl over one shoulder. Both Mrs Tubman and Vera were more modestly dressed in long frocks and matching coloured shoes.

Vera was waiting at the gate when a large black Mercedes Benz pulled up and out stepped a smartly dressed woman in a tailored trouser suit. She hugged Vera and both of them went over to meet the builders who had stopped work when they saw the car pull up.

So, this was the famous, rich Mrs Marsh. Sitting in Oscar's car, I tried to get a better glimpse of Mrs Marsh while he fussed about feeling in his pocket for the car's keys, talking to himself about how he hated to be rushed. "It was the same last year," he muttered under his breath, "When Mrs Marsh came. Only this year for some reason, which I can't fathom, we are being shunned out and missing the lovely afternoon tea with the chocolate cake. Last year, I had been invited to partake, but why not this year?"

He found the keys, and after a couple of attempts the engine started, and with the grating of the gears we moved off. I had a brief glimpse of the back of Vera and Mrs Marsh as they were talking to the builder.

On the way to Rangiora, I quizzed Oscar about what he knew about the visitor, but he had little to say. He'd found her a smart, well dressed woman in her sixties he thought, very with it and forthright. Not his type, too pushy for him, he added.

At Rangiora, we didn't like the sound of the film and neither of us wanted to shop which left the pub. The bar was a dark, cheerless space with a huge T.V. showing the horse races. Two men leaning on one of the high tables were watching, a half empty glass of beer in their hands. I ordered a glass of beer, but Oscar seeing he was driving asked for orange juice and sensing he was ill at ease and eager to leave, I restricted myself to just the one beer.

Oscar's little Honda car with its highly polished paint work and sporting rugs on its seats, revealed its true age as it coughed and spluttered its way back towards Waireka, at times threatening to give up altogether, when the engine died and then starting up again, but still complaining about having to go on such a long journey when its owner usually took it no further than to the store on wet days. "Had it since new, seen better days, but never lets me down," he said.

When we finally made it after many anxious moments thinking we'd be stranded on the side of the road somewhere, I was pleased to see that Mrs Marsh's car was still outside the Lodge. I was at last to get a close look at the famous Mrs Marsh in spite of Vera having done her best to keep me at a distance.

She recognised me first, coming to me as I got out of the car and peering closely at my face.

"For goodness sake. Jack Waldron of all people and here of all places. It must be years when we last saw each other," she said and throwing her arms around me she kissed me briefly on the lips and on both cheeks. I reciprocated and gave her an extra hug. We exchanged glances as we clung together like a replay of the pantomime which she had played in front of Vera when we were kids, knowing that Vera was looking then, and here she was today standing a few feet away. Back then of course it was performed solely to get her own back at Vera, and I doubted if it had much to do for any affectionate, she might have had towards me. Although I was embarrassed, back then it had awoken in me the first stirrings of love for another person. There was no mistaking her, with the same domed high forehead, flashing eyes and her jutting chin. Daphne had changed of course as age had left its mark underneath the thick makeup on her face and the thickening of her body, no longer the supple, athletic torso of old.

"What a coincidence," she said as we dropped our embrace of each other. "What on earth are you doing here. Vera tells me you are staying at the Lodge. Why here of all places and over fifty-five it must be, years later?"

"The earthquake destroyed my home, and I had to find somewhere to live in the meantime until the insurance is paid out and I can build again. I've lived in several different places since, and the insurance is only being settled now after nearly seven or so years."

She turned to Vera. "You must have recognised Jack surely even after all these years. Why didn't you tell me he was staying here? Never mind. Jack and I have a lot to catch up on with each other. We'll take a walk along our old haunts, just the two of us, if you don't mind Vera," she said.

"The sea is wild today, and the wind is up. It will be cold on the beach." Vera said.

"The wilder the better, I've always enjoyed it when it was like that," said Daphne. "Come on Jack let's go and face the sea in all its fury."

We went along forgotten paths to the beach chatting incessantly as we went. The full force of the wind hit us when we were out of the shelter of the sand dunes. Tears streamed from my eyes as the wind tore at my clothes. Daphne, her hair blown back from her forehead, her head held high stood with feet apart as if defying the wind, to do its best to stop her from going any further. I had never seen the sea like this before, as if in uncontrollable anger, it surged towards the beach with its waves lifted high by the wind, the foam of the white horses blown before them, an uncontrollable mass of tumbling dark water to crash with the noise of thunder on the beach and surge high over the sand towards us. We turned our back on it and sought the relative shelter of the sand dunes where we could hear each other's talk. She told me about her marriages, her first a mistake, an impetus affair that didn't work out and they divorced. The next was a more considered affair. There was money there and it wasn't to be ignored as she put it. There were parties, travelling, good times which led to infidelity on both sides of the coin and that ended in divorce also. Her last was to a much older man, with masses of money of course and a hotel magnate. "He died two years ago, and I now run the business, and I'm free again, but another marriage is not on the cards. One can have too much of a good thing," she said.

I told her about my life, my happy marriage, my daughter, and the business that I had built up and recently sold.

"And why did you bother to buy 'The Willows', as it was called when we were kids?" I asked.

She didn't answer for a moment, her lips pouted as she looked down at her feet. "You wouldn't believe me, but I bought it for Vera's sake."

She must have noticed my astonished look, as she went on to explain herself. "I know Nathan and I were horrid to Vera at times. Real little brats and you might remember I had it in for her when I saw her in my father's arms. I thought how could that insipid bitch take my mother's place and how could Daddy be so stupid to be taken in by her. I was incensed. It's amazing how things can change. After Nathan went missing, I ran away and stayed with my aunty in Christchurch until I left Girls' High. Mummy and Daddy lived in Wellington and then when Nathan's remains were found, and he had been murdered, Daddy became the prime suspect. For goodness sake how could anyone suspect Daddy of murder. It wasn't in his make-up. But nothing came of it, because Daddy had a number of heart attacks and finally died of a massive one before the case against him could be heard. No one has been tried since and I suppose the case is now closed after all this time. Mummy was devastated of course, and Vera returned from Australia and went to live with her to console her. Mummy lived a more contented life with Vera before she died. Like you Jack I'm the last of the family. I put Vera in charge of the Lodge partly because I felt so bad about the way I had treated her when we were kids and partly to thank her for looking after Mummy." We walked on in silence for a while until she spoke again, "Come on Jack see if I can still outrun you along the beach and jump further than you can from the top of the sand hills."

"And climb higher than me on the pine tree," I chipped in. "I doubt it. Neither of us look in good shape to do such energetic things any longer, and certainly not in a wind like this. It is as if wind and the sea want to deny us the beach." I said.

"These sand hills don't seem to be as tall as I remember them and the distance along the beach to Banks Peninsula looks even further away now."

We sat at the foot of a sand hill that we thought we remembered being our launching pad for jumps to the beach.

Further out to sea, a fishing boat was tossed about by the angry sea as it made its way back towards Lyttelton port with a swarm of sea gulls following in its wake swooping now and then to the sea behind the boat.

"The fish and chips boat we used to call it, remember," I said. Daphne seemed to be preoccupied with her own thoughts to answer.

"I didn't know that Nathan's remains had been found because I was living in England at the time," I said. "Had I been here I might have been able to offer some evidence that hadn't been considered in the case."

She had taken up a handful of sand and letting it pour between her fingers.

"It's all in the past Jack. I loved Nathan even though we fought like dogs at times, and I hated Vera when she was cruel to him. Daddy, as you probably know, wanted to have Nathan put in an Institution because he was becoming too difficult to handle at home, but Mummy wouldn't hear of it. She was closer to Nathan than she was to me. Daddy couldn't have ever thought of killing him just to get rid of him and if you think you have new evidence from back, then that might lead to an indictment against Daddy, I think you should keep it to yourself," she said.

I could see she was determined to let the whole matter go away as if it had never happened.

"Daphne, your father couldn't have killed Nathan, not that day at least, because he was sitting in his favourite place in his chair, fast asleep. I know because I saw him there at the end of what is now a car park at the far end of the village, you know in the shade of the large pine tree there. I remember we were together, but I left you and went out on the beach and saw Nathan further up the beach and Vera was following him. When he saw Vera coming towards him, he ran in the Pine Forest about opposite where my underground hut was. She followed him. I cut back from the beach and came out by the end of the road where Bert Saunders lived. He was outside digging in his garden and he came over to me when I appeared."

Daphne had turned away from me and was throwing her handfuls of sand out, which caught by the sea breeze sent it in my direction. I moved away and she stopped throwing sand in the air. She turned to face me with a look of annoyance in her eyes.

"Well, so what does that prove? Nathan may not have been killed that day and Daddy might have done it later. Drop it Jack I don't want to hear any more of this business."

"You still think your father might be guilty, then."

"What does it matter now. I didn't come here to listen to all this," she said with some acidity in her voice. "So put a stop to it. After all, when it all came to court you were on the other side of the world."

"That's the point, don't you see. While I was talking to Bert, Vera came out of the pine forest by Bert's place. I can still remember clearly how terrible she looked, her eyes bulging and her mouth wide open. She was covered in dirt and pine needles down the front of her dress, and there was something sticky on her hands. It could have been pine gum or perhaps, it was blood, but we couldn't tell because there was dirt all over it. Bert and I stared at her and she ran off down the road without saying anything."

Daphne's eyes had narrowed, her jaw thrust forward, her lips shut tightly. I could see that she was very upset by what I had told her. "And will Bert Saunders collaborate what you are implying," she hissed between her half-closed lips.

"Bert died a few years ago."

"Well, there it goes and who is going to believe what an eleven-year-old boy thinks what he saw fifty odd years ago especially one like you, Jack, who had a wild imagination in those days. "

"Make no mistake Daphne, I remembered what I saw that day. It has stayed with me ever since, her wild dishevelled look and all that stuff on her hands and dress."

"And now I suppose you will tell me she put Nathan's body in that underground hut of yours. If you had kept its existence a secret, then Vera wouldn't have known about it."

"Oh, she did, because a few days before Nathan disappeared, I went for a walk with your parents and Vera, and they found the hut because half of it had collapsed a little. I didn't let on I'd built the hut."

"Then why didn't we look there during all the searches that were carried out for weeks?"

"Because earlier when the Police were looking for that wanted man, they had looked in the hut which was partly collapsed at that time and found it empty. By the time we looked for Nathan, the whole hut had fallen in, and it looked like a hollow in the ground which it was before I dug it out a bit for my underground hut."

She had turned her back on me and was staring out to sea. I knew she was upset and was struggling to come to terms with what I had told her. Better now to get the whole thing off my chest to enlighten her even if her manner had become rather tetchy.

"Vera told me the other day that she was not interested in your father. It was your mother she loved."

Daphne remained looking out to sea. "I expected as much after Daddy died. I know that Mummy would never have let Nathan go from her if he had lived."

"And Vera knew that too." I said.

"I know what you are implying Jack, but you are well off the mark. For what it is worth, you may as well tell it to the sea gulls. They'll spread the word."

"Think about it Daphne? Vera would have a motive to get rid of Nathan."

She turned to face me. I recognised that look, eyes glazed, her jaw jutting out defiantly.

"So, you say, but how could you think that any of us would have wanted to kill anyone in our own family." She hesitated and looked down at her feet and in measured words she spoke slowly, "And I suppose you will tell the Police about

183

your suspicions and I can't stop you, but before you do hear me out. I felt as if I had unintentionally loosened the lid from a jar, which she had wanted to remain tightly shut, and I had released a genie. I stood up as a sea gull blown by the wind, swooped low overhead and landed at the water edge on the beach. Daphne was standing a few feet from me, half turned away, as if not wanting to face me while she talked.

"You may well have remembered seeing Vera come out of the forest in that dishevelled state, and on the day you said. She would have been too distressed to talk to you after what happened to her. I saw her like that too.

What you said you saw on the beach that day was properly right, but you didn't see me. Nathan and I were up to our old tricks, hiding to make Vera follow us into the forest. She never liked going in there, and we thought we would get her lost. Well, it all went as planned, until we thought we had got her lost all by herself and she would be scared, only it all went wrong. We heard her scream and when we crept up, she was on her knees and her clothes looked as if she had hastily rearranged them. She looked terrible, her face white, eyes and mouth wide open. A man with his back to us was standing by her, pulling up his trousers. I shouted out to him and he chased us. I ran one way and Nathan ran another way. When the man chased Nathan, I hid in the lupins and didn't come out for what seemed like ages, until I thought it was safe. I called out Nathan's name, but he didn't answer. I was too frightened to go deeper in the forest in the direction that Nathan had run, and I went back to find Vera, but she had gone, and you must have seen her when she came out of the forest. When I got back to the village, the car that had been parked along the road had gone. "

"Was it a Riley Kestrel?" I asked. I must have looked aghast, for I certainly felt mortified by what she was saying, for she was looking at me, now probably wondering how I was taking all this.

"How on earth would I know. It was a car. That's all."

"Did you tell the police?" I asked.

"I wanted to, but Vera felt too much shame to tell anyone. I now know she had been raped by this man."

"Did you know who he was?" I asked.

"No, I couldn't be sure. I never saw his face. I was too upset for Vera's sake to be certain. She was sobbing in her locked bedroom when I returned, but she let me in, and we talked for a long time. I promised not to say a word to anyone, and I haven't until now. She said she couldn't live with the disgrace of what had happened to her and I believed her then and still do today. Promise Jack, if you honour our old friendship, not to tell her or anyone else what I have told you."

She was looking at me closely watching for my reaction. I didn't answer immediately, still trying to take in what she had told me. She was looking a time closely and we held each other's gaze for a moment.

"And Nathan was never seen again after that day." I said.

"I can't remember for certain. It was such a long time ago, and I have tried to forget that dreadful day. Why on earth Jack did you want to bring all this up again?"

"Because don't you think that unidentified man might also be Nathan's murderer?"

She gave me a long hard look. "Leave it Jack. Nathan would have hidden when that man chased him. He had so many hiding places to go to ground. I doubt if the man could have found him." She hesitated and then as if something had occurred to her, she added, "Well you might be right Jack. But we don't know who he is, and it was years ago now. If Vera knew him, she has never told me, and to bring the whole lot up again would be too much for her to cope with. For goodness' sake, Jack forget it. I'm beginning to regret that I came with you on this nostalgic walk."

She thrust out her hand for me to shake, smiled briefly and then strode off back along the beach to the village.

I didn't follow immediately but sat down again by the sand dune and went over what she had told me. Maybe Daphne was right. I had no right to open up old wounds, but why was everyone reluctant to talk about Nathan's murder. After all I understand that the case is still open.

Maybe the truth is too horrible for them to face now. It could have been anyone of three people, two of whom I was once close to. Felix is not off the hook. Nor is Vera. Maybe her story about being raped was a cover up. She had a strong motive for killing Nathan. And there was Daphne herself. Why was she so reluctant to discuss the whole matter with me and insisted that I should forget about what I had thought I'd seen? Had she and Vera murdered him and concocted up this story of Vera being the victim of rape? And then there was this unidentified man, if he ever existed. I rather hoped he did, for I had a good idea who he might be. Bert had said that Nathan made those off noises of his in the forest because he was frightened of Len Hales who often went walking in there.

I wondered if Nathan was a victim too. Maybe I am prejudiced, but I like to think that Len Hales is the unidentified man.

I heard a car door slam, a car start up, and the sound of it as it left the village. The only sign I had of her leaving was the sight of the smoke from the exhaust of her Mercedes that lingered momentarily, before it dispersed.

Oscar was waiting at the gate. He greeted me. "Gone off in a huff if you ask me," he said. "Been inside with Miss Symington for the best part of an hour, and then without so much as a bye, she left in the car without acknowledging my farewell to her. You haven't upset her old bean. Have you made a pass at her? I couldn't blame you if you had. Fine looking woman and loads of cash."

I reassured him and made my way upstairs to my room.

We sat around the big table in the kitchen, which was still spread with the afternoon tea that had been prepared for Daphne's visit. Nothing had been eaten and tea had not been made previously. Oscar sat at one end of the table, with Miss Vera Symington at the other end, and Miss Clements and Mrs Tubman sat on the side opposite me. We sat in ominous silence while Mrs Tubman poured the tea and Vera cut the chocolate cake. We were waiting to hear about the owner's visit from Vera. She cut the cake in deliberate fashion, placing each slice on a plate before passing it around. We in turn thanked her and looked down at our plates, reluctant to eat it until Vera had put the knife down and picked up her cup. We did likewise with our cups. When Miss Clements dropped her teaspoon on the floor I went to pick it up and put it on the table beside me.

"Leave it just now if you don't mind," said Vera. "I have something to announce that will concern you all. Unfortunately, Mrs Marsh couldn't stay for tea. She was in a hurry to get to the airport. Pity, she would have liked to have tried your delicious cake, Mrs Tubman, and had time to talk to you all, but I'm afraid Mr Waldron took most of her time, apart from business that she had to discuss with me." She looked sternly at me, as if I had committed an unpardonable crime.

"Sorry about that," I said. "We had known each other before, and we had much to catch up with each other."

Vera cleared her voice and put her cup in her saucer before she looked up and spoke again.

"As you know, although perhaps, you don't, Mr Waldron, we usually close down over winter. This year in a month's time we will be closing which is little later than usual. Miss Clements and Mr Enright have their own arrangements during winter and Mrs Tubman is pleased to have a rest from working here. I, as you know, usually stay here over winter, but not this year. Mr Waldron, I take it you will make your own arrangements."

She poured herself another cup of tea and offered to do the same for anyone else. None of us took up her offer. I could sense an air of unease around the table, as if they expected her to say something else of importance to us.

It was as if, she was finding it difficult to say anything more until she had finished her second cup of tea. I had thought of her as being serene, rather remote from us and lacking confidence, but this afternoon she was making big effort to remain calm, but in control.

"As you know," she began in the same way as before which seemed to give her confidence to proceed. "Mrs Marsh had a long talk with me before she left this afternoon. She has decided to close the Lodge for good and make it into a holiday stay place with a restaurant, and with the new units being built, this place will become a holiday camp. I am not to stay, as she will appoint a manager to run the place, and I'm too old to do that work now. The Lodge will go on the market next year. I'm sorry, but I must ask you all to make other arrangements for your accommodation in the future. I know this is a shock to you all, but there's nothing I can do." She pushed back her chair and got up and left the kitchen.

Oscar and Miss Clements looked astounded, as if they couldn't believe what they had heard. After all they had been permanent lodgers here for some years now.

"This is a fine place indeed," Oscar said. "I suppose I'll have to consider living in one of those new-fangled Retirement Homes that I swore l would never do. What about you Miss Clements. Will you join me?"

I could see that she was shocked by such a proposal, but she soon recovered. "Thank you Major, but I will not accept your invitation. I haven't time to think about where I will go, but l certainly will not go to any Rest Home or place like that."

Vera was waiting for me at the bottom of the stairs, half blocking my passage.

"I'm sorry, Mr Jack Waldron, but what are you going to do now?" she asked.

"Oh, I don't know, probably find a place at the seaside to live, possibly Sumner. I've always liked Sumner. My wife died before the earthquake and our home was badly damaged later in the earthquake. I couldn't bear to do anything about it for years. It's in shambles now. I'll pull it down and sell the section, something like that. And you Miss Symington, even now I couldn't bring myself to call her Vera, what about you?"

"Like you Jack," she said with an emphasis on Jack, "I'm off to pastures new, to be housekeeper for Mrs Daphne Marsh in her home in Sydney. She has a wonderful home by the river."

Later that evening, when the wind had dropped, I went to the beach. The sky had clouded over, and the sea was calm now with the waves hardly breaking as they ran up the beach to the high tide line. In the past, the sea and I had never been compatible. As a child, I had often tried to swim to join Daphne beyond the breaking waves but time and again it tossed me back on the beach rejected like a piece of flotsam. I took off my shoes and waded in the slow-moving water feeling the slight tug of the outgoing wave under my feet, avoiding where I can the exposed ridges of protruding pipi shells from the sand. A sudden surge of water rose above my knees, as it raced to the beach. I braced myself against it as it flowed back, surging against my feet undermining them in the sand, as it made a feeble attempt to draw me back with it. I looked out to sea expecting another even bigger surge of water from a high breaking wave, but all was as calm as it had been before.